VIOLET KELLY AND THE JADE OWL

Fiona Britton is a Sydney writer, living and working on Bidjigal land. *Violet Kelly and the Jade Owl* is her first novel.

VIOLET KELLY

AND THE JADE OWL

FIONA BRITTON

ALLEN&UNWIN
SYDNEY•MELBOURNE•AUCKLAND•LONDON

First published in 2023

Allen & Unwin
Cammeraygal Country
83 Alexander Street
Crows Nest NSW 2065
Australia
Phone: (61 2) 8425 0100
Email: info@allenandunwin.com
Web: www.allenandunwin.com

Allen & Unwin acknowledges the Traditional Owners of the Country on which we live and work. We pay our respects to all Aboriginal and Torres Strait Islander Elders, past and present.

A catalogue record for this book is available from the National Library of Australia

ISBN 978 1 76106 746 4

Set in 12.7/17 pt Adobe Garamond Pro by Midland Typesetters, Australia

10 9 8 7 6 5 4 3 2 1

For Paul, Marlin, Henry and Shar,
who make room for a writer in the family.

And for Chloe, who pretends to be the sensible sibling.

CHAPTER 1

MADAME LOOKED RIGHT AND LEFT to check the hallway was empty, then stooped and pressed her eye to the brass keyhole of the Rose Room. Peeping wasn't altogether wrong, she reasoned. The lady proprietress of a gentleman's club must be well-informed, and certain information could only be learned in secret. Granted, the awkward bending was an affront to one's dignity and a strain on the knees. But all in all, spying through keyholes had served her well over the years and had saved more than one girl from a sticky end.

Mais oui, she thought, those girls trust me with their lives. We'll have no catastrophes in my house. *Quelle horreur* and all that.

Madame was working on her French.

She suppressed a sigh of sympathy for herself. Despite many years at the helm, the responsibilities of management remained a heavy burden. At La Maison des Fleurs, they walked a very fine line. It was important to appeal to a better class of chap. The notion that her girls had a certain *rare* quality added to their price.

But you don't want to turn too many men away either, she mused. Because we're not here for the good of our health, are we? And time waits for no-one, as they say. On that, she and the girls were agreed. Madame, now well into her fifth decade, was acquainted with the effects of time on one's person.

Madame focused her attention on the scene beyond the keyhole, being careful to stay silent. The man had paid good money for a private audience with Violet Kelly; better let him believe it was what he'd got.

She smiled in satisfaction at what she witnessed. Just as she'd hoped, Violet had taken charge of the situation and now the customer was being led, quite as if by Nature herself, through a practised set of moves. God, she was good.

Madame felt her knees beginning to seize. She straightened up in the doorway, joints protesting loudly as she unfolded her long frame. You can quit the melodramatics, she told her knees. Spry as a goat for fifty-five years, yet *now* you decide to give up? I don't think so. Not when the Marigold Room needs stripping and there's a shortage of champagne at the bar.

Curiosity satisfied, Madame set off down the carpeted hallway, chin in the air, to find her niece Bunny. There were half-a-dozen men in the downstairs parlour. Special guests, given rare early afternoon appointments. At this very moment they were probably reaching into their pockets to retrieve their wallets. Saints alive, it would be rude not to help them. She would return to Violet Kelly in half an hour. Or the full hour, Madame amended, in case Violet should decide to show off the *full* array of her skills.

Madame descended the back stairs slowly, in deference to her creaking knees. She deigned to grasp the banister to steady herself.

Violet Kelly was quite unlike any girl she'd encountered. Prepare yourselves for a convent blonde, Madame had told the men while drumming up interest for Violet's debut earlier that year. Legs up to her armpits and the 'touch-me-not' look of an English heiress. You've never seen anything like it, not in Paddington, not in Parramatta, not even in Paris! In the men's murmurs, Madame heard the clinking of coins.

The strategy worked. Now, some months later and well into the winter of 1930, Madame had noticed a pleasing surge in the takings of the house. Violet Kelly was quite simply raking it in.

Did Violet hear the chatter? It was hard to say. Surely the girl only had to glance in the gilt-edged hallway mirror to see she'd been showered with natural gifts. Those legs, the Folies Bergère smile. Any girl would be happy to be half so well endowed.

The thing is, Madame thought, Violet Kelly's got gifts the mirror doesn't reveal: she's as shrewd as a brown snake. Lord knows, if I was making a speech about it—though there's scant call for speeches in our trade, except at a graveside, more's the pity—I'd say that in the short time she's been here, she's picked up a bank manager's tact, a pirate's cunning and an alley cat's knack for landing on her feet.

Madame paused on the landing, leaning on the banister to catch her breath, and smiled to herself. Because right now Violet Kelly wasn't on her feet at all, was she? She was underneath a fat Dutch sea captain who reeked of ale and herring. But he positively *rattled* with unspent wages.

That girl would go far.

The thump of boots on the stairs broke her reverie. Albert—butcher's boy, occasional pleasure-house strong-arm and Violet's best friend from their orphanage days—thrust his head around the corner of the stairwell. 'Alright up there?'

'Albert, love, what are you doing here at this time of day?' Madame straightened.

'Come to see Violet, but she's busy. There's a man at the front door for you. I've left him in the hallway. And there's a new girl waiting in your office. Calls herself Mrs Brown. Top lip stiff as the clasp on a Scotsman's purse.'

'Good Lord. Alright.' Deserted or divorced, Madame had seen Mrs Brown's type before: fallen on hard times, a kid or two tucked away with an aunt or sister. Believed herself too dignified for their game but wanted the cash. It never worked out, and Mrs Brown would be sent away. 'Will you stay for tea?'

Albert shook his thick mop of brown hair. 'Nah, have to push off. I'll stop by the kitchen and see Charlie, then take myself out the back way.'

'Right you are.' I'll deal with the customer in the hallway first, thought Madame. With any luck, Mrs Brown will have come to her senses and fled to the Samaritans for a food parcel by the time I return.

But when she turned into the hallway in search of the customer, she gasped in surprise at the familiar face that greeted her instead. He was older now, the stern lines around his mouth and chin set more firmly into the flesh, yet his expression was as cool as ever.

Xiao Zhu spoke quickly, before she could recover herself sufficiently to demand an explanation for his unexpected appearance. 'Ah, good. You're here.' He raked his gaze over the expensive carpet, the fine glasswork of the chandelier. 'I hardly recognise the place . . . or you.' Now she felt his gaze travel her body, taking in her garnet necklace and the fine lace trim of her dress. 'I believe they call you Madame now.'

He turned away abruptly, ending any opportunity she might have seized to question him. He opened the front door and nodded to someone waiting in the street.

Madame peered over his shoulder. Two men were bundling a cloaked figure from the back of a sleek black saloon car parked on the street in front of the house. She saw a flash of scarlet embroidered slippers as the figure stumbled up the steps towards them.

Xiao pulled the cloaked figure into the hallway and closed the front door. The hood of her cloak fell away and Madame found herself staring at a beautiful young girl: an almond-eyed Celestial, whose face was etched with fear.

Madame steadied herself against the wall and opened her mouth to speak, but instead a ragged cough escaped her lungs.

'Tsk. You should see a doctor about that,' said Xiao impassively. 'Health is wealth. And one's riches must be protected.' He waved a hand, lazily describing an arc that took in her empire and every one of its souls. 'Wouldn't you agree?'

One's riches. The threat was made so casually. Xiao hadn't lost his knack for making an *ever-so-sharp* point.

She eyed the girl, who cringed and brought her hands to her face as if anticipating a blow. 'I don't know what this is, Xiao, but I forbid cruelty. You know that.'

'You ask what I know?' He blinked slowly and Madame felt a surge of terror. 'I'll tell you,' he continued. 'I know that it is unwise to refuse me. Let's go.'

CHAPTER 2

VIOLET KELLY FROWNED AND SHIFTED her position under the Dutch gentleman's stout torso. As luck would have it, her customer had arrived as the parlour clock struck the hour, at the very same time she'd hoped to meet Albert. Now she would have to wait until evening to hear the news her old friend was so desperate to impart. What's more, the sea captain seemed to be losing momentum. Heck, had she lost her touch, just as quickly as she'd acquired it?

It was time to move things along or risk a lecture from Madame on technique, and that spectacle, with its mangled French and eye-watering mime, was to be avoided at all costs. *Bien sûr!*

Accordingly, she clasped the Dutchman tighter and emitted a hearty moan, one from her catalogue, right in his pink ear. Honestly, the perfect gasp could really put the lead in a chap's pencil.

Sure enough, the sweaty captain found his rhythm.

After several minutes of this, Violet found herself being reminded of Madame's Delft clock. The Dutch captain was positively *metronomic*.

Violet stifled a yawn and smiled at the ornate ceiling. Before the frustrations of the last half-hour, she'd been feeling a particularly sweet sense of satisfaction at her achievements: here she was, at eighteen, a rich and sought-after professional nearing the zenith of her abilities. Installed in the finest room of the house, surrounded by the most beautiful things.

If one can learn the knack of enjoying life, she had thought, then I am a humble but *committed* student.

Now, however, her left calf was starting to cramp and she was in danger of being winded. She disliked having to try quite so hard. Of course, the captain had spent an hour in the downstairs parlour sampling Madame's best brandy and had struggled to find his land legs on La Maison des Fleurs' grand stairs.

Unhelpfully, her wandering thoughts alighted on the equally stout and odoriferous personage of the Reverend Mother, Sister Bernadette from her alma mater, the Orphanage School of the Church of Saint Michael in Darlinghurst.

Sister Bernadette got some things right, thought Violet, bracing against the mechanical Dutchman in a sudden return to the present.

'Girls like you end up working on their backs,' the Sister had told her. 'Wilful girls. Wicked girls.' This from a woman who couldn't keep the excitement from tugging on the corner of her lip when called upon to dole out the Sunday beatings.

Sensible Violet had hoped that the Sister's words were a premonition, even if they were intended as a curse. Any fool could see that, no matter her education and her wits, a girl like Violet faced dispiriting options. Who would want a parish orphan for anything but a drudge? What array of miseries awaited her? A life on one's back sounded rather better that a noble life on one's feet, if that life were spent with the crushing weight of misfortune forever weighing one down.

A year or so ago, when Violet and Albert were preparing to say their goodbyes to the other inmates at St Michael's Orphanage, they'd found themselves standing at the schoolyard gate, just as they had so many times before. They stared pensively at the small and grubby world they knew beyond it: the crumbling terraces, the dogs and newspaper. On that slate-grey winter day, when the wind was howling straight from the Tasman Sea, seventeen-year-old Violet, fresh from her final class as teaching assistant to sweet Sister Philomena, had brushed the chalk from her fingers, pulled her cardigan around her shoulders and twisted her freezing hands into the sleeves.

'I'm quitting misery,' she declared. 'From now on, I want to see beautiful things every day. I want to forget this ugly place. I want to forget I ever knew it.'

Even as she said the words, she knew it was an impossible wish. Who could forget the place that formed them?

Now she recalled the chill of that day and its sense of an ending and a beginning. The schoolyard gate marked the line they must cross. At their backs were sorrows that must stay in the past. Before them, an unknown world waited to receive them. With nothing but unhappiness in the past and no certainty of comfort in the future, save for the comfort they would make for themselves, Violet knew what they must do.

When she had turned to Albert, he'd seemed lost in thought, his knuckles grown white around the cold iron railings of the orphanage gate.

She nudged him. 'Struth, Albert. Just *look* at this place. You could slash your own throat and people wouldn't notice, they're so full of their own misery.' The crushing poverty caught people in its own relentless gyre. Families lost jobs, then homes. They lost children. Only a week before, a shop awning on Liverpool Street had fallen into the road, bringing the shopfront down with it and crushing the heads of two little boys playing noughts and crosses in the shaded dust below.

Looking out at the street, it was hard to imagine there was any pleasure in human existence. Violet kicked a toe in the dirt.

Albert rattled the iron bars. Eventually, he said, 'I want to eat beef every day. Really good steak. Brisket. Sausages. Every day.'

And now here they were, the butcher's boy and the concubine. There was poetry in the pragmatics of it.

Catching a breath, she made a quick inventory of herself. The sea captain was working his way rhythmically towards a successful arrival at port. Her blonde hair was cleverly set and unlikely to get too fussed if she kept her head still. She'd had the sense to tell the Dutchman not to smudge her lipstick before he took it into his drunken head to kiss her (because a girl must have her limits). Her long legs were stuck out at angles, to avoid the Dutchman's crushing thighs. She'd kept her shoes and stockings on, and now she caught a flash of her white patent-leather Mary Janes from the corner of her eye.

Goodness me, she thought, now there's a splendid shoe.

The little covered button that held the strap in place never failed to lift her spirits. Violet smiled. A low birth was no impediment to cultivating an eye for beauty, she mused. One can always appreciate aesthetics. Even if from awkward angles.

Next, she took in her surroundings. The Rose Room, Violet's boudoir, was Madame's finest. It was a source of great pride at

La Maison des Fleurs. The red-tasselled drapes were real silk velvet, delivered as a present to Madame by the Governor's valet. The garlanded carpet had come all the way from Turkey, bought for a song at the docks—and hardly singed at all from the dockyard fire! The bed was a brass half-tester from Mark Foy's; the sheets were softened linen, brand-new that week. In the corner, a claw-foot bath with brass taps and pipes stood on a raised marble slab. A trellis design dotted with faint pink miniature roses climbed the wallpaper. Above her, a Tiffany lampshade with a tortoise-shell rose hung low above the bed. All in all, it was a glorious display of decadence.

But gosh, her calf muscle was really hurting now.

Violet issued what she hoped was a rousing cry. The Dutchman's breathing began to slow, his body softened and his thrusting stopped abruptly. He broke into sudden heavy snores, loud enough to bring the ceiling down.

'Oh, double triple hecking heck,' Violet muttered. She wriggled herself free of his shrinking appendage, then heaved the man's portly frame aside. He rolled onto his back, snoring with his head thrown back and mouth open.

Sitting up, Violet reached for her silk nightgown and drew it carefully over her coiffed head. She whistled a hymn from her days in the St Michael's choir, the stirring Canticle of Simeon, as she rummaged in the Dutchman's coat and drew out a crushed packet of French cigarettes. She lit one from the cut-glass lighter on the bedside table.

'Better luck next time, champ,' she told the sleeping man, wiping her thighs with her nightgown.

It must be nice to be a captain, she thought. Telling other folks what to do. But let's face it, she mused, as she looked down at the supine walrus beside her, you still put your trousers on one leg at a time, just like any other bloke.

She drew on the lovely French cigarette and wondered what she might say to the formidable Sister Bernadette, if the five-foot gorgon were to break down the door at that moment, using the steel cap of her brogues.

Am I sorry, Sister Bernadette? No, I am not. Because I am lying in silk stockings. My hair is silver-blonde and done in finger waves, just like Esther Ralston's. And by this gent's brass pocket watch, I can see that Madame will be here in one and a half minutes to tell my steaming Dutchman to button his trousers and proceed to the back door.

She smiled at the ceiling. Blew a lazy smoke ring. Continued her imaginary conversation with her former nemesis.

After Madame comes in, her little niece Bunny will follow—Bunny for her soft brown eyes and her poorly rabbit lip—bringing clean sheets and a bottle of beer. And later, if the China ship's been in this week, we'll share a long pipe of Madame's special resin from abroad and have wonderful, magical dreams. When Bunny and I throw the clean sheets across the bed and the smell of Sunlight soap fills the room, I will think: silk stockings, hairdressers, bottled beer and Madame turning men away.

Sister Bernadette, these men would steal the change from the St Michael's collection plate for twenty minutes on the private side of my drawers.

So am I crying? Oh, no. I'm laughing myself silly. Really, I am.

Violet stubbed the cigarette out into the brass ashtray on the bedside table and sat up just as a knock on the door signalled Madame's arrival.

'Ah, sweet hell!' Madame exclaimed from the doorway. She bustled to the fog-horning Dutchman's side, looking dishevelled. 'What've you done to the stupid beggar?'

Not for the first time, Violet observed that Madame's Parisian accent gave way to Irish in times of stress.

'Keep your hair on, he'll be right,' Violet said. She jumped to her feet and stood beside Madame, grinning. 'Sleeping off his brewer's droop.' Men had died *in flagrante* at La Maison des Fleurs before now. It was testament to the skill of the girls.

'Thank God! I thought he was a goner.'

Violet peered at Madame, taking stock of her mentor. 'Are you alright? You look jumpy as a frog in a sock.'

Madame's coat-hanger shoulders hitched an inch closer to her ears. 'I'm fine, thank you, and you'll remember who you're speaking to!' Madame looked away, her chin set.

'To whom. And yes, Your Majesty.' Violet curtsied, vowing silently to keep an eye on Madame. It wouldn't be the first time she'd had to hide the brandy and call the doctor for a knockout draught. Being the favourite carried certain responsibilities.

Bunny appeared by Violet's side, her arms full of folded sheets. 'Aw, cripes. Susan has her bank manager arriving in ten minutes. You know he won't stand for being seen by a *sailor.*' She dumped the sheets on the foot of the bed.

Madame yanked the man's shirt down to cover his privates. 'For pity's sake, Bunny! Thirteen years old and all of married life's surprises spoiled. Look away, dear.'

Bunny sniggered and looked at the ceiling as commanded.

'Sorry, but it'll take the three of us, I reckon,' Violet said. She shook the Dutchman's shoulders and Bunny prodded his rounded thigh while maintaining a staunchly averted gaze.

The man stirred and grunted, then his rhythmic snoring resumed.

Tutting, Madame turned to the dresser and rummaged among the bottles and flasks. Finding what she sought, she opened a pot of pungent Chinese tiger balm and waved it beneath the man's prominent nose. Bunny sneezed loudly and the Dutchman woke with a start. The girl skittered out into the hallway, stifling her laughter, as her aunt thrust crumpled trousers at the startled Dutchman.

Madame coughed harshly into her handkerchief then cleared her throat. 'Ah, Monsieur is awake,' she purred in her front-of-house voice. 'Time to go, if you please.' She drew herself up to her full height and, in a trot that sometimes passed for elegance, joined Bunny in the hallway.

The door closed behind her. The man sat up.

Violet perched on the edge of the bed and patted the confused man's arm. He clutched the trousers and looked at her blankly.

'Well,' she exclaimed, 'you were . . . wow. Magnificent!' She rolled her eyes as if transported, and beamed at him. Flattery filled awkward moments like nothing else.

'Really?' He blinked.

Violet planted a crimson kiss on the Dutchman's damp brow. 'Oh, yes! Now, shall I help you with those?'

—

As she laced the drunk man's shoes, Violet's thoughts returned, once again, to her great good fortune.

It was all thanks to Madame.

Albert had it from the butcher that Madame's real name was Peggy O'Sheehan. 'Her soul's pure Blarney,' Albert had told Violet. 'That bony carcass has never been anywhere but the puddles of Kildare and here. Born to peat cutters, family came over before the war. Her sister Martha got away, went straight to the country to work, but the rest of 'em lived in a lodging house above the Argyle Cut—not exactly in a villa on the Seine. Sold bootleg cigarettes for a crust.'

Well, who among them could claim the distinction of a fine lineage? Not a soul, as far as Violet knew. La Maison des Fleurs was peopled with a dizzying array of beautiful cast-offs.

How many times had she been told the story of her own ignoble birth? Too many to count, because the nuns had taken pains to remind her that no amount of airs and graces could blanch the stain of illegitimacy.

Violet Kelly was conveyed into this world at two minutes to midnight on a brisk winter night in 1912, in the orphanage parlour. Shortly thereafter, Violet's twin—Iris—made her unexpected appearance, shunting into the midwife's unloving embrace at five minutes past the hour.

Poor Iris. As the nuns told it, the child's face was as blue as Sydney Harbour, and the twins' young mother bore her terror in silence while the midwife lay the limp infant on the chest of drawers and heaved her own tripe-and-onions breath into the baby's lungs.

Consequently, this surprise second child was yanked into the world and back from the brink. Hail Mary and so on.

Violet and Iris. The infant girls were handed swiftly over to the parish by their young mother, who fled. The babies were placed side by side next to the parlour fire, in a wooden apple crate that would serve just as well as a crib or coffin, depending on the Saviour's whim. Parish funds were already pinched. Reverend Mother Sister Bernadette was a practical woman.

But the girls lived. You might even say that, in spite of the nuns, they thrived, like dandelions that absorb the sunlight from a roothold in the cracks of the pavement.

But what would Sister Bernadette say now, Violet wondered, if she knew that Violet would cross the road to avoid her twin sister, should that scheming shrew ever cross Violet's path again?

Violet stood and regarded the Dutchman. 'Shipshape and Bristol fashion! Which means you're ready to disembark, my friend.'

—•—

After dispatching the Dutchman through a discreet side door and pocketing his lavish tip, Violet headed for the kitchen.

Li Ling Han was at the stove, stirring a large pot and enveloped in a cloud of savoury steam.

Charlie Han looked up from the kitchen table, where he was applying black tar paint to a cast-iron pot, which was placed on a pile of newspapers. 'Afternoon.' He dabbed the pot carefully with a ragged paintbrush.

'Afternoon, Charlie.'

Violet joined Li Ling at the stove, bent over the pot and peered in. Hearty ham bones jostled garlic cloves in a simmering spiced broth. The aroma was mouth-watering. 'Oh, Li Ling. I'm surprised you haven't lured all the men in Sydney here with that smell.'

Li Ling smiled proudly. 'This is love potion. Powerful magic to the right man.' She handed the ladle to Violet. Violet took it and risked a scalding sip, while Li Ling dried her hands and screwed the lid back on a jar containing paper spice packets.

'Oh, boy.' The broth was delicious.

'Look out, that's how she gets you,' said Charlie with a wink to Violet.

'Too late—Li Ling already has my heart.' Violet took another sip.

Li Ling snatched the ladle back from Violet. 'You better not be making a mess, Charlie Han. No soup for you if you get that paint on my table.' Li Ling's stern reply didn't quite hide her look of satisfaction.

'Do I look like a gambling man?' replied Charlie, earning him a swipe over the head, aimed to miss, from his wife.

'So?' asked Violet, flopping into one of the worn wooden kitchen chairs and resting her elbows on the table. 'I missed Albert. Did he tell you why he's got such a bee in his bonnet?'

Charlie paused his careful dabs with the paintbrush and cast his wife a wary glance. 'Ah, Albert. He's got a lot on his mind.'

'What does that mean?'

Charlie set the paintbrush down on the pile of newspapers. 'He said to tell you to take care of yourself.' Charlie leaned forward. 'He reckons there's someone watching the place.'

Violet narrowed her eyes impatiently. Her old friend could be *too* vigilant sometimes. 'Albert's letting his imagination get the better of him, again. He's convinced we'll all end up knifed in an alley someday and he's determined that I should take more care. If someone's watching, I bet it'll be another one of Susan's soppy customers. That girl knows how to keep 'em loyal.'

She smiled at the thought of a lovelorn admirer lurking in the shadows. The girls of La Maison des Fleurs were *adored*! If the house was being watched by a tormented suitor, this would hardly raise pulses; the girls were used to it.

To be fair, thought Violet, we *encourage* it. Desperation was good for business.

Li Ling turned to the table, interrupting Violet's pleasant daydream. 'Ahem. No, it's not Susan. Not this time. Albert says the person's spying on you.'

'Phhht, what?' Violet exclaimed. Li Ling's look of concern was unsettling. 'Li Ling, I'm sure he's just spooked. His new pals have put ideas in his head.'

According to Albert, on his first day at the butcher's, he'd delivered a crate of pigs' trotters to a certain Nico and Arlo, brothers who ran a Stanley Street delicatessen and a list of side interests. As the brothers had tossed the trotters into salting barrels, they had admired Albert's splendid arms, thumped his broad shoulders. These were dangerous times, they'd said. The streets weren't safe for a young man without friends. They would teach him how to look after himself. But what, Violet had wondered, did they expect in return?

And were these men now responsible for Albert's jittery nerves?

Charlie gave Violet an apologetic shrug, hands raised. 'Albert seemed very sure it's you who's being watched. He said he saw this person looking up at your window.'

How, wondered Violet, could he possibly know that? Perhaps Albert was trying to frighten her into taking his warnings seriously. 'He's been wrong before, Charlie,' she said. 'When half of St Michael's went down with measles, Albert was *sure* we'd avoid it if we drank a bottle of castor oil. That was a bad day for the nuns on bathroom duty.'

'Ooh,' Charlie winced.

'Indeed, and we still got measles, something fierce. Anyway, why on earth would someone spy on me?' Yet even as she asked the question aloud, a small, internal voice cried out: only a fool would believe she was entirely without enemies. For the second unpleasant time that day, Sister Bernadette came to mind—although

Violet dismissed the idea of the old nun taking up espionage. Nevertheless, she silently admitted that even *her* closet might contain a skeleton or two.

She put the thought aside hastily: Albert was clearly getting to her.

Li Ling patted her shoulder. 'It's probably nothing. Just silly rumours.'

Charlie clapped his hands. 'Hey, Li Ling! Remember that time we heard that Violet could say "it's the biggest I've seen" in seven languages?'

'Yes!' Li Ling slapped her thigh, creasing up at Charlie's squeaky imitation of Violet.

Charlie gave another hoot. 'And remember that time we heard she was double jointed?'

Li Ling doubled over, dabbing her eyes with her apron. 'Yes!'

'Okay, Punch and Judy!' Violet shouted as Li Ling collapsed into a kitchen chair. 'I'm right *here*, you realise?' She pursed her lips. 'Am I to blame if my reputation precedes me?'

This triggered fresh gales. Violet couldn't supress a smile.

Yet it was perplexing. Albert liked to believe he was the eyes and ears of La Maison des Fleurs: what if he was right, and their delightful existence was under threat? Sydney's notorious Kings Cross was a battleground. But the pleasure house had always drifted above the unpleasantness, a suburb (and a world) away in Paddington.

'What else did Albert say?' asked Violet warily.

Charlie snapped his fingers, remembering. 'He said you *have* to go to Nico's this afternoon and pick up your package. He said Nico was sticking his neck out for you. What does that mean, sticking his neck out?'

'Albert means Nico is doing me a favour,' said Violet. A favour

I hardly want or need, she thought. Albert had been at her for days to visit Nico to pick up this mysterious gift, a late eighteenth birthday present. She had some idea of what might be in such a package: a gun or a flick knife, perhaps.

Now she felt a surge of irritation. *Albert* was the problem! He was the ant in the jam jar! The toast crumb in the butter! Her goal was to enjoy a luxurious life with unbridled enthusiasm. This afternoon, for example, she'd made a plan that involved lying in the Rose Room with Bunny, looking at *Australian Home Journal* and drinking cherry liqueur. Playing with hairstyles, trying on dresses, perfecting her smoke rings. It sounded trivial now. Was it wrong to wish for such things?

'Hecking heck,' she said crossly, getting to her feet. She caught the fleeting raised eyebrow from Li Ling. 'I'll go to Nico's, if only to shut Albert up.'

Charlie shrugged. 'He just wants you to be safe, Violet.'

'This is a storm in a tea cup, I tell you.'

Violet looked from Charlie to Li Ling as the last of their gaiety drained away.

Li Ling got to her feet and moved to the stove. After a clattering of pots and dishes, she turned back to the table with a steaming bowl of broth and noodles in her hand. She placed it on the table in front of Violet. 'It's bad luck to leave with a fire in your belly and nothing else. You sit back down and eat.'

'Ah, at last! Something we can agree on!' Violet resumed her seat gratefully and accepted chopsticks from Li Ling. 'I forgive you for making terrible jokes at my expense.'

'Can you blame us, when you make it so easy?' Charlie quipped.

His grasp of English was clearly coming along rather better than Violet had assumed. She took note.

The group fell into a companionable silence while Violet ate. In her heart, she knew what kept Albert awake: of course, he couldn't bear to lose Violet. But he also believed they'd worked too hard to obtain this life to lose it now. He wanted her to defend herself and retain the life she'd made.

She would go to Nico's. She didn't *want* to. But as she ate, Li Ling and Charlie's pensive stares were enough to convince her. After all, did she want to be the one who shattered the perfect peace of La Maison des Fleurs for everyone?

CHAPTER 3

MADAME CHECKED HER WATCH: it was just after 3 pm. She followed Bunny down the hallway, then paused in shadow at the top of the narrow servants' stairs and watched her niece disappear in the kitchen below. She pulled her velvet kimono jacket around her and nuzzled the soft pile of the collar.

It's just an ordinary day, she told herself. Girls. Drinks. Men. One be-bunioned foot in front of the other. In shoes you regret by 8 pm and have to wear until midnight.

But it was useless to pretend.

You old fool, she scolded herself. You've made a shameful bargain and there's nothing for it now except to look yourself in the eye and admit it. You know what you've done.

She sagged against the wallpaper, a cough escaping her chest in a racking spasm, disturbing her train of thought. She clutched the handkerchief to her mouth, gagging. Come on, she told herself. Get it over with. Let's see the damning evidence.

She crushed the handkerchief in her palm. There would be spots of blood on it, she knew. No need to even look.

But she did, opening the vile linen square in her palm. The scarlet spatter confirmed what she had already guessed: her lungs were getting worse.

Pocketing the handkerchief, she shuddered at the enormous fun the parish gossips would have with the story of her unhappy end. The garish clichés practically wrote themselves. *Ageing Courtesan Perishes from Consumption.* Et cetera.

Look at this place, she thought, taking in her fine surroundings. I should have known I'd never be allowed to get away with a life so well lived. Xiao wasn't the only one who would use her success against her. That venal lot from St Canice's, her very own parish: they'd expect her to suffer. What use was their moral superiority otherwise?

Madame let out a sigh. Maybe this girl of Xiao's was a form of punishment. A rehearsal for the special hell kept for deal-makers, where every day she would be faced with the same question: *Will you turn a blind eye to the suffering of one to protect the others?*

For there was no doubt about Xiao's threat. Refusing to take his frightened girl would have meant certain danger for her and *her* girls.

Now she felt a surge of anger.

After she died, her life would be reduced to a tawdry morality play by those women of the parish and others who disapproved of her; that was to be expected. But what really stung was that she doubted the people who judged her had been forced to make the choices she had. Had they known true fear and desperation? Had they had their own love used against them?

Right now, those parish women were probably doling out soup to the unemployed, smugly quoting psalms while harbouring the petty viciousness and jealousy that rotted a person from the inside out.

'Penitence, my arse,' she muttered aloud, straightening. I'd rather take myself down to Central and lie in front of a train than give the church gossips the satisfaction of claiming me in death, she decided, when they've been so bloody despicable to me in my life.

Hell or no hell.

She trudged downstairs. As arranged, Doc Flanagan was waiting for her in her office, ready to deliver his medical verdict.

Pony up, Peg, she told herself. Here comes more bad news.

—

'Well, Peg, it's not TB.'

Doctor Percival Flanagan Esquire leaned his portly frame forward, pulled a wooden footstool closer to his chair and elevated a stockinged foot with a wince. 'Damned varicose veins!'

His shoes were lined up neatly beside his chair.

You can take the man out of the army, Madame mused. 'Not TB. That's something.' She sat down behind her leather-topped desk and smoothed her fingertips along its cool surface. 'But?'

'Cancer, probably. Wouldn't you rather we go to your suite? Then I could examine you properly.'

'Not today.' She hoped he didn't notice her slight shiver.

Doc Flanagan folded his plump hands across his striped waistcoat. 'We need to send you up to St Vincent's for tests, of course. But look on the bright side. You may as well think of this as your notice of retirement. Your gold watch and your handshake. You've got some money put aside, I assume?'

'Well, fetch me my pipe and slippers, and wheel over the bathchair, why don't you?'

'Come on now, Peg. Don't be like that.'

'Have you seen what it takes to keep this place going?' To be having this conversation today of all days, when the mantle of responsibility felt more like a yoke.

The doctor looked at Madame over his wire-rimmed spectacles. 'You're walking into your grave, pet.'

She opened a drawer in the desk and pulled out a flat half-bottle. 'It was ever thus. Pass me those glasses.'

The doc obliged, reaching for two crystal tumblers on the shelf beside him.

She poured herself a quick nip and knocked it back, then poured them both a second, larger drink. 'Anyway, I have other plans apart from dying.'

'I see. Am I involved in these plans? I sense a trap.'

She passed him his glass. 'I thought I might get meself a car, and you could teach me how to drive it.' She ventured a smile. He was doing his best, and he was a dear friend.

Doc Flanagan took the brandy and laughed, his multiple chins jiggling. 'A car, you say? I knew you had a death wish. Why in the world do you want a car? Where would you go?'

Madame rested her head against the back of the chair. 'Anywhere. That's the point. So, will you teach me?'

'I swore an oath against doing harm!'

'Oh, come on, Perce.'

He laughed. 'Alright. I'd rather like to see you have your road trip.' He raised his glass. 'To anywhere. You can't be unhappy once you've had a chance to take to the open road. This is God's country, this.'

'Oh, come off it—you don't believe in God, Percy Flanagan.'

He hooted with laughter. 'Who says I don't? Might have me a wager in both directions and let the devil take the hindmost!'

Madame stood, drained her glass, went to the window and peered out. 'It mightn't be such a bad thing to escape the city for a while. I've never seen Sydney so down at heel, Perce. So tight in the grip of the gangs. You have to wonder who's pulling the strings. I mean, someone's making a living but it isn't the poor wretches out there.'

Actually, someone's making a *killing*, she thought, the terror on the face of Xiao's girl returning to her mind. She closed her eyes, thankful that her back was still to the doctor.

'Don't be so shocked,' Doc Flanagan said. 'It was greed that drove the stock market into a flamin' spin last year. Greed and speculation. It might be a new decade, but people haven't changed a bit.'

'I still like to believe this is a better world that the one we were born into,' said Madame. You have to believe it, she thought, otherwise what was the point?

Doc reached for his shoes and bent forward over his considerable paunch to lace them. 'Oooft. When did my arms get shorter, eh? Listen, my father was born and raised in a two-room hovel outside of Southampton and my mam not much better. No different to yours, Peg. The only way is up when your beginnings are a dirt floor and stone soup.'

'I s'pose.' She turned back to him, the hot scald of brandy numbing her pleasantly. 'Will you stay for the evening?'

Doc straightened up, puffing from the effort of bending, and wagged a finger. 'Tempt me not! I have an appointment with a dog's eye from the Sail and Anchor.'

'Beef and Guinness?'

'The very one.'

'Well, a doctor must keep his appointments.' She felt such a flush of fondness for the doctor she wanted to reach for him, clutch him to her tightly. Every now and again they risked the odd clinch, but only after a fine night of cocktails and cocaine, when the sun was rising, the parlour was empty at last, and a bleary-eyed embrace with a good friend was just what the doctor—and his patient—ordered.

But in the cold light of day, the image of it almost made her laugh aloud: her bony body, sharp as a bag of elbows, against his short, rounded one. 'Come on, you old goat. I'll show you to the door.'

—◆—

After farewelling the doctor, Madame stepped out the front door and stood on the steps of the building, looking down the street. Watching his bobbing figure amble away, she felt her spirits sink once more. A strangled sob tugged at her throat.

How she longed to sit on the steps. To wrap her arms around her knees and hug herself, like she would have as a girl. To surrender her frame to the stone and to cradle her own sore chest.

But a madame doesn't sit, she thought. A madame doesn't fecking collapse.

The doctor had turned into Five Ways and disappeared from view. Now she watched strangers. Working men trudged home along pavements streaked with afternoon shadows. A lone, hunched pedestrian looked up at her, tipped his hat and walked on, head down.

There, she thought. Some respect. She issued him a wan smile.

Still, a moment later she found herself fighting back tears, wrapping her velvet jacket around her as she watched the trickle of traffic along the path. By 7 pm there would be a crowd of men in the street, all waiting to be admitted, and an electric buzz in the air from their keen anticipation. If you had to have a house of sin on your street, you could do a hell of a lot worse than La Maison des Fleurs. We know our worth here, she thought.

Xiao had complimented her taste, her success. She knew these were veiled threats but he wasn't wrong: hers was the best pleasure house in Sydney. It was truly elegant: a three-storey terrace, smartly painted and boasting flower boxes in every window. In a well-heeled part of Paddington, too, tucked away from all the nastiness occurring in other parts of town. Why, you could hardly take a step in nearby Kings Cross and Darlinghurst without having a cold razor held to your throat.

At La Maison des Fleurs there was singing in the parlour and proper drinks, like champagne and vermouth and crème de cassis. Her girls were spoiled, Madame saw to that. The fine reputation of La Maison des Fleurs meant that she could hold out her gossamer net and catch girls like Violet Kelly who, despite a dazzling academic report from one of the less awful city orphanages, would have been destined for the boneyard—after a downward fall so fast, it'd make the hardiest slum rat brace for impact—had Madame not intervened.

She'd seen it before. A girl's life could be fearfully short.

And there were boys like Albert McAllister, who came in handy for guarding the door of La Maison des Fleurs on weekends and so avoided getting mixed up with the violence in Kings Cross. There were Li Ling and Charlie Han, who had appeared at her back door wearing matching threadbare pants one Sunday, selling perfect radishes and lettuce. They'd stayed on to run the kitchen and scullery and had become beloved members of La Maison's family.

And Bunny, of course. Her ward and niece from her dead sister Martha.

She sighed. It wasn't perfect. You couldn't claim it was Christian charity. But the house was a kind of shelter. Now, if there was a gun battle in Kellett Street, Albert was safe from it. If the magpies pecked the foil tops off the milk bottles on the orphanage step and the lot went sour, then it was hard luck for some kids but not for her Violet. If the fleapits of Surry Hills were lousy with sly grog and slashers, crooked cops and the clap, then Bunny and the rest of them—Susan, Anne, Doris, Elsie, Ruby, Theodora—could count themselves saved. The world of Madame and her charges was a luxurious bubble.

There it is, thought Madame. The point. Life gives you girls like Violet, boys like Albert. People who've been let down, left behind. You give them a future better than they dared to imagine.

Oh, Xiao, she thought. You knew I wouldn't stand to have them put in danger.

The last of the clear afternoon light was leaching away and the street was descending quickly into gloom. Damn Sydney winter, thought Madame. Days shorter than a policeman's temper.

A movement in the gathering darkness opposite, in the recessed entrance outside Petersen's workshop, made her freeze.

Had she imagined it, or was that inky shadow a human shape?

She peered across the street. Again, a tiny movement in the gloom caught her eye: it was as if someone were flattening themselves against the tall doors of the workshop, deep in the shadows.

Madame felt a shudder travel the length of her body. She turned abruptly and went inside, closing the door behind her, feeling the gnawing return to her gut as she pressed her back against the heavy wooden door.

Of course, it made sense that Xiao would have stationed someone to watch over his charge. The idea of unseen eyes gazing at her, judging her, sent a second tremor down her spine. What did the watcher see? Did he read the shame she felt, having accepted Xiao's terms?

What a time to discover someone watching, she thought: at the moment you realise you can no longer look at yourself.

—

With the remaining afternoon customers now dispatched, Madame entered the parlour to find it full of chattering girls seated around Li Ling and a small card table covered in a fringed shawl that was littered with her fortune-telling paraphernalia. The girls, dressed in robes and curlers, pulled cushions onto the floor and surrounded Li Ling, who was enveloped in scented smoke.

Madame hung back in the doorway, watching the scene. Bunny was so excited she could hardly sit still; the girl flitted around collecting the ash from the incense sticks and filling cups with Li Ling's special oolong tea. One by one, Li Ling let the girls select from the pile of tools—her cards, her Cantonese astrology books, her fortune-telling sticks and her book of Chinese proverbs.

Eventually, Bunny spotted Madame in the doorway and beckoned her in. Madame entered the room quietly and perched on the satin stool in front of the piano, clutching her hands to her aching chest.

Her lungs burned and it felt like a punishment. Nausea stopped the breath in her throat. She felt bilious from the sweet incense, and the noise in the parlour threatened to bring on a headache.

But Li Ling and the girls didn't seem to notice her anguish. Madame felt the grip of it release a fraction, amid their chatter and laughter.

Li Ling was patient with the girls, explaining her methods as she went. When Susan's tea-leaves produced a particularly cryptic result, they called out to Charlie, who joined them from the kitchen. He mimed the words neither he nor Li Ling could translate, to much applause. Bunny was laughing so hard she knocked a teacup onto the floor and drenched Ruby's satin slippers.

The incense and brandy had made Madame drowsy. She felt her eyelids growing heavy as the anxiety left her body, leaving exhaustion in its place.

Then Madame heard her name being called. Li Ling was waving her over to the table.

She straightened up, wide awake suddenly. 'Me? Heavens no, Li Ling. Don't take this the wrong way, but I'm afraid your Oriental claptrap isn't for me.'

Bunny pouted. 'That's a bit rude, don't you think? If you asked her, Li Ling would light a candle in St Canice's. Wouldn't you, Li Ling?'

The woman shrugged. 'No harm in a candle. No harm in tea-leaves. No harm in this.' She waved the bamboo tube of numbered sticks.

'Go on, Madame,' said Susan, shaking out her long yellow-blonde hair. 'It's just a bit of fun.'

Grumbling, Madame stood. Around her, the girls' faces were turned up to hers in delighted anticipation, their happiness and excitement causing a pang of sentimental pride.

She crossed the room and sat down. 'Alright, let's have it then.'

She took Li Ling's bamboo tube in her hands and clasped it tightly, focusing her mind on a single question. She shook the tube until a single stick fell to the floor.

Li Ling left her chair and bent to pick up the stick, searching for the number printed on the side. Then she returned to her chair and flicked through the book of 'lottery poems' until she found the corresponding number. Madame saw a cloud of discomfort pass across Li Ling's calm features as she read Madame's poem from her book.

The mother sparrow builds with clay against a storm
The traveller struggles against the driving rain
Her fledglings huddle inside the nest
But the clay melts and falls, all efforts futile.

All efforts futile. The words rang in Madame's head and she suppressed a shiver. Her question had been simple: was the future of La Maison des Fleurs in doubt?

Panic surged in her chest. She stood and smoothed down her wiry hair with clammy palms. 'What a load of nonsense. Sparrows, for pity's sake. Shouldn't you girls be resting? We open at seven sharp, don't forget.'

Clutching her kimono to her, she strode in the direction of her office, sensing Li Ling's eyes on her back.

As she reached the hallway, the Chinese girl's face appeared in her mind once more, the terror staring from her black eyes. A further doubt seized Madame. She had made a deal. But was Xiao's word worth anything—anything at all?

She was overcome by a sudden breathlessness, and panic raced through her like an electrical charge. Gasping, she careened through the hallway and opened the front door. The very last slanting rays of afternoon sun blinded her momentarily and she sucked in a lungful of oxygen.

Her house, her girls. All of it built on a debt that belonged in the past. Was any of it safe, now Xiao was back to collect what he felt he was owed?

CHAPTER 4

AS SHE STEPPED OUT THE front door of La Maison des Fleurs, Violet felt an unexpected chill of apprehension. In the comfort of the kitchen, it had been easy to shrug off the idea of an observer, hidden in the shadows. But as she pulled the heavy wooden door closed behind her, she felt quite disturbed by the notion—so much so that she almost tripped and fell headlong down the front steps in her haste to leave. Perhaps Albert was right, she considered, steadying herself. Perhaps her determination to enjoy life at La Maison *had* deadened her wits.

Whatever the truth of her situation, those eyes on her back— real or imagined—felt as hot as a westerly straight off the Hay Plains. She hurried out of the junction at Five Ways onto Oxford Street, and soon her thoughts were distracted by the world around her. The thoroughfare was alive with traffic and people. Across the road, three men were unloading goods from a square-backed motor van while shouting to one another in a guttural tongue. She stopped to allow a stout pony to pull a cart of boxed cauliflowers across her path and two boys passed her on bicycles, no more than a foot away, causing an eddy of dust and grit to cover her shoes.

She looked about her. It had been a dry winter and the street was windblown. She began to pick her way along the pavement to avoid the knots of ragged yellow grass.

Stepping cautiously, she made her way past an alley where two men were tugging on the reins of an anxious, threadbare horse, whose bony hips protruded through his dusty flanks. The horse's eyes were rolling in terror and pain.

You didn't learn much about horses in a place like St Michael's, but even she could see that the nag would get a bullet before sundown.

She walked on in subdued spirits, past a cluster of ragged children, who were lingering on a corner outside a boarded-up lodging house. She pulled her coat collar more closely to her neck.

The tinkle of a tiny bell announced her arrival as she opened the screen door to Nico's Stanley Street delicatessen and stepped inside, overcome at once by the rich, foreign smell of continental meats and cheeses, and by the throng of people.

The little shop was crowded. The atmosphere was jolly and the conversations loud and convivial. The shelves were ranged with unfamiliar imported foods. She took in the long zinc counter covered in glass domes, the strange dried sausages hanging in clusters from the rafters.

It's me who's out of place here, Violet realised, looking around. Her beaded purse felt slippery in her sweaty hands and her coat began to feel unbearably hot.

She fidgeted among the shoppers in the afternoon crush. The heady smell was making her feel slightly nauseated.

'Nico's got it good,' Albert had told her admiringly. 'He fences for Tilly's mob and for the Lewis brothers, *and* he's got a secret bar above his family's delicatessen in Stanley Street. He's got two mistresses as well as a wife.'

'Listen to you! You're better off making sausages, Albert,' she had said.

'Wait till you meet him, Violet. See if you agree with me then. There's something about him.'

We'll see about that, she thought, eyeing the handsome, dark-haired man behind the counter. With efficient grace, he weaved among the baskets, domes and jars. He reached for items from the shelves behind him, all the while maintaining conversation with his customers. He held up a wheel of cheese and described it to a customer in rapid Italian. The women at the front of the queue were laughing with him. Violet felt Nico's warmth and charisma even at a distance.

One by one, most of the afternoon customers were served and departed with a tinkling of the bell above the door. Violet found herself at the front of a short queue of people. When Nico lifted his face to hers across the zinc counter to ask what she wanted, she replied, as instructed, that her name was Violet and that she was picking up olives for her friend Albert.

Nico's face broke into a smile, revealing beautiful front teeth separated by a charming gap. He grinned across at her, as if selling a gun to a teenage girl was an everyday matter. 'Miss Violet! You wait five minutes? I help you then, no problem.'

She felt his easy charm and wished she could relax, even a little. Albert was right: there was something about him. She withdrew to the shadows at the back of the shop, among the racks of herbs and pots of salted anchovy.

When the last customer was served, Nico locked the door and turned the window sign to *Closed*.

'Come, sit.' He beckoned her to a small wooden table in the front window of the shop, looking out into the parched dust of Stanley Street. She sat as he pulled the green baize blind closed.

'*Un momento,*' he said, returning to the counter. He called out in Italian to someone on the other side of the beaded curtain at the back of the shop. A woman responded, sounding irritated.

Nico returned to the table where Violet waited with a plate of sliced meats, which he described in turn—olive-studded mortadella, luscious salami and fennel-flavoured *ventricina*. From behind the beaded curtain appeared a girl of around ten, with chestnut hair and plump cheeks. She placed a little dish of pickled vegetables and a small loaf of crusty bread in front of Violet.

Nico seized the child and kissed the top of her head. '*Grazie*, Isabella! Now go, play with your sister.' The girl laughed and ran back into the family's quarters behind the curtain.

Nico sat. He began a tender description of how to best enjoy the delicacies before her. Violet listened and accepted the small morsels of food that Nico handed her. As she nibbled apprehensively, she glimpsed a second small and grubby face watching them from behind the wooden bead curtain in the delicatessen. Large dark eyes, a small hand on the doorframe.

'Now. You like coffee?' Nico asked.

She nodded. Her appetite had deserted her.

He returned to the counter and made tiny cups of coffee from his noisy espresso machine. When he returned to the table, he stood behind her chair, placed a little cup before her on the table and dropped a grubby canvas drawstring bag in her lap. Taking a seat, he nodded. 'Open it.'

Under his nonchalant gaze, she unwrapped a dainty pistol, oiled and deadly.

Her hands were clammy and trembling as she lifted it. The gun was heavy for such a small object. She let it fall into her lap and saw that it was very beautiful—in the same way that a racing car or a bird of prey is beautiful. Lethal, spare. Every part of itself turned towards a single purpose.

Nico finished his espresso in a gulp and drew his chair close to hers. Violet's heart hammered in her chest.

He reached forward and, covering her hands with his own, looked into her eyes: 'Every gun must 'ave a name. You will use it to protect your life, so you must honour its strength. First, you name it. Then you begin to understand the power it 'olds over you.'

She withdrew her hands and clasped them primly in her lap so that he would not see them trembling. She was annoyed with Albert for sending her to this man, who treated her like an ignorant child.

'A gun doesn't have power; *I* have power,' she said. 'I'm the person who'll fire it.'

He smiled, lines appearing around his eyes. 'A gun changes things. You must understand that?'

'But I might not use it.'

'True. But now that you have it, you know you *can* use it. You will take this knowledge into every conversation, every argument, every conflict. You don't see this now, but you will come to understand. Can you shoot?'

Violet hesitated. Should she admit she'd never held a gun before, let alone fired one?

'No matter. Meet your Beretta.' Nico pronounced the unfamiliar word with a flourish, then quickly showed her how to clean and store the gun. How to load and how to fire it.

'This tiny gun, when I fire it, I aim for the eye. Bam.' He mimed the action, the weapon held out in front of him and his right eye narrowed. He looked at her squarely. 'But not you. Your 'ands will shake, so it is better you should aim for a big part of the body. You get lucky, you kill your enemy with a bullet in the chest. Better still, your enemy takes a bullet in the gut and dies slowly, 'is insides beside 'im on the floor.'

At this vivid image, Violet felt the blood drain from her face. Nico's shop began to swim before her eyes—again, she felt overpowered by the smells, the sheer heavy truth of the gun. She took a deep breath.

Nico handed her the gun with a sad smile. 'Well, that's it. Ciao, little princess.'

Violet stood hastily, stumbling a little.

Nico stood too, frowning. 'You're upset. I didn't mean to upset you.'

Violet stiffened. 'I'm not upset. I don't really need a gun, you see. I'm just taking precautions.' Damn you Albert, she thought. Damn you and your 'safety'.

'Yes, of course.' Nico nodded.

'I won't fire it. Probably not, anyway.'

'As you say. But the gun is yours now. I do this favour to Albert because he asks it. But I'm a man of peace. It's better to make amends, I believe.'

'Yes.' She pushed the image of the leaking body out of her mind and walked to the door.

'Be safe. Be brave!' Nico called to her as she pushed her way into the evening chill.

Violet left the shop with tears of anger beading in her eyes. Albert had sent her here, to be treated like an idiot, over a gun she didn't even want.

The Beretta was tucked into her coat pocket. She trudged home, feeling Nico's words sink in. I'm in charge, she insisted to herself. I decide what happens! But Nico's words roiled in her mind. *A gun changes things.* Was the gun now written into the script of her life, just as surely as her legs, her hair and the magnificent Rose Room?

Nevertheless, her distaste for the gun didn't stop her ruminating on the name she would choose for it. Still distracted, she stopped at the pub on the corner to pick up a bottle of stout and left, instead, with a bottle of Resch's lager. As Violet waited to collect a portion of chips at a fish shop to share with Bunny, she was so distracted, the lad had to wave the paper parcel before her eyes.

When the name came to her, it was as if the gun itself had suggested it.

Sister Philomena had introduced Violet to the legend of Artemis. The nun, blue eyes round at the prospect of being caught straying from the curriculum, had pressed a battered book of Greek mythology into Violet's hands, the relevant pages dog-eared for reference. A goddess of women and nature, the Sister had whispered; a girl who fought for other girls. It was important to learn the pagan gods, she said, in a louder voice meant for the whole class, should one be called upon to indict them.

Violet knew that Albert was prone to seeing threats where there were none. He was alert to dangers that Violet believed were figments of fantasy. But in one sense he was right: one can hunt or be hunted.

She would name the beautiful weapon Artemis. The hunter.

—◆—

Back at La Maison, Violet took the back entrance via the laneway that ran along the side of the building. She trotted up the kitchen steps and stepped into the kitchen. Finding the kitchen empty, she deposited the chips and beer on the table and took the servants stairs to the first floor. Then she walked quietly along the hallway to the Rose Room, hoping to avoid the other girls, and, taking the gun from her pocket, shoved it into a drawer of her dressing table.

There, she said to herself, it's done. Now Albert can calm down and with any luck the horrid thing'll stay exactly where it is until I retire a fat and wealthy woman.

With a sigh of relief, she replaced her kitten heels with slippers, then returned to the kitchen.

Li Ling had left the kitchen's Kookaburra stove alight and, with a little encouragement, Violet managed to get it blazing. It was nearing 6 pm and the doors were still closed to guests but, nevertheless, she heard laughter coming from the parlour next door.

Violet jumped as the door to the parlour flew open and Bunny pushed her way in, arms full of cake plates.

'Where'd you disappear to?' asked Bunny, sliding the stack of plates onto the draining board beside the sink.

Violet tore open the newspaper parcel of chips then flipped the lid on the cold bottle of Resch's and took a long pull. 'Had to see a man about a dog. What's going on in there?'

'Li Ling's telling fortunes.'

Violet bit her lip as she remembered Albert's troubling message about the spy on the street. 'Anything about bad times ahead?'

'Nope. Mostly just porkies about tall, handsome strangers.'

'There's a shortage of them. Good grief, sometimes there's nothing so perfectly perfect as a cold beer.' Violet took another swig then pushed the bottle across the table towards Bunny. She was so thankful to be home, to put the uncomfortable ordeal of Nico behind her, that she felt suddenly elated.

Bunny took the bottle gratefully and sat. 'But I'm only thirteen and all of married life's surprises have been spoiled for me!' she squeaked, in a perfect echo of Madame's Irish-tinted French.

Violet laughed, a little more of the afternoon's worries lifting from her shoulders. Standing, she stretched her arms above her head. It was time she bathed and prepared herself for the night's activities. 'I really ought to get upstairs. You can have the rest of the chips.'

'I can't eat all these!' Bunny glanced at the clock above the stove. 'You've got ten minutes to spare. We could take a quick look?' She picked up the newspaper from the table and waved it.

Violet hesitated, then resumed her seat and accepted the beer bottle back. 'Oh, alright. Quickly, though, before Madame comes in.'

'Oh, don't worry about her. Her knickers'll untwist once she's started on her evening brandies.'

Violet snorted with laughter, and beer shot from her nostrils. She wiped her face with the back of her hand. 'I suppose we could be working for a real dragon. You know, some hatchet-faced matron. Yes ma'am, no ma'am. Emptying ladies' chamber-pots and the like.'

'Or we could be wiping creepy old men's arses.'

'Or selling our own teeth.'

'Or cutting off our own legs so we can beg.' Bunny seized the bottle and took another swig.

Violet laughed but knew it was true: they were lucky.

When Bunny's mother Martha had died, she would have been left to fend for herself without Madame. The girl was another outcast. She'd been raised in a strict Christian household in Bathurst and taught to abhor her degenerate aunt. It didn't stop the girl turning up here, looking for work, after selling her mother's few possessions and buying a ticket to the big smoke.

'It's fine. No man'll want me, not with this,' she'd told Violet, pointing to her lip, spilt to the septum and fleshy as a wound.

So, Madame had been convinced to let Bunny earn her keep, as a part of the machinery in the background of La Maison des Fleurs. She helped Charlie Han to fix things and lent Li Ling a hand in the kitchen. She stripped beds, replaced towels and filled buckets with ice for champagne. As far as Violet was concerned, Bunny was living proof that *everyone* had a place in the rather perfect world of La Maison des Fleurs.

Violet felt the sudden urge to celebrate her good fortune. Putting Albert's discomfiting assertion about the spy to the back of her mind, she got to her feet, brandishing the beer bottle. 'Come on, let's make a toast.'

'Who to?'

'To Madame. To La Maison des Fleurs. To the men of Sydney, who pay our way.'

'Cheers! And now let's read the paper.' Ceremoniously, Bunny unfolded the classified section of the newspaper on the wooden tabletop.

Violet sat and stuffed four chips into her mouth then wiped her hands on a tea towel. 'Well?' As usual, she was impatient for a very particular sort of news.

'Hold yer horses.' Bunny turned to the inside back page, with its list of births, deaths and marriages.

Violet tapped her foot and gnawed a fingernail impatiently. Bunny had no idea that the daily local newspaper, with its reports of hatchings and matchings, stabbings and funerals, was a lifeline of information: information that might one day reveal details about her sister, who was, at this moment, *locus incognita*.

One of these days, I'll tell Bunny about Iris, she promised herself. Keeping a secret so important went against the grain when she and Bunny shared so much. But how would she explain her sister's terrible act, the true reason they were parted?

Oh, belt up, she told herself crossly, watching Bunny scan the newspaper. You sound like a character from a penny novelette.

But the thoughts came creeping back: was Iris sitting in a pretty room, reading the newspaper, searching for her sister? Was she the head of a smart household, admired by a dashing husband for her cleverness, her kindness, her fine manners? Was she a model citizen, fair and wise? Violet hated to admit it, but she wanted to know. Desperately.

Madame tottered in and sank into a seat at the table, letting her French phrasebook fall into her lap. Violet braced for a bad-tempered sideswipe, but Madame only rolled her eyes when she saw Bunny with the open newspaper.

'Oh, for crying out loud, Violet,' Madame said. 'You should just tell us who you're looking for. Every day it's the same. Who is it you're so keen to find?'

Violet blinked in surprise. Was she so obvious? 'Who says I'm looking for someone?' She tried to hide the flush of embarrassment that came over her by snatching the phrasebook up from Madame's lap to fan herself. 'Gosh, it's hot in here.'

Madame shrugged. 'Orphanage girls are always looking for someone. And if you wanted news, you'd read the *Herald*.'

Violet took another handful of chips and snuck a glance at Madame. The older woman's eyes bore the telltale glaze of an afternoon tipple. 'You've got me all wrong, Madame. I'm just here for the scandal and gossip.'

Bunny shushed her excitedly. 'Wait up, here's a local marriage.'

'Tell us!'

Bunny read aloud: '*Iris and Walter Bourke of St Catherine's parish Waverley announce their wedding.* Oh. Held last Saturday.'

Violet gave a start. 'Did you say Iris? Does it say anything else? Give it here.' She dropped the phrasebook, seized the paper and scanned the page. The recently married Iris was twenty-five years old. Not her sister, then.

She handed the paper back, making sure to hide her disappointment.

Madame gave a peremptory sniff. 'If they're Waverley Bourkes, they might be Ulster Bourkes. Protestants. Nasty. Give us a chip.' She helped herself, then continued: 'I don't know what you're up to, Violet, but if you decide to approach these people, you'd better take Albert with you. Be on the safe side, pet. There are all kinds of unpleasant types out there.'

'I'm not up to anything, I swear.'

'Well, mind yourself. Think about everything you've already got, before you go around chasing phantoms.' These words were spoken with such conviction that Violet opened her mouth to reply, then changed her mind.

Bunny sent a quizzical glance her way. Violet shrugged in response.

Warily, Bunny pushed the last of the chips towards her aunt. 'There are plenty of perfectly nice people in the world too, Aunty. Just think how lucky we are to have found each other!'

Madame stirred from contemplation and raised her head. 'Lucky indeed.'

'You're in a strange mood today,' her niece observed. 'Would you like me to rub your feet?'

This did the trick.

'Hell's teeth, Bunny, do you want a clip around the ear? You should know by now I can't bear to have anyone touch my feet.'

Bunny giggled, sliding Violet a triumphant glance. Nothing returned Madame to herself faster than a poke in the dignity.

Madame stood up, took the phrasebook from Violet's lap and frowned down at them. 'I'm tired is all. You girls don't know what it's like to be in charge.' She turned to Violet. 'You'd better get your evening dress on, *cherie.*'

She was using her French: break time was over.

Madame coughed into her handkerchief. Violet saw a flicker of pain crease the older woman's brow for a moment. Was she ill? Could that be the reason for her strange behaviour?

'As for you, Bunny,' Madame continued, 'I want you to get one of them roses from the vase in the drawing room and put it in Violet's hair. And you can bring a pot of cha to my office in half an hour. *Adieu.*' She sashayed out.

Madame might have her moods, but Violet knew that Madame's defiant swagger said: *I am still in control of things, thank you very much.*

———

Bunny drew Violet's bath in the Rose Room and launched into a breathless description of the funeral procession she'd seen that morning.

'You should've seen the brass on the horses,' Bunny said. 'And the coffin, Violet—it was a tiny white one. For a kid, you know? I felt a shudder go right through me! The poor, poor thing . . . There was a giant pile of flowers in the back of the cart, and they kept falling into the road, leaving this terrible white trail. And you should've heard the wails of the mother in the open carriage behind the hearse. Honestly, the whole thing gave me the creeps.'

Violet sat on the edge of the bath, only half-listening, observing Bunny as the girl opened new bottles of bath scent one by one.

Bunny offered a bottle to Violet. 'How about this one? Oil of orange and cloves.'

Violet screwed up her nose. 'A bit Christmassy. I'll reek like a boiled pudding. What else is there?'

'Rose. Lavender.' Bunny squinted at the smeared labels.

'Let's have a bit of both. Then scarper if you want to get a rest.'

Bunny stood and wiped her hands on her apron. 'Thanks, Vi. I'm half dead from the early starts this week.' She pointed to a beautiful gown laid out on the bed. 'Your pink chiffon. And I haven't forgotten about the rose. I'll be back to put your hair up in twenty minutes. Don't get it wet.'

'I won't, I promise!'

Bunny closed the door quietly behind her. Violet slipped into the bath, the hot water sending a pleasant thrill along her spine. She closed her eyes and slipped lower, until the aromatic bathwater filled her ears and cancelled the murmuring sounds of the house. In the echoing underwater, she heard her own heartbeat thud.

Madame's words came drifting back. *Orphanage girls are always looking for someone.*

It was true, of course. Every morning, when Violet woke in the beautiful Rose Room, she wondered if today she would read a newspaper notice that told her where Iris had gone. Every evening before dressing, she wondered if tonight she would meet a man who looked her over and exclaimed that she looked just like another girl he knew—Iris the schoolmistress or Iris the greengrocer or Iris the banker's wife.

Iris was the missing glove, the lost earring, the dropped knitting needle. The absent half.

As the heat of the bathwater loosened her thoughts, Violet's mind wandered to the gun, heavy and cool in her dressing-table drawer. If a gun changes everything, she wondered, does that mean it changes me? Unbidden, an image flitted into her mind of her aiming the gun at her sister, as if shooting an evil version of herself.

Admit it, she thought. You hate Iris. And you miss her like a maimed soldier misses a limb.

Violet gave a sigh. There were men outside waiting to be entertained, so she climbed out of the bath, stood on the Turkish rug and dried herself slowly, enjoying the deep pile of one of Madame's bath sheets. Then she sat before the dresser and applied cream to her face, followed by face powder that made her skin glow. She painted her eyes with dark Indian kohl, bought from Paddy's Markets. She drew an arched line along the top of each eyebrow. Then she applied red lipstick, being careful around the edges. Lastly, she curled her eyelashes with Vaseline, just like Madame taught her.

She batted her eyes coquettishly at her reflection then stood and began rummaging in the top drawer for underwear.

She pulled out a pale and frothy silk garment and held it against her body, eyeing herself in the mirror. Was her sister wearing silk and furs? Pearls and powder?

It didn't pay to dwell—not when downstairs there were crisp banknotes in rich men's pockets, ready to be unfolded.

She rustled into her ivory slip. Every banknote she pocketed was a message to her thieving sister: *You didn't win.*

CHAPTER 5

THE AFTERNOON SHADOWS HAD LONG ago stretched into darkness and the watcher was cold. The street outside La Maison des Fleurs was suddenly still. The watcher knew this to be the halting moment between the end of the day and the start of the night's entertainment. In ten minutes or so, men would begin to file into the street to wait for the doors to open.

It was time to go.

The idea of spying on La Maison des Fleurs, disguised in a digger's coat and hat, had seemed a good one. In reality, the ground was chilly beneath bare feet and it was difficult to stand still for so long. A spell of fidgeting had already caused the tall, nervous woman in charge of the place to peer a little too intently into the shadows that afternoon. No, it wasn't a perfect plan; far from it.

But it had some merits. Information, to be exact.

Things the watcher could tell the woman in charge.

The woman in charge didn't know that the same man who had tipped his hat to her, causing her to smile and straighten with pride, had now paced the street six times. Three times north and, returning, three times south, his hat pulled down to cover the razor scars on his face. Scars that told you straight away the company he kept.

The woman didn't know that the black saloon car returned every hour or so to take the man's reports of the comings and goings at La Maison des Fleurs.

And the woman didn't know that the man had approached the littlest girl, the sweet brown-haired one with the bung lip, as the girl had emptied ash from a saucer into the drain beside the front step.

He'd seen the girl from the corner and quickened his pace to intercept her. Stepping up, nice as you like, he'd asked the girl for a light. She'd smiled and handed him a box of matches from her apron pocket, then pointed to the dusk sky, where the bats swooped overhead, following the sunset. The girl's laugh had tripped like water over stone: easy, natural.

He had followed her gaze, squinting at the flying creatures.

'Keep the Redheads, mate,' the girl had said. 'I got loads more inside.'

The man's fingers gripped the matchbox; his eyes were hooded under his hat.

Oh, some things could make you colder than a flagstone floor.

And did the woman in charge know that Violet had sneaked out that afternoon, running off in her fancy shoes? Probably not.

But the watcher knew.

She knew that Violet had snuck back in via the laneway, wearing the same furtive look that she'd had when she left. That meant Violet had a secret.

She knew that right now Violet was in her room, dressing for the night ahead. And she suspected, from the way the strange man in the hat behaved, that the whole place was in some sort of trouble.

Which is just what my lousy sister deserves, Iris decided.

CHAPTER 6

BY 7 PM, THE FRONT PARLOUR of the La Maison was alive with the hum of voices and the strains of Susan and Anne attempting a duet on Madame's upright Beale piano.

Violet stood in the doorway and surveyed the scene. She spotted redheaded Ruby at the bar and crossed the room to join her friend.

Ruby could balance on her hands while her elegant feet dangled over her head. She could stand on the tiptoes of one foot and twirl a silver hoop above her head on the tip of the other. She'd come to La Maison after missing her berth on the train to join Ashton's Circus in Broken Hill—a mishap that made Violet's heart glad. Ruby was supple as a stripling and soft as butter, and prone to demonstrating these qualities while not wearing so much as a stitch.

Ruby greeted Violet with a Chinese bow, hands clasped in prayer, followed by a voluptuous squeeze and a kiss on the lips.

She stepped back and smoothed her dress, a scarlet cheong-sam. 'Do you like it? It's from Li Ling's sister in Shanghai. We had to unpick the darts at the front to get these in.' She squeezed her breasts with a peal of laughter.

Violet smiled. 'I love it. This dress is so tight I'm walking like a man in shackles. By the way, I heard that the circus sent an agent to get you back.' It was Violet's favourite tease.

'Yes. Alas, the beard gave her away,' Ruby replied. 'I heard that the orphanage sent a nun to get you back.'

'Yes, but the beard gave her away.'

They laughed, foreheads pressed together.

Ruby pulled away and slapped a palm to her cheek. 'Drat! Can you do martinis? Regular Edgar claimed to be gagging for one and that was ten minutes ago. If we don't hurry, the poor man'll expire before his thirst is quenched.'

Regular Edgar: he was ninety if he was a day, yet he showed up every night at the door of La Maison des Fleurs at seven on the dot. Rumour had it that he was some by-blow of a remnant British aristocrat, exiled to New South Wales to see out his dwindling days far from prying eyes. The girls fussed over him as if he were a loyal Labrador who, after years of service, deserved a comfortable decline. This week, he appeared to be enjoying Ruby's numerous charms. Violet surveyed the room for him; Edgar acknowledged her with a doddering wave from the chesterfield banquette beside the piano.

Violet took the gin bottle from Ruby with a wink. 'Can I make a martini? Does the pope wear a dress, darling?'

She measured spirits into the cocktail shaker. Susan and Anne reached a shrill crescendo, prompting applause from the floor.

Madame's taste for luxury and excess was nowhere more evident than in La Maison des Fleurs' parlour. In each of the four corners of the room stood an enormous urn, filled with peacock feathers and bird of paradise stems. Elegant palms flanked the glass doors that led to the hallway and the stairs. The walls were draped with long silk panels that were gathered into swags and knotted with strands of glass beads. Against the walls were elegant polished-leather banquettes. Atop the piano sat a gilded birdcage with a matched pair of budgerigars, Dido and Aeneas.

The parlour lamps were in the latest Art Deco style and imported from France: each one featured a different bronze nude carrying a rounded glass orb. Large cushions and rugs were dotted around the floor. Madame's girls lay draped on couches; they languished on love seats with their legs entangled; they were propped on the laps of guests. Smoke from Major Davidson's pipe lent a pleasant haze to the scene.

Ruby nudged her. 'See that handsome gent in the corner by the palm? That's Hector Poulos, also known as Helena. Hector wears a suit and a moustache and drives his companion Betty up and down George Street.'

'No!'

'True story. He has a leather whatsit too. The girls say you can't hardly tell the difference.'

'Never!'

'Scout's honour.' Ruby pinched Violet's cheek. 'You convent girls! So delightfully naive.'

They smirked at each other. Violet handed an olive-bedecked martini to Ruby with a flourish and scanned the crowded parlour. Major Davidson appeared to be acting out a hunting expedition for Elsie and Doris with the inanimate assistance of one of the elegant palm trees.

Madame appeared by Violet's side. Her face seemed pinched and pale.

'You alright?' Violet asked. 'Maybe the doc can give you something for that chest.'

'Concern yourself with your own chest, Violet Kelly.'

Violet wriggled in her constricting satin dress. 'Oh, believe me, I am. Thanks to this dress I think I've stopped breathing altogether. I can't wait to get out of it.'

'That's lucky, because your half-past-seven appointment has arrived. Philip Chandler, Englishman. Diplomat or what-have-you. So offer him something clever. Poetry recitation. Painting.' She waved her hand distractedly. 'You know.'

'Painting? Blimey.' Violet raised a pencilled eyebrow. 'We really do cater for all tastes here.' As far as art was concerned, a convent education barely stretched beyond arranging the flowers for Sunday mass.

Madame patted her arm unsteadily. 'Champagne's in a bucket on the bar. I'll be in my office if anyone needs me.'

Violet turned and eyed the crowd, looking for her illustrious visitor. Her gaze alighted on a tall man wearing a very fine cream linen suit. He was waiting at the bar, holding a pair of champagne glasses. His dark hair was a little longer than was usual and fell across his forehead.

He was handsome, damn it. She felt a shock of pure desire as she caught his eye and he returned her gaze. Then he raised his hand and waved.

So. Philip Chandler. Violet composed herself and approached him. Slipping into her accustomed role was as easy as slipping a hand into a silk glove.

On reaching him, she said, 'Goodness, are *both* of those glasses for me? I hope so, because I'm parched.' She took the glasses.

He smiled. 'It is rather good champagne.'

'My point exactly. If you're lucky, I'll save you a drop.'

He cocked his head to one side and appraised her again. She felt an unaccustomed flush rising in her cheeks.

'That's good, because I'm feeling lucky,' he said. His eyes were pale blue. Did they actually just twinkle?

She caught the end of his tie between her fingers and leaned in. 'Madame suggested I bowl you over with my skill in recitation, but I can only do Wordsworth. Not exactly a heart starter.'

'Recitation is an excellent idea.' He affected seriousness. 'I'm a fan of good diction. But Wordsworth? Are you planning to bore me rigid?'

Violet rolled her eyes at the double *entendre*. She took the champagne glasses, momentarily pressing close enough to his linen pleated trousers so that their thighs touched. She felt his hand slide around her hip to skim her *derrière*.

'Fortunately for you, I also know some edifying limericks,' she said. 'Shall we?'

Philip Chandler followed Violet from the room, holding a silver ice bucket in one hand and maintaining the lightest hold on her fingertips with the other.

She reached the foot of the stairs and turned to face her customer, only to find his face—his lips—were inches from her own.

She raised a warning finger. 'I'm afraid kissing isn't—'

'Of course. Forgive me. But we're not kissing.' His gaze travelled the outline of her cheekbone, her jaw, her mouth. He didn't move.

'We should go upstairs.' Violet was finding it increasingly difficult to keep a clear head and she couldn't yet blame the champagne.

Philip took the glasses from her hands, his gaze finishing its long slow journey around the contours of her face before meeting her eye. A faint smile. 'Why Violet?'

She blinked at the question, drawing away slightly. 'Pardon?'

'Why Violet? I mean, why did you choose Violet as your parlour name?'

She felt unexpectedly exposed. Should she be sharing intimacies with a virtual stranger? Worse—should she admit that she *wanted* to?

'Violet is my real name,' she said. She leaned close to Philip and kissed him softly on the lips. If you were going to break the rules, it was smart to do it in the darkened hallway where Madame couldn't see you.

He drew in a sharp breath, his eyes still fixed on hers. Then he laughed. 'Oh dear. Miss Violet, I think—metaphorically speaking, of course—that your slip is showing.'

She stiffened. '*Au contraire*, Mr Chandler. What you've failed to understand is that I'm in complete control of who sees my slip and when it is seen. And don't for a second believe that I can be shamed out of enjoying myself.'

Was there something new in his gaze? Warmth, perhaps?

'I would never attempt such a thing,' he said. 'I take back the tease. I'm at your command.'

'Then we understand each other.' She turned and proceeded up the stairs.

There were rules, and the rules were important. Yet, she mused as she climbed the stairs, acutely aware of Philip Chandler behind her, some rules were more important than others.

The rules had a purpose, and that purpose was protection. In the peach-tinted light of the Rose Room, however, she found herself turning to stare at him again: his smooth face, his broad shoulders. Her resolve appeared to be deserting her once more.

She guessed he must be twenty-five. Judging by the weight of his solid gold cufflinks and the expensive cut of his suit, he was as rich as Croesus. And then there was his accent.

He strode over to a small table by the window and placed the glasses and the champagne bucket down. The window offered up a smudged view of the oily night sky. He poured foaming champagne into a flute and handed it to her.

Violet took it, sat on the bed and began to unbutton her shoes. He hurried over. 'Oh! Wait.'

He took a sip from his brimming glass then, placing it on the floor beside him, kneeled on the carpet with loose-limbed ease. 'Let me do that.'

Carefully, he unbuttoned the first white patent-leather shoe and slipped it slowly from her stockinged foot. He turned it around in his hands as if it were a priceless Ming vase.

'Magnificent,' he declared, his eyes full of amusement. He kissed the shoe in mock reverence. 'If only it had a companion. But wait—it does! What providential luck!'

He placed the first shoe on the floor and began to unbutton the second one, smiling wickedly.

Violet stuck out her chin a little and pursed her lips. 'You know, I can actually be quite serious when it comes to shoes,' she said, with maximum hauteur. 'These beauties in particular.'

He took the second shoe in his hands, slipped it from her foot and held it up with the first, frowning at them studiously. 'You're absolutely right, Violet of La Maison des Fleurs. These shoes are no laughing matter. I would challenge any man who says otherwise. I am, in fact, a sworn defender of the footwear realm.'

'Is that so?'

'It is. I took a solemn vow in my youth. I've actually fought duels over footwear. Killed a man with a stiletto over a—'

'A pair of stilettos?'

'It was a matter of honour.' He drew a line across his throat with the heel of her shoe.

'You be careful with that,' she said.

Taking the shoe from his hand, she kissed him. Properly this time. Tonight, the rules can go hang, she thought as he returned her kiss.

She opened her eyes but kept her lips against his. 'Are you staying just for the hour?'

He kissed her again. 'That's a very bad idea, isn't it?'

'A very bad idea,' she repeated.

—

An hour later, Violet opened the door and took another bottle of champagne and another ice bucket from Bunny's silver tray, nudging the Rose Room door closed with her foot. The diplomat sat up, tossing aside the rumpled sheets and revealing his pleasing naked form.

She lingered a foot away from the bed. It was a pity—nay, a crime—to squander such a sight.

'Where does your Madame get her marvellous plonk? I should tell the embassy,' Philip said, stretching muscled arms above his head.

She hefted the ice bucket against a bare hip and crossed the room. 'No idea. Half the grog in Sydney's illegal, I know that much for sure. For all I know, these bubbles fell off the back of a cart on their way to the home of the Governor-General himself.' She flashed him a grin and handed him the bottle.

'I'm shocked, my dear. To think they told me this was a decent place.' He popped the cork, poured fizz into their glasses and handed her one.

'Mostly respectable, but never decent.' She slid into the bed beside him, balancing her glass with care. She aimed the pointed tip of her tongue at the whorl of his ear but, sensing her, he turned and surprised her with a soft, rather chaste kiss that sent an unexpected pang through her heart.

How was this man able to disarm her so completely? It was unnerving. Unwanted yearning stirred in her heart again and she squirmed to be free of it. It didn't pay to be tempted by a deeper connection with a man like the one beside her in the bed. Better, as Ruby put it, to keep things gymnastic.

Yet it was hard to maintain her vigilance against connection when she felt such a heavy languor, a delicious velvety calm, stealing over her body. Drowsily, she sank lower and rested her head against his chest, where his free hand rested, and idly examined the rings on his fingers.

His hands were square and expressive, the fingers long. A wedding band, she noted. Well, that was to be expected.

She reached for a small gold ring with a carved inset of onyx, which adorned his little finger. She twisted it between her fingers. 'What's this one?'

He placed his champagne glass on the bedside table then slipped off the ring and placed it in her palm. 'See the engraving? That's our family seal.'

'A seal? Settle down, Rockefeller.'

'Oh, let me tell you the story. My great-grandfather Silas made a packet selling pig iron to the British railways. Bought land and a title off some mad, syphilitic earl.'

'You can do that?' she broke in. 'Buy titles?'

He shrugged. 'As we both know, just because you're not *allowed* to do something doesn't mean it never happens.'

'Quite right.' She sank a fraction lower, allowing a little more of her body weight to rest on his fine, long torso. It was lovely to listen to rumble of his voice inside the cage of his ribs.

He continued. 'I think the earl had to adopt my great-grandfather or something. Anyway, Silas wanted all the things a noble gent should have, so he commissioned this.'

She studied the engraving on the flat onyx disc, frowning. 'It's a sword and a shield.'

He shrugged. 'See? Pig iron maker. Not an ounce of imagination.'

She handed him the ring, then twisted to face him, her cheek against the fine hair on his chest. 'So let me guess: you grew up in a castle and everybody had to call you "sir". They made you wear dresses until you were five. You cried when they sent you off to boarding school because they wouldn't let you take your favourite polo pony.'

'Oh, so close! My great grandfather left an absolute fortune—'

'I knew it.' She thumped his chest.

'Ah, but wait. The family fortunes were fine until they landed in the hands of my mother and father. She lost all the cash by gambling with the true aristocracy. That lot have had generations to perfect their cheating. *He* drowned in the bath after a bottle of navy rum and a vigorous caning from his mistress.'

'No!'

'All true. Mama was carted off after she threw herself out the drawing room window and only succeeded in breaking her ankles. After she died, I was brought up by aunts. School paid for by the church. Spat on by the real posh boys, despised by anyone who was actually born to rule.'

'See? I read you like a book.'

'Your powers are uncanny.'

'Actually, that's a terrible story. I'm sorry.' She gave him a squeeze.

He wrapped his arms around her, resting his chin on the top of her head. 'Don't you want to know how the story ends, though?'

'Let me guess: *Depraved diplomat dies from heart attack in boudoir of sought-after* fille de joie?'

'*Fille de joie*? Now you're just showing off.'

'It's how I pays the bills.'

'Also note: I'm not dead yet. You're good but not that good.'

'How dare you! Alright, tell me the rest of the story.'

He kissed the top of her head. 'It turns out the miserly aunts had invested in a little venture called the East India Company. After they died, I inherited everything. So if there's a moral, it's that you just never bloody know when fortune's going to favour you.'

'Says the stinking rich man.'

'But true nevertheless, my flower.'

She traced a finger along his collarbone. 'So, you've travelled the world?'

'Some of it, yes.'

'And you've been to the Orient?'

'Well, yes, I've travelled the Subcontinent. And China.'

'I expect you've seen certain texts, then. Certain sacred, illustrated texts, shall we say.'

'Oh, you mean *those* kind of texts.'

'Exactly.' She unwrapped herself from his embrace and settled her head on the silk pillowcase, stretching luxuriously. 'So . . . why don't you impress me with your knowledge of foreign parts?'

—

Violet woke early the next morning and lay still, her eyes closed and her lips tingling from last night's kisses.

Philip Chandler had stayed for nearly four hours, by which time they were both quite exhausted, from the thrill of repartee as much as from pleasure. They drank a quantity of champagne too—that accounted for her current headache and her dry mouth. She had dismissed him with a fervent kiss at La Maison's back door. Four hours. What a delectable ordeal.

Ruby, passing them in the hall, had issued an undignified howl as she observed Violet kissing Philip as she pushed him out the door.

'Steady on, Violet, he's not paying to take your tonsils out,' Ruby called. Ruby, it could be said, didn't show much regard for *any* of the rules.

Rolling to one side, Violet now wrapped her arms around her chest and tried to conjure the previous evening's pleasant feelings, to hang on to the sensation as long as possible.

It hadn't been easy to rejoin the flowers in the noisy parlour after such an unexpected pleasure. When Violet returned downstairs, Madame was nowhere to be seen. The crowd was on the verge of becoming rowdy. Albert had taken up his usual position in the hallway and, at Violet's signal, he performed a few subduing laps of the room until the hubbub died down a little.

At midnight, Violet had found herself marshalling a tipsy Ruby and Anne upstairs with a pair of country boys who were rather the worse for wear from a night at the Randwick race-track. Given the sorry absence of a sober force among them, how the four of them managed business was a story she would extract from Ruby in due course.

Then she herself was called upon to spend a tedious hour with the retired principal of a South Coast school who needed every minute of that time to overcome his crippling shyness.

At 2 am she performed a striptease, with all the vigour and sauce she could muster, for a cheerful unit of off-duty firemen who tipped her generously and told Madame, who had reappeared, that poor Violet looked done in and wasn't it time they all went home to bed?

Now Violet sat up in bed to reach for a glass of water, thinking once again of Philip's teeth against her neck, his fingers in her hair . . .

'Christ on a bike!' Violet shrieked.

Bunny was sitting on the end of her bed, her face sunk in misery.

Violet shook her head and groaned. 'Jesus, Bunny, I was flat out like a lizard drinking until past three. I'm bushed! If you're getting in, get in.'

She lifted the blankets so that Bunny could crawl into the bed and draw some of the warmth. The poor girl's ice-cold feet tangled themselves in Violet's.

'Heck, you're bloody freezing.'

Bunny gave a sniff. 'There's something.'

'Something what? And this better be good if you're spoiling my shut-eye.'

'Something I found. I need to tell you.'

'Well, out with it then.' Violet sat up reluctantly and faced the girl.

Bunny lay still for a moment. Then she wriggled into a sitting position. 'Li Ling mended Madame's broderie anglaise pillowcase yesterday, so I thought I'd just pop up and put it on the spare bed in Madame's rooms this mornin'. You know how Aunty likes to keep that room nice? Anyway'—she took a deep breath—'I don't know what it means, but Madame's got a girl up there. A Chinese girl, all covered in tattoos. And that's not all.' Now Bunny's lip quivered and tears sprang into her eyes. 'She's chained to the bedpost in the spare room, scared as a whipped dog.'

CHAPTER 7

VIOLET PUT HER FINGERS TO her lips and paused on the landing. Bunny, seeing the gesture, nodded and halted behind her.

At the end of an ordinary night, Madame could be expected either to select a bed partner from among the suitors who presented themselves, or she would take herself to bed with a pipe of opium from the Chinese merchants down at the docks.

Let's hope that whichever she chose, she's now fast asleep, thought Violet.

They tiptoed up the stairs to Madame's apartments on the top floor. As they went, Violet racked her brains to remember which of Madame's suitors had been present last night.

Bunny bit her thumbnail and whispered as they climbed, 'What about Vito from the Sail and Anchor?'

'Nope.'

'Hmm. That Mickey Munro or his brother? Or Gary the Knife?'

'No. And no.'

It was useless. For Violet, much of the previous night was a blur, especially when you factored in the hours with Philip Chandler. She felt another twinge, which was followed closely by a guilty shiver. Perhaps she ought to give herself a refresher on Madame's rules. The old girl might be tricky but she knew how to go the distance in a tough business.

They reached the locked door to Madame's private rooms. Bunny rummaged for the ring of keys in her apron pocket.

Violet nodded encouragement. 'If she wakes up, we'll tell her we found a leak in the Rose Room ceiling and we came to check. Couldn't have the roof caving in, could we?'

Bunny nodded. They pushed their way through the door as quietly as possible, entering Madame's private sitting room.

They needn't have worried: Madame was sprawled on the divan in her sitting room, out like a light—alone—with the opium pipe beside her. Glowing embers in the grate indicated she'd been up until dawn.

'With any luck she'll sleep till the afternoon,' Bunny whispered. 'This stuff doesn't usually wear off fast.'

Violet nodded. 'Cross fingers, eh?'

They clasped hands and hurried through to the hallway beyond, casting nervous backward glances at the figure on the divan. Violet gave silent thanks for the carpet underfoot.

The first door off the hallway led to Madame's sleeping quarters—her bedroom, bathroom and dressing room. Beyond that was the second, smaller room, reserved for guests.

They stopped in front of the door.

'Come on, let's have a look, shall we?' Violet sounded braver than she felt.

She turned the door handle slowly. A muffled cry came from

inside the room, making the hairs on Violet's arms stand on end. She exchanged a wide-eyed glance with Bunny. Cautiously, they stepped into darkness, to the dreadful sound of a body—a person, a real live person—scurrying to the furthest corner of the room, accompanied by the awful clanking of chain.

Bunny swore and fumbled for the light switch.

Blinking in the sudden harsh burst of light, Violet and Bunny stared into the room. There was a prisoner, just as Bunny had said. She was fixed by a single manacle to a post at the head of the iron bed.

Violet gasped and several thoughts spun and coalesced at once. The girl in the far corner of the room was the most beautiful creature Violet had ever seen; yet she was brutally manacled by her wrist and weighed down by a heavy chain at her throat—like a Canaanite slave in Violet's colour-plate edition of the Old Testament.

The implications of the scene rushed at her: what God-awful trouble had Madame got herself into?

Violet took a step towards the chained girl and Bunny choked back a cry of alarm. Violet shushed her.

The captive was tall and slim, and her hair was long: the glossy tresses fell all the way to her hips in a black cascade. Apart from her face, every exposed inch of her skin—her arms, her hands, her shapely legs, her neck—was decorated with elaborate tattoo work: turquoise dragons, chrysanthemum flowers, purple creeping vines. She was wearing a blue dress in the cheongsam style, similar to Ruby's, with fabric buttons across the chest and a high collar. On Ruby, the dress had exaggerated her natural curves; on this girl, however, the dress skimmed the straight lines of her body. Her face, too, had a delicate symmetry. Violet took in her exquisitely arched brows, her lash-fringed almond eyes, her rosebud mouth.

The contrast between the girl's delicate frame and the thick chain around her neck made Violet's stomach turn and she wanted to look away—the iron links were connected by a locked hasp from which hung an ornate green pendant in the shape of a bird. Surely it must be painful, Violet thought, stepping closer. Painful and demeaning.

The look in the poor girl's eyes was one of pure fear.

Violet held out her hand. 'We're here to help you,' she whispered.

The girl abruptly lifted her hand to halt Violet's approach and shouted in desperate, clipped English: 'No! Not help. Not come close!'

She shook her head desperately. Then she fell to her knees in the corner of the room and sobbed in terror. Violet winced as she noticed the red raw chafing around the girl's wrist from the manacle. Bruises had bloomed on the girl's neck from the ghastly chain. She was a heart-rending sight.

Slowly, Violet stepped back and joined Bunny in the doorway. The sobbing girl lifted her head and shook it sadly. 'Not help.'

Violet felt hot tears welling. 'But you *need* help!'

'No!' The girl was shouting again, struggling to her feet under the weight of her monstrous collar. 'You help, you die. You die too.'

What did she mean *too?*

Then the girl's eyes widened in terror, and she let out a piercing scream.

A gasp from the hallway made Bunny and Violet turn. There they saw the source of the chained girl's distress. It was Madame: face a rictus of horror, hair as wild as a bird's nest.

'Oh sweet Jesus, Violet Kelly,' Madame whispered hoarsely. 'Swear to me in God's name that you didn't lay a finger on her. Because if you did, we're all dead.'

They turned to the sound of a thump as Bunny dropped to the floor in a dead faint.

The prisoner shrieked, her free hand drawn to her mouth as she stared at Bunny unconscious on the floor. Tears spilled down her cheeks.

'*Zuzhou*,' the prisoner whispered, gesturing at Bunny. '*Zuzhou*. Curse!'

Violet immediately dropped to Bunny's side and shook her vigorously.

Bunny stirred and struggled to sit up. Madame, tight-lipped and stricken, helped Bunny to her feet.

Violet drew Bunny away from Madame and held the girl to her side. Outrage surged through her. 'What's the meaning of this? This, here, in La Maison des Fleurs?' She gestured at the captive. 'This girl is in pain! Shame on you, Madame!'

Madame staggered forward and crumpled into a chair by the dresser. 'Violet Kelly, I command you to take Bunny downstairs. This is a grave situation and you cannot get involved.'

'No way. You'll tell us what's going on here, before we even so much as twitch.'

'I'm warning you,' Madame said ominously, 'this doesn't concern you.'

'Don't be ridiculous. We're here, aren't we? So it does concern us. What is she doing here, chained up like a dog?'

Madame slumped forward in the chair, her elbows on her knees. 'You don't understand. It's like the girl said herself. She's been cursed.'

Violet shook her blonde head. 'I don't believe in anything so . . . so *medieval* as curses. And if you do, you deserve to be cursed yourself for keeping a young woman prisoner like this.' She released Bunny and went to stand in front of Madame.

She held out her hand. 'You must have a key for the manacle somewhere. Where is it?'

Wearily, Madame reached into her dressing-gown pocket. She produced a small brass key, which Violet snatched from her.

'The man said it was a death curse,' Madame began. 'If you even touch her—'

'Don't be ridiculous.'

Quietly, Violet approached the girl, who was shaking now and whispering over and over: 'No . . . please, no.'

The prisoner tried once more to repel Violet, making shooing gestures as Violet drew near, but her strength seemed drained. Her hands fell into her lap and her head dropped forward. Her tears continued to fall as Violet knelt beside her.

After a moment, she allowed Violet to reach over and lift her adorned wrist. As gently as possible, Violet turned the cruel manacle over and found the lock. The chain fell to the ground, dragging the manacle with it. The girl's wrist slipped free and she tucked both hands under her chin. She stood, then sank onto the bed and lay curled up, sobbing into the pillow and nursing her chafed wrist.

Violet placed a hand on the weeping girl's shoulder and winced as the prisoner flinched at her touch. 'Hush now, don't be afraid. What's your name?'

The girl fell quiet. Then she turned her head and held out her hand to Violet. 'Shen. I am Shen.'

Violet took the hand and repeated the whispered name. 'Shen, I'm Violet, and I don't believe in curses.'

Shen shook her head slowly. Violet inched closer and, with her fingertips, touched the chain that encircled the girl's neck. Shen's eyes widened in terror again as Violet's fingers traced the outline of the green pendant. It was an owl and Violet recognised the green stone as the same jade that Li Ling wore in tiny beads around her wrist.

Bunny, finding her courage, joined them. 'A jade owl. What does it mean?' she whispered.

Madame's choked voice reached them from the chair by the dresser. 'Please, Bunny, don't touch it! I couldn't live with myself if anything happened to you.'

Shen clasped the jade owl in her fingers, eyes full of sorrow. '*Zuzhou*. My curse. Your curse now.'

Violet Kelly shook her head sadly. How could she explain to Shen that she was imperturbably, irrevocably lucky? That she had endured the deprivations of St Michael's Orphanage and the separation from her sister, and was now taking immense enjoyment in living out the worst of Sister Bernadette's hellfire predictions? What was a jade owl to Violet Kelly?

Violet smiled. 'Bunny, run and get Madame's mercurochrome and a bandage from the bathroom cabinet. Madame, I suggest you give us an explanation—but I recommend you pour us one of your fine brandies first. And no skimping.'

Madame heaved herself to a standing position and shuffled into the hallway. Violet heard the clinking of glasses and the hiss of gas being released from a soda siphon.

She turned to the almond-eyed girl curled on the bed. 'Now, Shen, what are we going to do with you?'

—

Violet positioned herself beside the bed. Bunny, arriving promptly with dressings and antiseptic, carefully tended to the girl's wounded wrist. Bunny's gift for rambling now came to the fore: as she cleaned and soothed, she whittered on softly, describing Shen's beautiful tattoos and telling her, without cease, how fortunate she was to find herself in a house so pleasant as La Maison des Fleurs.

As Bunny ran back and forth from Madame's tiny kitchenette, fetching water, Bex powders and anything else that might offer Shen relief, Violet stood, observing Shen. The girl was silent and obliging but she had the inward focus, the silent composure, of someone accustomed to pain.

Violet didn't leave Shen's side until she saw the girl's tense shoulders relax a little. Then she asked Bunny to fetch another chair and she placed this one next to Shen's bedside.

She sat and reached for Shen's hand and clasped it in her own.

When Madame reappeared with brandy five minutes later, Shen raised imploring eyes to Violet's tumbler, so Madame was requested to return with another.

When she returned with the full glass, Madame held it far out in front of her to avoid drawing close to Shen. Shen's whisper of thanks caused Madame to flush and cross herself. She made her way shakily to the chair beside the dresser, where she sat, her gaze averted into the hallway.

It was chilling to see Madame behave this way—crestfallen, wrought with anxiety and unsure of herself. How we rely on her confidence, her front, thought Violet. She's the prow of the ship.

But not today.

Violet drained her brandy. A girl was in trouble and they were wasting time. 'Come on then, Madame, out with it. What in the world is going on here?'

CHAPTER 8

THE CONVERSATION SWIRLED AROUND MADAME. She understood it was time to speak. Instead, she found herself somewhere else completely.

Was it the past? Was it a *place*?

She saw a shade of green so bright it seemed a trick of light. A mossy grey-stoned village hall, next to the crooked iron railings of a churchyard. The slope of the hill behind a house (was it her mother's house?).

Madame wondered if these images were cribbed from somewhere, or invented to fill a void. Whose memories are these? she wondered. Whose past have I fled to, if not my own?

It was the drugs, of course. Still affecting her, making the room swim. The pictures in her head were as bright as the plates of her illustrated histories. And the urge to be somewhere else was so great she felt it almost lifting her out of her chair.

Ah, but that was the singular joy of opium. You could just conjure up those colours and shapes, and the sensation came along with it. A bit of peace. Your body flying out.

Nausea swept over her and the hard wooden seat of the chair against the bones of her arse told her she was back. She raised her head and risked a glance around the room: the girls were staring at her, awaiting an answer.

Madame drew a long breath, felt it catch at the back of her throat, and coughed into the sleeve of her gown. There it was: her punishment, manifest in her lungs. She could barely lift her gaze to face her questioners. 'Gimme a minute. Please.'

Moments like these, she thought suddenly, are the points on which life pivots.

At last, she lifted her gaze and looked across at Violet and Bunny.

Violet shifted in her seat impatiently. 'Come *on*. Tell us what Shen's doing here.'

Madame swallowed hard and began.

There was another house, many years ago, she told them. Even as she spoke, the clenching terror of the time returned.

It was where her Da had brought her when the family's ship from Liverpool docked at last. When she, her sister and her brother were still small enough to sleep head to toe on a single cot.

They'd begun the journey as five, but one wet night, not long after the boat left the dock, Shelagh O'Sheehan left her berth, took off her shoes and slipped under the railing and into a grey sea.

'The crew said it was an accident but there was always doubt in my mind,' Madame said. 'There were few escapes from the old man's fury, and that sea, the colour of rain itself, must have called to Ma, the way ice calls when you have a fever.'

So, she went on: it was little Peggy, solemn Martha and their big brother Ronan, an enormous dolt of a boy, who disembarked at the Quarantine Station with their Da, missing a mother and with scarcely a penny between them.

Martha, aged twelve and clever enough to be afraid, took her leave almost immediately. She went west as hired help, attaching herself to a school governor and his wife from the ship.

That left just the three of them—Da, Ronan and Peggy—to find their way.

And what they found was a sliver of a shop with a kitchen behind and a bedroom above, set in a terrace in The Rocks. The locals called it the Halfmoon. From the time she could count, it was Peggy's job to sit behind the window of the ground-floor Halfmoon shop and sell phony Pall Malls, lollies, pints of milk and copies of *The Evening News*. She would talk sweet to the coppers who passed by, so they'd turn a blind eye to the book-making and graft taking place upstairs. All day, men traipsed up and down the stairs behind her to visit Da and Ronan.

Bookmaking was a gentleman's art, her Da told her. It was supposed to make them rich, but Da had no knack for keeping money. Money flowed down the stairs and out the door. Her brother Ronan was no better than Da: he struggled with basic sums and clapped her about the head with his meaty fists for being the smart one.

The debts piled up. Bruises too. Oh, there was violence she couldn't bring herself to speak of.

'I had one friend at this time,' she said. 'A strange boy called Jian Zhu.'

At the sound of the Chinese name, Shen gave a murmur.

Madame nodded. 'That's right, Jian Zhu. Young Jian Zhu came past the Halfmoon shop every afternoon with his stern brother Xiao Zhu, who wheeled a merchant's cart. They sold everything from matches to vegetables to fireworks.'

Some afternoons Jian would join Peggy in the shop and they would dust and rearrange the tiny shelves of Velvet soap and biscuits tins together. Sometimes he would sneak a firecracker from his brother Xiao's cart, and after dark they would run to the water's edge on Hickson Road to let them off.

'Jian Zhu's English was bad, which suited me,' said Madame.

She liked the quiet hours they spent together in the dusty light of the tiny shop, the sweet humour in his eyes. She had grown used to men who had heavy footsteps and roaring voices. Jian wanted nothing but her company, her laughter.

When she filled out to become a beautiful sixteen-year-old, there were men who expected new favours from Peggy. Her Da told her to take the money and think herself lucky that she had charms to spare.

Da was wild-eyed and mad by then, Madame explained, and her brother half-cut all day, every day. The debts were crippling. She found out from one of her father's friends that Da and Ronan had managed to upset some of the local standover men. Day and night they would be visited by vicious brutes threatening all sorts of cruelties.

'So, they dreamed up a plan, Da and Ronan,' she said. 'A plan they said would save us all.'

Madame swallowed hard and took a sip of her brandy, only to find the glass empty. She let it slip from her fingers into her lap.

'They told me that they wanted to make good with one of the men, buy themselves a bit of time. I'd be saving the family if I played my part and just did what I was told. "It'll be just fine," Da said. "Pay the man a little attention and let us worry about the rest."'

Madame stopped. It was coming back to her, like always, in strange little moments: the blinding light pouring into the kitchen. Running past her father and tripping, almost falling upstairs. Counting to a hundred.

The warm blood, the cold knife.

She sighed. There was no reason not to tell it now.

'I was told to wait in the kitchen. It was cold in there—as cold as the night Ma went into the sea. The breeze from under the door cut me in the legs. Then Da came down the stairs. He said there was a man waiting for me upstairs. I should be a good girl and do what was required.' She paused, closed her eyes briefly. 'It wasn't the first time.'

She cleared her throat to continue. 'It was dark and quiet in the room when I got up there, not even a candle alight on the sill. I slipped under the covers and it took me a minute or two to realise the body next to me wasn't moving, not even to breathe.

'Before I knew it, the spilled blood had soaked through my nightie, even through my skin, or so I thought. When I reached down to grasp the cold hard thing against my thigh, I knew I'd done much more than even Da and Ronan could have hoped. I'd placed my fingerprints on the knife that killed him.'

Oh, the shock of betrayal when she realised that her own brother and father were long gone, and had left her to take the blame.

Madame met Violet's gaze. When she spoke next, her voice was flat, tired. 'They killed a man and framed me so as to escape their debts,' she said. 'They disappeared that night. God knows how, but it was Jian who came when I screamed. Jian who dragged me out of the room and ran with me through the night streets. Who helped me wash away the blood.'

Madame took a breath. 'Everything changed after that,' she said.

Australia went to war, she told them wearily. She went first to a seamstress who offered work and board for girls, but she soon drifted, like so many girls before her, into the more lucrative business of the fleshpots. Jian begged her not to but she was sick of hard times and saw it as a way out.

'You all know that choice, I suppose,' she said. Madame risked a glance at Shen, who blinked at her from the bed.

'Xiao!' Shen whispered.

Madame nodded. 'Oh, yes, Shen, my dear. That brings us back to Xiao.'

She put her brandy glass down on the floor beside her and rested her arms on her knees.

'Well, I loved Jian,' she said. 'Pure and simple. And he loved me too. But his family wouldn't allow us to marry. Instead, Jian was provided with a wife of their choosing, a nice Chinese girl, recently arrived. In a year they had two babies already, nine months apart. Irish twins they call it. Ironic, eh? Irish twins?'

She continued. 'But he would visit me in secret. He felt guilty, I think, for leaving me alone. I was the loneliest person alive.'

The war dragged on. In the meantime, Xiao's business interests flourished. Gone were the days of the handcart in the street: now he had warehouses in Woolloomooloo and a growing empire. Jian too. He did his duty by his family and grew rich, working alongside his brother. When he was just twenty years old he bought a certain three-storey terrace at the finer end of Paddington for his growing family.

'This place!' said Violet, incredulous.

Madame nodded. In 1919 Jian and his family took a trip to Singapore. On the return visit their passenger ship was intercepted by authorities and Jian and all of his family were found to have contracted Spanish flu. The four of them died in a quarantine centre in Adelaide.

'In the week after,' Madame said, 'I received a visit from Jian's mother and Xiao, the powerful brother.'

Xiao translated his mother's words: Jian had left Madame the house and she was welcome to it. No mother could bear to live with such ghosts.

But then Xiao spoke to her coldly in English, knowing his mother would not understand. 'You may have the house and I won't stand in your way,' he said. 'But we know what your family did. We know that blood was spilled. You came to my brother with dirty hands. Now he is dead, his bride and babies too. One day I will expect a favour and you will not refuse me. The police still seek the killers of the man who died in the room above the Halfmoon and they will pay handsomely to learn of your whereabouts.'

Madame lifted her eyes to meet those of her audience.

'But what about Shen?' Bunny asked.

Madame nodded, then exclaimed, 'In the name of the blessed infant, Bunny! I forgot you were listening.'

'C'mon, Aunty, you're killing us here!' said Bunny.

Madame continued, with a catch in her voice. 'So, Shen is that favour.'

Xiao's power and empire had grown in the intervening years, she now explained. These days it was illustrious and his businesses tastes were more refined.

'Specialised, if you catch my drift,' said Madame. 'Things you can't get in an ordinary shop. Antiques and the like.'

A consignment of goods had been sent on the latest ship to Melbourne from Shanghai. This consignment included a treasure by the name of Shen, a decorated angel of that famous city's pleasure houses and a favourite of Pu Yi himself, the great emperor-in-exile, who sometimes journeyed in secrecy from his quarters to visit her. Shen was a great prize, and Xiao and his associates planned to tour with her around the world, offering her to the rich and immoral for their private delectation. For the right price, there was nothing Shen wouldn't be made to do. After all, her tattoos would conceal so much.

Madame watched as, hearing this, Violet tightened her grip on the captive girl's hand.

But now, Madame said, it turned out that Xiao was himself slave to a certain lust: he liked to gamble. Last night, Xiao had paid a surprise visit, and had told her of the trouble he found himself in.

During a three-day game of cards in a private club in the city, playing against a man more powerful than himself, he arrived at a point where he had nothing left to stake. His house was gone, his money and his assets too.

In desperation, he offered the man a share in Shen. They could work her together, in exchange for the man returning his business assets. If he were to win, Xiao reasoned, he could restore himself to prosperity.

This man—a white ghost-man, a *gweilo* with the soul of a demon whose name Xiao didn't disclose—was the kind of man to strike fear into even the stoutest of hearts. The man proposed a counteroffer: Xiao could win everything back if he agreed to raise the stakes. The man wanted Shen all to himself. He wanted her as a blood prize.

Now, Xiao knew what a blood prize was, although he was

shocked to hear this powerful man suggest it. It was beyond anything even Xiao would offer his customers.

This man told him that he had desires that could not be inflicted upon people in the general sense. He could see that Shen was indeed a treasure, an exquisite ornament. It would be an immeasurable pleasure to take such a life. If the work was as beautiful as everyone described, then her tattooed skin, for example, would be a priceless ornament in its own right. Even the idea filled him with strength.

Xiao had told this to Madame with a look of naked terror in his eyes. Shen was worth more to this man dead than alive. And Xiao, if he won, would be restored to his own modest greatness. Yet this meant offering up Shen to be tortured for pleasure and, eventually, killed as some kind of sacrifice. Could Xiao live with himself?

Apparently, he could. Inevitably, he lost.

In the silence that followed, Madame cleared her throat. Xiao had told her that she was now called upon to house Shen in Sydney until he received his instructions from the mysterious 'ghost-man'. They did not know when this man would call for his prize. Shen should be kept chained, at the man's insistence. Her subjugation should begin at once.

Madame told them, 'Xiao said, "Do not make this worse for yourself. Do not touch her; she is marked for death. In my family, we take this very seriously. You must observe the customs."'

On no account should Madame attempt to remove the chain around Shen's neck, he warned. This was the solemn emblem of Xiao's unbreakable promise to the ghost-man. She wore the jade owl: the harbinger of death, the eternal watcher. This was Shen's curse and it would be the curse of any fool who attempted to free her.

Only Xiao and the white man had a key to unlock the hasp with the jade owl pendant.

'You see,' Madame said to the silent room as she stood to leave, 'Shen is as good as dead already.'

CHAPTER 9

VIOLET WAS OUT OF HER CHAIR and following Madame down the stairs in an instant. 'Oh, no, you don't! Come back here!'

Surely Madame could see that they couldn't hand Shen over to a monster who meant to torture and kill her? How would they live with themselves?

Madame stopped on the landing, her chest heaving, and turned towards Violet, her eyes red and wild. 'There's nothing we can do. Don't you see?' She wiped away her tears and hurried on.

Violet stared after her mentor with a mixture of shock and disbelief, then followed her, taking the stairs two at a time. Her mind was racing. Of course Madame had agreed to Xiao's demands: if she had refused him, he would have taken his information about the murder in the Halfmoon to the police and condemned Madame forever. If that happened, La Maison des

Fleurs would be finished. Madame was sparing Bunny, Violet, Charlie, Li Ling—all of them.

But how, thought Violet, can we stand by and allow an innocent girl to be sacrificed? Madame's enemies were terrifying, Violet could see that. But there had to be a better way—one that meant Shen could live. *Surely*.

They would find it.

'I'm going to help Shen,' said Violet. 'You should too. Imagine if it were Bunny in Shen's place!'

At this, Madame stopped and steadied herself against the banister. 'Stop that.' The look of horror on her face told Violet she had struck a nerve.

'Stop what? Shen belongs to people—people who are just like you or me. You would see it my way if you didn't feel so . . . so ashamed.'

Madame turned her face away. It was clear that Violet's words had bit deep. She sobbed, 'You can't—'

'I can and I will. I'm sorry for what you've been through. No girl deserves such cruelty. Which is why we can't let this . . . this "ghost-man" take Shen. You must see that?'

Madame shook her head tearfully. 'You walk into this and you'll put yourself and the rest of us in danger. Don't you see? If we meddle, we'll all be targets! I've worked too hard for that. You've been safe here. I've kept you all safe!'

'But what's the point of any of it if you can't save a girl like Shen? A girl who needs you more than anyone?'

But Madame just gave a sob, then turned and continued to the bottom of the stairs.

When Violet joined her, Madame was reaching for her coat and cramming her feet into her church shoes.

She'll be going to confession, Violet thought, for all the good it'll do her. 'I'm coming with you,' she called after Madame. Violet was wearing a faded cotton house dress and hadn't so much as brushed her hair. But she'd have to do. She ran to pull her coat from the peg and her outdoor shoes from the rack by the back door.

As Violet hurried through the parlour, she discovered Albert asleep on the couch with his face buried in a pink satin nightgown.

She pulled up short. Yesterday, she'd decided that Albert was the cause of all the friction in her life. She had judged his caution to be overzealous and his stories about the threats to La Maison to be far-fetched. Plus, there had been the wretched visit to Nico's! Yes, Albert was very much still *in the bad books*.

But now it seemed that he may have had a point. The sun had, indeed, risen on a world that wasn't perfect, and her beloved La Maison was in trouble. She bit her lip. She did *so* hate to be wrong. But in the circumstances, she needed Albert on her side.

Violet shook his shoulder roughly. 'Get up, you!'

He jolted awake. 'Christ, Vi—'

She held up a hand and crouched next to him. 'Shut up and listen.'

'Oh. Okay.'

Violet scowled and jabbed a finger into his chest. 'Firstly, I don't want a gun. I'm going to throw it in the harbour, the first chance I get.'

'But—'

'But nothing! Secondly, I won't have you frightening Charlie and Li Ling with stories about spies.'

'It's not a story, I swear,' he whispered. 'You see—'

'No! It doesn't matter now because we have a more immediate problem, one involving a prisoner in Madame's quarters.'

'A prisoner?' Albert sat up groggily and pulled his rumpled cap over his tousled hair. He looked confused. 'I wasn't expecting that.'

'Well, if you're shocked, imagine how I feel. Not all of us have your imagination for intrigue. Anyway, you have to go down to Chinatown on the tram to get Li Ling and Charlie Han and bring 'em back here, right away. They can translate for our Chinese captive.'

'Chinese? Blimey. But fair go, Violet. I've never been to Charlie's place. How will I find him?'

'Just ask someone. They live on Sussex Street above a shop, I think. Get them, Albert.'

'Violet, I need to tell you—'

'No! If I don't leave straight away, I'll miss Madame at St Canice's.' Violet shook her head in exasperation. 'Besides, I'm still furious with you. Whatever it is, it'll have to wait. Will you go to Chinatown?'

'Orright.' He sighed, reached for his boots and began to tug them onto his feet. 'Heck, I could murder a cup of tea. Is Bunny about?'

Violet called over her shoulder. 'Make it yourself. I'll be back in an hour.'

—

Madame was already more than halfway to St Canice's church by the time Violet caught up with her. People moved aside when they saw Violet approach—darting up the street with her coat unbuttoned, her head down and her hair flying behind her.

A year ago, when Violet arrived on the doorstep of La Maison des Fleurs to throw herself on Madame's mercy, with nothing besides a battered cardboard suitcase and her now-famous legs,

Violet promised herself she'd watch Madame and learn how an ordinary girl could become a rich and powerful woman with a place of her own.

Thus, Violet had paid attention to Madame's every move.

She learned that Madame liked her tea stewed and her breakfast bacon in a wedge of brown bread. She learned that Madame liked the old songs, so she taught herself 'The Wearing of the Green' and 'Rose of Tralee' and hammed it up in the parlour when Madame was in the mood.

And when Madame needed help with her sums and her books, Violet stepped in. While St Michael's Orphanage School had failed to turn out a devout servant of the church, they'd done a fine job teaching Violet how to read and reason, how to do sums, how to write a good letter and how to conduct oneself around people with education.

Madame had come to rely on her.

Violet ran the last block of Barcom Avenue and caught up with Madame on the wide footpath of William Street. Wind blew dust into her eyes as she seized Madame's sleeve.

'Oh!' Madame stopped, clutched her chest and broke into ragged coughing.

Violet put her arm around Madame's shoulders and tried to catch her own breath.

'Listen,' she panted. 'You don't need to have Shen's life on your conscience. Just let me talk to Li Ling and Charlie. Perhaps they can find a Chinese family to hide her for a bit. Just let me find a way to get her out of La Maison!'

Madame shook her head. 'Jesus himself, girl. You don't know who you're dealing with.' Her voice was filled with dread.

Violet considered her for a moment as a car passed close by, startling two police horses walking uphill on the other side of the street. She pulled her coat around herself and crossed her arms. 'I'm not stupid. I know these men you speak of are dangerous. But I don't care.'

She sounded more certain than she felt. It strengthened her resolve, to say the brave words aloud.

Madame sniffed. 'You're a fool. I'm going to church now, if you'll excuse me.'

'Say a prayer for Shen,' Violet said. She turned to go. 'Better put in a good word upstairs for yourself, come to think of it. Sins do weigh a person down.'

Madame shook her head, exasperated. 'You beat all, Violet Kelly! Will you be asking for the Pope's blessing next?'

'I wouldn't go that far,' said Violet evenly.

Madame held a handkerchief to her nose and mouth, stifling another ragged cough. 'You're leading us into trouble.' She trotted into the road, avoiding the sheets of newspaper blowing up the hill from Rushcutters Bay.

'Bollocks. I'm saving you as well as Shen.'

'I didn't ask for your help.'

'Are you mad? Madame, if you let them take Shen, it'll kill you—I know it will! Then I'll have you on my conscience too. Just let me find a way.'

'If there was a way, I would have taken it.' Madame turned.

'Let me try!' Violet cried, watching her mentor rush across the road, head down into the wind. She decided take Madame's silence as permission to carry on. She would find a way to solve their dilemma.

Violet turned back towards Paddington. Her mind was racing as she considered their predicament. To compensate, she used a trick the nuns had taught them: you walked slowly, in measured steps. After a while your thoughts slowed down too, and your breathing. Around and around the nuns went, in their little cloistered square between St Michael's church and the schoolroom. Their shoe soles must have been worn to paper.

Violet retraced her route along the winding Paddington street with deliberate steps, her coat buttoned to her throat.

Finding her mind a little clearer, Violet allowed her thoughts to return to Shen. Madame's fear of Shen's captors was proof enough that these were very bad men. Everyone knew Madame faced down the boys from Kings Cross once a week, exchanging a pile of cash for their dubious 'protection', just to keep the doors open. It was a cost of doing business.

It followed that if Madame judged this ghost-man to be a different class of cold-blooded killer, then she was probably right.

But knowing that didn't change things, Violet decided. There were some lines you couldn't cross. Shen mustn't be handed over.

The Chinese girl would have bathed by now and be tucked up between fresh sheets, enjoying Bunny's earnest care. Perhaps Bunny was brushing Shen's lustrous hair.

She had time to detour by Five Ways to collect a lemon tart for lunch. She added a fresh loaf of bread to her mental shopping list. That would please Albert, whose belly always needed filling.

As she walked, Violet turned the pressing question over in her mind: where could one hide a uniquely identifiable girl from a man who had the money and networks to search high and low, and the scruples to kill without pausing to blink?

Violet frowned. She didn't know the answer. Not yet. But she hoped Charlie and Li Ling Han would have an idea.

She turned into Glenmore Road as a tram rattled past, the overhead lines hissing and zapping.

Mrs Moran's daughter Averil was up a wooden ladder out on

the pavement, cleaning the window of Moran's bread shop. Averil nodded primly to Violet as she passed.

Violet paused before the plate-glass window. Across the road, a large group of men had formed outside the pub. They were dirty and rough-looking. Their voices rose in agitation and Violet recoiled a little in fear. As she watched, a man emerged from the crowd on the pavement pulling a small handcart with one hand. The man's other sleeve hung limp at his side and his broken shoes were tied to his feet with string. Behind him, a young woman shuffled awkwardly, leading two small children. Her children's feet were bare and they cried pitifully.

Averil climbed down from her ladder and joined Violet on the footpath. She whistled through her teeth and nodded towards the family.

'Chucked out for not payin' the rent. There's no work for a man with two good arms, let alone for a man come back from the war with just one. So much for Lest we Forget.'

The men clapped the one-armed man on the back and solemnly moved aside so the family could make their way through the throng and continue up the street. One or two of the men placed small items—a bottle of beer or a coin—in the handcart as they passed.

Then a change of mood appeared to stir the crowd. The family's shame and despair had roused the men's anger. A bottle smashed against the kerb. There was a scuffle. Then, just as suddenly, the men turned away from each other listlessly.

Violet shook her head. The papers talked about nothing but poverty and desperation. She'd seen the families in Surry Hills and Darlinghurst lined up at the door of St Michael's begging for scraps. She didn't dare walk the Hungry Mile herself, not even with Albert by her side, but she knew that the men were lined up down there by the wharves around the clock, waiting for a day's work to feed a wife and a clutch of kids at home. Things seemed to be getting worse. She crossed her arms, hugging her warm woollen coat around her. She gave silent thanks for the luxury of La Maison des Fleurs.

'Where will the family go?' Violet asked Averil.

Averil shrugged. 'Most go to the parish first and ask for help. Then some go down to the worst bits of Surry Hills and don't get any further, 'cos of the grog and all that. But some are heading out La Perouse way and putting up shacks in the dunes.'

'Sounds miserable,' Violet murmured, shaking her head. She turned away and pushed open the door to Moran's shop. The bell chimed above her.

Averil called after her, suddenly hostile. 'Hey! Don't you go getting any high ideas about yourself. We all know what you've been doing to get them nice clothes.'

Violet blushed and walked quickly inside.

Inside the dark shop, the loaves of bread were stacked high on the wooden counter, wrapped in paper. Violet took one and, in a rush, asked Mrs Moran for the lemon tart. As the woman wrapped the delicacy, Violet hurried to find her purse and collect her change before turning to push her way out of the shop, her arms laden.

On the doorstep outside, she pulled up short.

In the middle of the road stood a girl. The girl was watching Violent intently. She was the same height as Violet. The same build, the same age. Her face was the same oval shape and her blonde hair curled around her shoulders the way Violet's curled, only the other girl's hair was wild, matted. She wore a frayed felt hat pulled down low over her eyes and a stained, tatty coat. She was barefoot.

Violet's heart was thumping. She blinked in disbelief.

Iris.

Before Violet could react, the girl turned and darted up the street and into a laneway.

Averil Moran came to stand at Violet's side, staring across the street in the direction the girl had gone. 'Well, now I've seen everything. There's bloody two of you.'

Violet opened her mouth to reply but found herself speechless. Was that really her sister, the twin who had left her for dead in that godforsaken orphanage? A wave of dizziness passed over her and she grasped the sleeve of Averil's cotton blouse to steady herself.

Averil shook off her hand and spat on the pavement. She gave Violet's fine coat and shoes a pointed once-over. 'Question is, who really came out on top, eh?'

Violet walked away quickly to the sound of the shop bell clanging and Mrs Moran chastising her slovenly daughter from the step.

As she neared La Maison, Violet slowed to a halt. Her thoughts were in a scramble. Could that really have been Iris? What on earth had happened to her?

Rather than entering La Maison by the grand front door, Violet walked slowly to the laneway behind and stood for five long minutes in a patch of sun beside the bins and discarded crates. She was trembling like a blade of grass.

She leaned against the grey fence palings that lined the alley and looked up at the sky, where a bright sun was nearing its midday position.

At ten years old, with Iris gone and only Albert to share the daily misery of the orphanage, Violet had wished herself dead. In the tormented years of adolescence that came after, she knew vaguely that there might be no coming back from the dark place to which she had been forced.

It was shameful to admit, but thoughts of revenge had been a spark in her darkness. Iris would be made to pay for what she did.

But revenge corroded too, burned itself along a terrible path. And seeing Iris—if it was indeed Iris—looking wild and dressed in rags . . . Well, that changed things.

At last, she let herself in the back gate of La Maison des Fleurs' yard to find Charlie Han and Albert arguing by the kitchen door.

As she watched, Albert took off his cap and rubbed his forehead with the back of his hand. 'She can't do you any harm, Charlie,' he was saying. 'She's just a girl.' Albert's frustration was clear in his voice.

As Violet reached the two men, Charlie was shaking his head. 'Albert, Shen is a big problem.'

Albert looked at Violet sadly. 'Thank goodness you're back, Violet. We haven't been here long. But Li Ling took one look at Shen and hightailed it back downstairs. Charlie spoke to Shen long enough to find out what was going on, and now he's told me her story. For Pete's sake, Vi! What are you getting yourself involved in?'

Violet handed him the cake box and the bread. 'Albert Reginald McAllister, have you forgotten where you're from? You of all people should know that when someone needs help, we do what we can.'

Albert adjusted his grip on the parcels. 'Well, I don't fancy getting shanked by some big standover man, thanks very much. Or cursed by some fancy Chinese witchcraft.' He shuddered.

'Now you're just being ignorant, Albert.' She wasn't sure she believed herself, but Violet said the words with conviction.

'So, what are we going to do? Li Ling won't come out of the bathroom. She says Shen's a death-bringer!'

Charlie took a step forward and held out both hands to Violet. 'I'm sorry. Shen says you have the heart of an ox. You want to help. But she begs you to leave her alone now. She wants to die a clean death.'

Violet felt hot anger colouring her cheeks. 'There's no such thing.'

Charlie smiled serenely. 'Oh, yes! Clean death means no more hurt. No more harm.'

Violet pulled away from Charlie. Shen would not be handed over to those awful men.

'No-one is going to die,' she said. 'Shen will live, we will help and Shen will know that we do this freely, and that we are not afraid of the consequences. Albert, come inside with me—we need to talk.'

Albert gave Charlie an awkward pat on the shoulder then followed Violet through the back door.

She waited for Albert to drop the parcels on the kitchen bench then led him into the parlour. Once there, Violet turned and stopped Albert abruptly, a hand against his chest. She looked squarely into his brown eyes.

'You knew it was Iris watching, didn't you.' It was a statement, not a question.

'Oh, crikey, Yes. Ah, shit!' Albert looked down at his boots.

She landed a heavy punch on his shoulder. '*That's* for not telling me straight. She's following me. I almost came face to face with her at the bakery.'

'I tried to tell you! I just wanted to give you the news myself. When I missed you yesterday I thought I'd leave a message with part of the story, just the bit about being watched. Figured you might work it out.'

This stung, as she remembered how she had pushed the

thoughts about skeletons in her closet aside. 'I've had other things on my mind. How long have you known about Iris?'

'A few days.'

Violet crossed her arms. 'Go on.'

'She found me at the butcher's. She's living like a tramp and the lads she's with are trouble, trust me.'

A terrible thought dawned. 'Don't tell me you sent me to Nico's for the gun because of Iris?'

Albert shook his head sadly. 'The gun's been sitting in Nico's drawer for weeks. I wanted you to have a way to protect yourself against those . . . those *pigs* who come in here every day!'

Violet felt her throat seize with emotion. Tears of embarrassment had collected in Albert's eyes. He wiped them away angrily.

'It's not that bad, Albert. I promise,' she said softly. 'You needn't worry. I'm having the time of my life, remember?'

He sighed. 'What if Iris has come to make trouble?' asked Albert, sniffing. 'Don't you want to protect everything you've worked for?'

'With a gun? You've got to be kidding.'

'But look at what you have!'

The words were scalding. 'It was never about *things*.'

'Violet, I'm sorry!'

Her heart felt as if it might break. 'Where's Iris staying now?'

Albert shifted uneasily. 'Last night I let her stay out the back of the butcher's shop, in Mr Cavendish's woodshed. I gave her a feed, but she was gone by dawn.'

'It's only a matter of time before she shows up at the front door.'

Albert reached for her hand, bewildered. 'I thought you wanted to find her.'

Violet pulled free of his grip and backed away. 'Not like this.'

She turned and walked to the foot of the back stairs but a sound made her pause before the door of the ground-floor bathroom. She heard Li Ling crying from within. Violet's heart felt terribly heavy.

She turned back to her friend, who stood hunched in the hallway. 'Albert, if you want to help, you can talk Li Ling around. Tell her this isn't a matter of curses. We have to save Shen, we have to protect Madame and we have to take care of ourselves. Iris can wait. Will you talk to Li Ling?'

He nodded.

'And Albert?'

'Yes?'

'I can see now that you were trying to tell me. I'm sorry.'

He rubbed his shoulder. 'You might look fancy these days but you still punch like a street brawler.'

'Don't you forget it.'

Clinging to the banister, Violet hauled herself up onto the bottom step. Her legs were leaden with a new kind of weight. She recognised it from the darkest days of childhood. It was fear, pressing down on her.

She climbed to the third floor and entered Madame's apartment, pausing outside the spare room as, to her surprise, she heard merry voices and laughter coming from inside.

At that moment, Bunny slipped out the doorway and into the hall. 'Violet! You're back!' Bunny sounded excited. 'I had an idea. I hope you don't mind.' Bunny bit her lip, eager for Violet's approval.

'Tell me.'

'I thought Ruby might be able to help. Maybe she could hide Shen in the circus? So, I brought her up here. She's in on the secret now.'

Violet nodded wearily. 'You mustn't tell any more people after this. I suppose we can trust Ruby.' She wasn't sure that was completely true: Ruby had a wonderful warm heart but a tendency to vagueness and a committed disregard for rules. Could she be relied on to keep the secret of Shen?

It was too late now.

Bunny gave an exaggerated sigh of relief. 'Oh, thank goodness! I didn't want you to be cross with me. Why don't you go in and see them? They're playing gin rummy.'

Violet entered the room. It was a pleasing scene: Shen was laughing as Ruby spread the cards before her. Ruby was evidently trying to explain the game.

The girls looked up.

'There you are,' Ruby said. 'I've found out a few things. Shen is nineteen. She was born in a village but doesn't remember where. She travelled here by boat. Oh—and unless we save her some man is going to kill her.'

Not just kill her, Violet thought. First he would flay her. Torture her.

Violet flopped onto the bed beside Shen. The girl was watching her carefully, Violet noted. Her dark eyes seemed to be full of pain or yearning, in spite of her smile.

Shen reached over and touched Violet's cheek. 'So kind,' she said, in faltering English.

Violet held Shen's hand and squeezed it. She wanted to tell Shen she knew how it felt to be alone. To be told your life was worth nothing.

Instead, she kissed Shen on the cheek and turned to Ruby. 'Deal me in and we'll come up with a plan.'

A knock on the door made Shen gasp and cower. Bunny opened the door, revealing Li Ling and Charlie Han beside her in the doorway. Violet and Bunny exchanged glances, and Bunny shrugged.

Charlie stepped forward. 'We changed our minds. Li Ling has an idea to help Shen.'

Li Ling now came forward, her eyes apprehensive but her face proud. Lowering her gaze, she murmured to Shen in Chinese then gave a shallow bow.

Charlie nodded towards his wife. 'Li Ling is sorry for Shen. She says the old superstitions make us afraid. But no-one deserves to die as a blood prize. We will help.'

Violet sprang to her feet and went to Li Ling. She embraced the woman briefly then drew back. 'Please tell us your plan.'

CHAPTER 10

MADAME STEPPED OUT OF THE darkness of the church onto the bright sandstone step. Two local women slipped in through the doorway behind her, arms full of fresh lilies and eyes averted. The irritating tap of their tasteful shoes against the tiled floor of the nave set her teeth on edge.

I see—waiting until I left, she thought. Cowards.

'Beg pardon, ladies,' she called to their retreating figures. 'The priest's all warmed up, if it's confession you're after. You look like you could do with unburdening yourselves.'

Won't be seen breathing the same air as a sinner like me, she thought. Pair of toadies.

'Lilies are poisonous, you know!' she added.

Poisonous to animals, Peg, she reminded herself. Settle down; you sound like a mad woman.

Merde.

She reached into a pocket for the flattened packet of Craven A and lit one using her brass lighter.

How good it must feel, she thought, sending a stream of smoke towards the stone ceiling of the porch, to simply believe that the devil capers about on goat's hooves and carries a pitchfork. Because the moment you know that ordinary evil—selfishness, cowardice and complacency—lurks in every heart, the whole world is a darker place.

She looked out across the churchyard and over the street, and pursed her lips. Sydney could be so pretty sometimes. Even in winter, with the plane trees as nude as telegraph poles and the kids all shoeless and forlorn. She took another drag on her cigarette and exhaled, watching the smoke drift away.

A car engine idled and a horn tooted in the street below the steps, disturbing her thoughts. She peered through the cropped branches of the churchyard crepe myrtle trees. 'Percy? What the devil are you doing here?'

Doc Flanagan leaned out of the open door of a green-painted grocer's van that had seen better days. 'Morning! Albert said I could find you here. Your carriage awaits, Madame!'

She dropped her cigarette, giving the parish widows something to sweep up, and trotted down the steps and along the path to the kerb. 'What on earth are you doing in this death trap?'

'My pal Chicken's selling up. Off to his daughter's place in Wagga Wagga, doesn't want the bother of a car down there. I delivered that daughter and the other four besides, so he says he'll give it to us cheap.'

She surveyed the ancient vehicle. 'I was hoping for something a bit more stylish, Percy. Can't a girl have a bit of dignity?'

Doc laughed. 'Whatever for? I thought you enjoyed offending the middle classes. Come on, let's take her for a spin and you can let me know how much you'd be prepared to offer Chicken, eh?'

Madame folded her arms. 'Five daughters? That's a lot of hair ribbons and face cream.'

'What are you getting at?'

'Perce, this car would barely sell for scrap! If anyone's getting a favour here, it's Chicken,' Madame replied. She drew herself up. 'But I do believe I'd like to take this *ve-hicle* for a spin with you, Doctor.'

Madame, chin elevated, opened the door of the van with a gloved hand. Losing only a little of her poise, she slid sideways onto the bench seat.

Doc Flanagan tilted his hat towards her. 'Where shall we go?'

'Bondi. We can watch the ships line up for port and dream of better places.'

He peered at her. 'Are you alright? I've seen that look before.'

'Hmph. I've been thinking.' She slid him a look.

'Uh-oh.'

She turned in her seat. 'Might need to defend meself. Thought I might look at one of your medical books. Find out the best way to stab a man. In the neck, do you think?'

He let out a sigh, both hands on the wheel before him. 'And here's me thinking: *Go and find Peggy O'Sheehan. She'll want distracting from the fact she's dying. Poor Peg, all sad and torn up inside.*'

'Ah, yes. Well, I'm not rapt about that, it's true.'

'Yet here you are, talking about stabbing a fella. Tell me: does my head rattle when I move? 'Cos I reckon I must have rocks inside it to be hanging about with you.'

'I've often wondered. Might explain your attachment to me, Perce.' She scratched her nose. 'What about poisoning? Might be cleaner and more secret. I could get in and do it before the enemy strikes a blow, as it were.'

'Oh, for heaven's sake. Are you going to tell me what's going on?'

She puffed out her cheeks and looked at him. 'Alright. But it'll be you getting your neck wrung if you so much as breathe a word to another soul. And you'll have to promise you won't see me any different once you know.'

He placed his hand on her gloved one. 'Don't insult me.'

'Alright, drive.'

—

They drove all the way to Bondi and back, the gearstick of the van wobbling between them. But Doc Flanagan turned out to be a dead loss when it came to advice on murder or self-defence.

Get a dog, he had told her. A German shepherd. Terrific judges of character.

A guard dog won't help us now, Madame told herself as she waved him off, then trudged up the steps to La Maison des Fleurs' front door. Not now the enemy's got one foot inside the gate.

CHAPTER 11

IT WAS NEVER ABOUT THINGS.

It was about hope. Optimism. It was about a future for Violet and Albert that looked different to the only life they'd known. You needed to see people experience happiness to imagine the same happiness for yourself. At La Maison des Fleurs, people were happy.

Violet felt sick at the thought of Artemis the gun, shoved at the bottom of her knicker drawer.

Oh God, Iris. What *happened*?

Bunny broke her train of thought. 'How much you got in there?' She nodded at the Bushells tea tin full of pound notes and coins, which rattled on Violet's lap as the tram clattered along Anzac Parade. Violet's life savings, to buy the life of a girl.

'Don't know. Ten pounds or thereabouts?'

'Struth. Will it be enough?'

Violet looked at Li Ling, who shrugged. 'I've got no idea,' said Li Ling.

The tram to La Perouse took Bunny, Li Ling and Violet from the cramped inner city all the way into a stark landscape of white dunes studded with tin shacks and lean-tos. Li Ling's plan was a stroke of genius. She'd explained that the Chinese market gardeners opted for long shirts, gloves, pants and their characteristic woven hats, to avoid the sun. In such an outfit, Shen's tattoos would be concealed and she could hide in plain sight among the Chinese folk out in the La Perouse settlement. All that remained was to convince old Mr Ming, the unofficial leader of the market gardeners, to harbour their fugitive.

The tram approached a turning circle at the end of Anzac Parade and, brakes squealing, came to a stop. As the women exited the tram, Bunny stumbled on the step.

A young Aboriginal man dressed in vicar's robes stepped forward from the tram stop to offer his hand to help her down. Bunny accepted the man's proffered hand, but her face registered her shock at his dark skin.

'Thanks, mister,' Bunny said primly, pulling away.

'Actually, it's Father. Father Eddie Gibbs.' He doffed an imaginary cap to Bunny, who shrank back a little.

He reached up to help Violet, who took his hand gratefully, hefting a heavy basket containing food and gifts and the tin of money onto one hip.

'Thanks. Gosh, it's turning warm today,' she said, landing awkwardly next to him.

He laughed. 'This is warm? Please tell me it gets warmer than this.'

'You're not from here?'

'Nope, from out past Broken Hill. Just shy of the state line. Hot as a furnace in the summer.'

'Well, Father Eddie, I hope spring comes to Sydney soon and warms things up for you.'

The pastor looked to be in his mid-twenties. He had a warm and friendly face, but on one side a long scar puckered his cheek from his temple all the way to his chin.

'Actually, maybe you could help us to locate the man we're here to see,' Violet said.

He shrugged. 'What kind of man are you after? Out here we've got the Russkies, the Poles, the blackfellas, the Old Chow and a whole stack of folks who come from nowhere and don't have nowhere else to be.'

'Old Chow—is that the Chinese? We're after a Chinaman. Mr Ming. Living in the market garden camps.'

Father Eddie looked at his watch. 'I've got ten minutes until this old trundler heads back into town. Just enough time to take you to old man Ming. You might even get him to talk to you.'

'What do you mean?'

The pastor raised an eyebrow. 'You'll see.'

'Brilliant. Here.' Violet handed Father Eddie one of the crisp new apples from the top of her basket. 'For your trouble.'

'Don't mind if I do.'

He led them off the road and onto a track that wove neatly through the small settlement lining the street. Up close, Violet saw that the yards were swept and fenced—though the fences were made from iron bedheads and car parts and the like. A vegetable garden swept up the hill behind one of the larger houses, which sported a brick chimney and an outdoor privy. Chickens pecked in the dust behind the back door.

Father Eddie followed her gaze. 'Maclean's place. Keeps it as neat as a pin. Got ten kids and they all help in the garden. Chicken shit, that's his secret. Best tomatoes I ever tasted!'

Violet laughed. They walked on.

After a couple of minutes Father Eddie stopped and pointed. 'That one, that's Ming's.'

Ming lived in a big house in the rolling dunes beyond the rise. Behind the house, trim market gardens stretched out in a patchwork of green hues. Smaller dwellings, roughly made from board and sacking and rusting tin sheets, were dotted against the sand.

Father Eddie turned to Li Ling. 'You might need to translate for your friends. Ming's a cranky bugger, but it helps if you speak his native tongue.'

Li Ling nodded.

Violet regarded Ming's place. It looked like it had been added to over many years with sheets of corrugated tin and planks, like many of the other shanty houses. But the central structure was older and made from hewn sandstone blocks. The roof of the old part of the house was made of clay tiles, and the sandstone of the broad chimney glowed in the bright morning sun. Ming's was one of the grand houses of the camp, she realised.

Father Eddie patted Bunny on the back. 'See you, kid.' He turned to Violet. 'Look after yourselves. I've gotta get that tram.'

They watched as he hastened down the sandy path.

Bunny whistled, looking after him. 'Did you ever see a chap so black? And what about that scar, eh?'

Violet sighed crossly. 'I thought you'd be used to all kinds of folks by now, Bunny.'

They set off along the path, Li Ling in the lead.

Bunny shaded her eyes from the sun. 'When I was growing up, my mum didn't let me talk to the darkies, not even the little kids who lived a couple of doors up. That's what she called 'em—darkies.'

She fell silent. It was rare for Bunny to mention her mother.

Violet shifted the weight of her basket to her other hip. 'Well, look around you, Bunny. This is what the world is: people getting by, all kinds of people. It makes no more sense to be afraid of a person for their skin colour than to be afraid of them because their face is put together different.'

Bunny's hand flew swiftly to her cleft upper lip.

'Be afraid of the people who truly mean you harm, Bunny.' Violet felt a shudder go through her as she remembered the words Madame had flung at her: *You're leading us into trouble.* She brushed the thought aside. 'Anyway, Father Eddie seemed like a good egg to me.'

Bunny shrugged. 'I suppose.'

'Let's hope this man Ming turns out to be another good egg, eh?' Violet said, as they arrived at the house.

She set the basket of food and gifts on the ground at Ming's front door and stepped back to allow Li Ling to take the lead. Bunny hovered at Violet's side, her hand across her mouth.

A man stood blocking the doorway, scowling. He wore woollen army pants and leather boots and his neck was as thick as a cedar trunk.

Li Ling spoke rapidly, but the man's expression didn't change. She turned to look at Violet.

'Try again,' Violet urged.

Li Ling took a slow, deep breath, then addressed the man again. It sounded as if she was pleading with him. Still he stood silently, sizing them up.

Eventually he spoke, his voice low and rumbling.

Li Ling gave an exasperated sigh. 'He asks why he should help us. He doesn't know us. He doesn't know the girl's family. He says you only ask him because one Chinese person is just like all the other Chinese people to you.'

'Shen can *hide* here among other Chinese people. That's the whole point. We'd hide her ourselves if we could, but this is the best solution we could come up with.'

A girl of eight or nine slipped past the old man and rolled her eyes at him, tutting impatiently. She wore a high-collared traditional Chinese jacket over a long cotton dress. Her feet were bare.

'Don't worry about Grandpa,' the little girl said. 'It's not that he hates white people particularly. He doesn't like anyone much.'

Bunny smothered a giggle and Violet nudged her. 'What's your name, clever clogs?'

The girls smiled proudly. 'Eliza. Not very Chinese, is it?'

'It suits you down to the dirt, Eliza. Please tell your grandpa we only ask his help for a short while, maybe just a couple of days. He'll be saving a girl's life. Plus, we can pay.' She bent to retrieve the tin of money from the basket and shook it. 'My money's the same as his money, right?'

Eliza turned to her grandfather and delivered what appeared to be a stern talking to. Li Ling chuckled.

A hint of a smile crossed old Ming's face. 'Alright. You'd better come in,' he said.

The inside of the cottage was surprisingly bright. Winter sun poured through windows that ran along the side of the building. Violet saw crashing waves out beyond the undulating dunes.

At Ming's instruction, they sat at benches on either side of the scored kitchen table. He brewed jasmine tea from a pot boiling on the range, and served it in tiny cups made of the finest porcelain, decorated with delicate blue brushwork. They cradled the cups and sipped as Ming emptied the tin of money in front of them and counted out his fee.

Then he scooped the remainder back into the tin and pushed it across to Violet. 'We will take the girl for a few days,' he said. 'There's a small worker's shed along the path. We have clothes she can wear to cover her. A hat, gloves, jacket. Bring her tonight.'

Violet let out a sigh. 'Oh, thank goodness. We're ever so grateful.'

Ming peered at her, his hands folded in front of him. 'You know these men who brought Shen to you?'

'No, not at all.'

'What do you think they will do when they find Shen gone?'

Violet stiffened. 'I have a gun.' She heard Bunny gasp.

The old man's face softened and he finished his tea in a gulp.

Li Ling pulled the Bushells tea tin towards her and opened it. 'You only took five pounds!'

Ming replied to her in Chinese as he got to his feet. The meeting was over.

'What did he say?' asked Violet, standing.

Li Ling busied herself tying a shoelace. 'Nothing really. Told me he left some money to buy Shen some work boots.'

'Liar!' piped up Eliza. She turned to meet Violet's eye. 'He said it was to pay for your funeral.'

CHAPTER 12

THEY MADE THE RETURN TRIP in silence, Violet's companions as reluctant to consider the implications of Ming's words as she was.

There was no opportunity to rest when they reached La Maison. Bunny helped Violet into her tight blue evening gown, its bodice appliquéd with seed pearls. The gown was made of silk satin and smelled of Shalimar perfume. It was fitted to her torso then swung in short, revealing panels from her hips. Its shoestring straps were adorned with dainty diamantés.

Violet sat patiently in front of the dresser as Bunny wrestled her hair into orderly curls. Her mind was far away, however, turning over the many problems still to be resolved: Iris's sudden reappearance, their plan for Shen's disappearance . . . Shen's neck chain and the lock with the jade owl was an issue. It would surely arouse the interest, if not suspicion, of the market gardeners.

How could it not? Shen would have to be sure to button her collar to her chin.

Ruby said she knew a man who picked padlocks with just a toothpick between his teeth. He was on his way home from touring in the Ashton's Circus sideshow, apparently. Ruby would ask for his help to remove the chain.

Now Bunny patted Violet's coiffed head. 'All done. Better than Carole Lombard in *High Voltage*.'

Violet turned her head from side to side, admiring Bunny's work. 'You're really good at this, you know.'

Bunny shrugged the compliment away. 'Well, if it all goes tits up here I can get a job down in the David Jones salon, I suppose. I've got to go get Ruby's taffeta ironed for her nine o'clock. Some visiting American with lots of money.'

Violet stood as Bunny bustled to the door. Should she tell her about Iris?

'Wait.'

'What is it?' Bunny looked back at Violet from the doorway, her eyes shining with her customary optimism.

It nearly broke Violet's heart. She couldn't tell Bunny about Iris's terrible, lousy coat. Her fraying hat. 'Nothing, pet. I was proud to be your friend today, seeing the way you looked after Shen. That's all.'

Bunny giggled. 'You getting jealous, Violet Kelly? Don't worry, I'm still your Bunny.'

She swept out of the room, her arms full of jars of hairpins, towels and rollers.

Violet opened her cupboard. Which shoes to wear? Her gaze rested on the white patent-leather buckled heels and her thoughts drifted inevitably to Philip Chandler, the shoe connoisseur.

Enough of that, she told herself. It didn't pay to get mixed up with a client. She chose a dazzling pair of silver stilettos—murder to walk in but always a hit with the crowd.

Before heading downstairs, Violet tiptoed up the stairs to Madame's quarters, carrying her shoes in her hands.

She found Shen asleep, the light beside her turned down low. Shen stirred as Violet came in, then awoke with a cry of terror.

'Shh, it's just me.' Violet kneeled beside the bed.

Shen reached out a hand to clasp Violet's.

Violet lifted the manacle and chain from the floor and fastened it once again around Shen's wrist. She whispered, 'We have to make sure you're secured, as Xiao left you. Just in case. Charlie will come. You understand?'

Shen blinked drowsily but nodded. 'Charlie.' Shen frowned. 'You?'

Violet shook her head. 'I will come to see you tomorrow.' Violet knew Shen didn't understand. Charlie could explain, perhaps.

Shen reached out to stroke Violet's eyebrow and cheekbone with her fingertips. In the dim light, Violet watched Shen's beautiful dark eyes as they travelled her face, her jaw, her lip.

Shen leaned forward and kissed her. Lightly at first but then more deeply. Violet felt herself sinking into the soft luxury of Shen's sensuous lips. The girl drew close to her and, responding, Violet reached out to stroke Shen's hair. The kiss seemed to go on for minutes.

Shen withdrew first. 'You save me,' she said softly. 'Now you have me.'

Violet shook her head, dismayed. 'Oh! No, Shen. It's not like that.'

Shen smiled. 'I'm happy. I belong to you.'

Violet felt her throat constrict and found herself on the verge of tears. To be kissed because Shen believed she owed her something! It was shameful.

Violet collected herself. She had work to do and she could not explain this to Shen now. She stood, then bent to bestow a solemn and chaste farewell kiss on Shen's cheek. 'Goodbye, Shen.'

—◆—

In the parlour, the mood appeared relaxed—on the surface, at least. Madame had wound the gramophone and was playing Duke Ellington at an immoderate volume. She sat perched beside the bar with a tumbler of brandy in her hand and her eyes closed, swaying to the music.

Albert appeared at Violet's elbow. 'Everything's ready for us to get Shen out,' he said in a low voice. 'Charlie's out the back.'

She nodded. 'Good. It's up to you now. Don't forget Xiao might have someone watching the place. Use the laneway and make sure she's covered. She mustn't be seen.'

'Gotcha. When should we bring her down?'

Violet folded her arms. 'Not before nine. If we have to risk moving her through the hallways, we want to be sure the customers are drunk as lords first. Then they won't notice a thing.'

Albert gave her the thumbs-up and slipped back out into the passageway. Violet straightened her shoulders and prepared to face the night.

Ruby would be down any minute wearing the red taffeta dress reserved for her American gent. Susan circulated with a jug of iced Pimm's. Doris and Elsie were playing a quiet game of backgammon. Violet counted six men in the room—most of whom were clustered around Doris and Elsie.

One man sat alone reading a book, his face obscured from view. He lifted his eyes and Violet's stomach flipped: it was Philip Chandler, handsome as ever.

Spying Violet, he promptly closed the paperback, shoved it into his jacket pocket and rose to his feet. On his way across the room, he collected two glasses of Pimm's from Susan's tray.

He presented one to Violet. 'Evening. I hope you don't mind a repeat visit.'

Violet took the glass and appraised him over its rim as she took a sip. 'Heavens, you don't waste time, do you?'

'Not when I know what I want.' He raised his eyebrows rakishly.

She led him to an empty love seat under an oil painting depicting a flock of doves against a crimson sunset. 'What are you reading?'

He fished the book from his jacket pocket. '*The Waste Land.* I brought it for you, actually. Decided you could do with some real poetry.' He placed it on the seat between them.

She laughed and picked up the book. 'Modern poetry! The nuns at school didn't approve of anything written after 1700.'

'Nor should they. Nuns have absolutely no business reading poetry. It should be a condition of their vows. Read it. Tell me what you think.' He clinked his glass against hers and leaned a little closer. 'By the way, I've noticed those deadly weapons on your feet.'

Violet smiled. 'Aren't they quite the thing?'

'Do I need to fight anyone else for the right to enjoy them?'

She hesitated. 'Not for the next hour or so.' Violet reached over and caressed his cheek. 'But perhaps you ought to see someone else tonight, Mr Chandler. It'd be a shame to travel all the way from England and not see *all* the sights. What about

Ruby? She's so flexible she can almost . . . light her own gun-powder.' She winked.

'Amusing as that sounds, it has to be you.'

She smiled. 'Come on then.'

Madame's eyes flicked open as Violet led Philip Chandler to the door. *That woman can sense an impending breach of the rules from a hundred paces*, thought Violet.

—

She lay on her bed in the Rose Room with her head in the crook of his arm, sipping Pimm's. From here, she could study the sharp angle of his jaw, the rise and fall of his chest.

'Right, my turn,' he said. 'You're the secret love child of a Russian tsar, whisked away to the colonies as a babe in arms, raised in a house of humble means by a loving family who treated you as their own and never questioned your taste for beetroot and vodka.'

'Oh, so close!' *I could stay here all night*, she thought.

'Tell me.' His fingers trailed along her neck.

'I'm an orphan, like you—although I didn't have your luck with aunts. Raised in a local orphanage and I have a twin.'

'No!'

'It's true. But we're no longer in touch.' *It wasn't a complete lie*, she reasoned.

'How can you bear that?'

'You ask too many questions.'

'I'm sorry. It's none of my business. Here, I brought you some-thing else.' He sat up with a groan and reached for his jacket, which was crumpled beside the bed, and pulled a small box from the top pocket.

'You already gave me a book!' She wriggled to sitting, her head against the brass bedhead.

'This is something special. A violet amethyst. The Ancient Greeks drank out of cups carved from it because they thought it prevented drunkenness. One look at *their* poetry and you can see it failed.'

He handed her the little jewellery box and she opened it. Inside was a silver brooch in the shape of a peacock, in the French Art Nouveau style, studded with coloured stones—the largest of which was a large amethyst set at the centre of the peacock's forehead.

'Oh, it's beautiful. Not just amethyst, these are topaz and sapphires! And those peacock eyes look like diamonds. *Philip.*'

'Tiny diamonds. Specks, really.'

'I love it. But . . .'

'But what?'

'Are you leaving town? Is that why you're in such a rush?'

He hesitated. 'It's how I pays the bills.'

'*Touché.*'

'A diplomat's job is to do what he's told, go where he's sent and not complain. It's a perfectly British occupation.' He threw the sheets from his legs and turned away from her to sit up.

She placed a palm flat on his back, along the spine. 'Where to?'

'Back to London to begin with. Then, I suspect, India.'

'When?'

'Any day now. The London office is trying to get me on the next boat going around the Horn of Africa in the right direction.' He pulled on his trousers and turned to face her.

'Who's waiting for you at home?' she asked.

'Now who's asking too many questions?' He let out a sigh. 'My wife Mary is at home. Mary, who's clever, beautiful, titled, rich and completely in love with Eleanor, her companion. I'm only in the picture for appearances' sake.'

'But what about you? What about love?'

'Who needs love? I have adventure!'

Violet reached up to him and he tugged her to her feet, then pulled her close.

'If you really believed that, you wouldn't be giving beautiful jewels to young ladies you hardly know,' she said. 'And if you don't hurry, you'll end up adventuring your way onto Madame's blacklist.'

'Violet, may I come back tomorrow?'

'You know I'll be here.'

'That's not what I asked.' He looked at her directly, his clear blue eyes devoid of sarcasm.

'I'd like that,' she said.

—

Violet showed Philip Chandler to the door and farewelled him tenderly, yet she felt conflicted.

It was delicious to be with him. But it was dangerous too. Jewels are lovely, she thought, as she closed the door behind him, but are they payment enough if I become aware of my own loneliness?

He was leaving, after all. She pushed aside the unfamiliar feelings aroused by him, the vulnerability and sweet yearning. There's naked, she thought, and then there's *naked*.

As she returned through the hallway she was surprised by Albert.

'There you are,' he said, sounding agitated. 'It's nearly nine. Shen's ready to go. I've checked the back lane and the front, and I think it's all clear.'

'Alright. Good luck!' She gave him a sisterly peck on the check, which he wiped away with his fist.

Her heart troubled, Violet returned to stand by Madame's side at the piano. Dido and Aeneas chirped in the brass cage, while Susan picked out a tune with one hand in the piano's tinkling high register. Violet's nerves felt jangled and she shifted from foot to foot anxiously. Madame's eyes opened to slits and she raised a large brandy.

'Is it done? Has that cursed girl been removed?'

'Not yet. Soon.'

'Better watch yerself with that diplomat. Saw you over there, talking books and whatnot.'

Violet crossed her arms and stared out into the boisterous room. 'Well, Peggy, I've been thinking. It occurs to me our Mr Chandler might come in handy, if we need to pull some official strings.'

Madame drew herself up to her full height and wheeled to face Violet. 'Violet Kelly, you impertinent so-and-so! Don't you dare call me—oh, saints preserve us!'

'What?' Violet turned to see what had caused the look of alarm on Madame's face.

'It's Xiao! He's come to check on us.'

'Oh heck, Shen and Albert!' Violet turned and hurried for the door.

CHAPTER 13

MADAME STEPPED INTO XIAO'S PATH, calling once again on the mercy of the saints and her dwindling reserves of composure. 'Xiao. We weren't expecting you again so soon!'

He must suspect *nothing*.

He appraised her silently and the sight of him sent a wave of confusion through her; in the mature lines of his face, she now detected a shadow of Jian, the younger brother she had loved so long ago. Xiao wore a well-cut dinner jacket with satin lapels and a sky-blue cravat. His black-and-white patent-leather shoes tapered to elegant points. His skin was burnished in the soft gold of the lamplight.

Oh, this is a cruel torment, she thought. Jian, how I wish it was you and not this bloodthirsty leech. It was dizzying, the way the past came crashing into the present.

She pulled herself together and smiled at Xiao. 'Let me guess:

you're so taken with the place, you've come back to ask for the name of my decorator?'

'I'm here to make the necessary checks, of course.'

She swiped a glass of champagne from a passing tray, took his arm and leaned in close. 'Come, come. There's no need to sneak up on us, Xiao. You have my word that Shen is confined.'

He sniffed. 'How quaint. But your word is nothing. Only proof will suffice. My business partner sends his regards, by the way. He remarked on how pretty your niece is, but for that lip.'

Putain! She gave a sharp gasp then shook her head in disgust at the provocation. 'No wonder you lost at cards, Xiao. You show your hand, so. You'll remember that you're a visitor in my house.'

Casting around for any sign of Violet, she led Xiao to a chaise in the corner of the room. 'It's quiet here. We can talk.'

Xiao sat, legs apart and hands on his knees. 'You wish to talk? What do you and I have to talk about?'

Her confidence drained away at this final dismaying remark. Was there no way to stall him? He glanced around the room, sizing it up. Once again, Madame saw the luxury of the place through Xiao's appraising eyes. The man seemed to be calculating as he watched, noting the expensive decor, the well-stocked bar. The girls.

'Actually, I believe I will trouble you for a whisky,' he said unexpectedly. 'Then you can take me to see the girl.'

'Of course.' Seizing the chance to buy precious time, Madame hailed Ruby, who was lingering nearby, and whispered in her ear. Ruby left for the bar and returned swiftly with a bottle, a fine glass and a chrome jug of ice.

At that moment, Madame caught sight of Doctor Flanagan's white hair and flushed cheeks amid the crowd. Saved, she thought.

Percy pushed his way towards them through the throng, waving his hand in an exaggerated greeting. 'I say! Hello, Pegs—I mean, Madame.' He pulled up short in front of the seated, frowning Chinese man. 'Oh heavens, terribly sorry! I was just hoping to, ahem, join the party.' He looked imploringly at Madame, who moved swiftly to capitalise.

'Not at all, Doctor. Ruby, bring us the card table, will you? Now look at that. We have a four for bridge if you join us, doctor.'

Thank heavens for Percival Flanagan, she thought. When he's not lancing boils or terminating pregnancies, he's saving me from a spot so tight I can feel the grip of it crushing my lungs.

Before Xiao could object, Ruby slid the card table in front of him and, with a theatrical flick, unfurled a lace cloth.

Doc Flanagan shoved his hand out to Xiao. 'Percy. How do and all that. Well, before we start the cards, tell me if I'm right: you look like a man who follows the cricket. Yes? Wonderful game. Do you Orientals have something like it?'

Seeing her opportunity, Madame excused herself for a moment, got to her feet and edged away, craning to see over the heads of the crowd. Where the hell was Violet Kelly?

At last Violet appeared in the doorway, her face flushed. She caught the attention of Ruby, who was now circulating with champagne, and whispered in her ear. Madame watched as Ruby edged through the crowd, greeting familiar faces as she went, coming to a stop by Madame's side, where she whispered, 'Ten more minutes. They're heading up the back stairs now and they have to get Shen into her old clothes and back into that evil contraption. She's ever so distressed.'

'And that's why,' concluded Doc loudly, 'the British use willow for cricket bats and not some other wood. *Fascinating*, don't you think?'

Not bothering to repress his impatience, Xiao tossed down the glass of whisky and got to his feet. 'Take me to your apartments now, Madame,' he demanded.

'Not before you've shaken my hand, I hope.' Violet materialised before them, beaming her Folies Bergère smile and showing an indecent amount of upper thigh through the split satin of her dress. '*Enchanté* and pleased to make your acquaintance, sir,' said Violet with a slight curtsy, eyes lowered.

As she straightened up, Madame caught the fierce look in Violet's eye. The girl stared unblinkingly at Xiao as he crudely assessed her.

He turned to Madame, eyes stony. 'How much?'

Madame saw the tiniest flinch ripple Violet's sanguine facade.

'It's our custom to keep business discussions to a minimum in the parlour,' said Madame. 'We like to establish an affinity with guests first. *Salut!*' Still as crude as a barrow boy, she thought, as she raised her champagne flute to him.

He shrugged. 'Why make it difficult? Everything in this room has a price. So, I ask again: how much for her?'

Madame attempted a laugh. 'Xiao, come now. My girls are entertainers. Hostesses. They are much more than just a fee.'

'Are they? Yet you hire them out by the hour. How eager you are to affect etiquette and pretty talk, for the sake of your conscience. Yet at the core, you and I are no different, Peggy. Romantic notions can cloud one's grasp of the truth.'

'Truth depends on your perspective, Xiao. I believe we trade in notions here at La Maison des Fleurs. They are our currency. Here, a certain truth is created through illusion and performance. I sense you've already been affected. I wonder what it is about Violet that takes your fancy? What notions evade the head but stir the heart of a man like yourself, hmm?'

Violet slipped between Madame and Xiao, placing a hand on the sleeve of his jacket. 'Xiao, I'm free now. Let's go to my room, where we can settle the matter of money. Bunny, fetch me a bottle. I'd like to drink champagne with our visitor and we'll need fresh glasses.'

Madame looked at her sharply. 'Are you sure?'

Violet cocked her head. 'Whyever not? Come.'

Madame watched Violet lead him away, her mouth dry. She reached for Doc Flanagan's hand and grasped it. She didn't dare to think what Xiao would expect from her, once the door of the Rose Room closed behind them. That girl's courage would be her undoing.

CHAPTER 14

VIOLET PLACED THE CHAMPAGNE BOTTLE on the dressing table, closed the door of the Rose Room and took a moment to compose herself. She took a deep breath, steadying herself against the table, then turned to face Xiao.

'So . . .'

'You must be important, to have a room so luxurious,' he observed.

Violent shrugged. 'Not really.'

As he took in the room, she made a slow study of his face: he was handsome, although the square planes of his jaw had grown heavy in mid-life. The expression in his eyes was guarded (a gambler's face, she thought, with its practised look of detachment), but his eyebrows were thin and expressive.

He arched an eyebrow, tilting his head to one side. 'I see you staring. You don't seem like the others.'

'I'm not sure what you mean. Girls like me are ten a penny in this town.' Girls you would happily harm for sport, she thought.

She hid her shiver. Before her stood a man who cared nothing for people's misery. Just knowing that made her afraid of him. But tonight, when she'd heard him speak in the parlour about her price, she'd felt a visceral recoil. No girl was safe around a man who regarded her in such terms. Chains or no chains.

'I think you're being modest,' he said. 'A girl like you might go far in business, if you were clever about it. I could use someone with your'—he paused, searching for the phrase—'*industry knowledge.*'

'Oh, you've got me all wrong. I'm just here for a good time.' She handed the bottle to him so he could pop the cork, again scrutinising his face.

At school you learn about devils and demons, she mused. You think monsters are mystical. But the day you look evil in the eye you recognise it. It wears a dark suit, and smells of cedarwood and single malt.

He smiled; it was chilling. The cork hit the ceiling. The champagne fizzed and emitted a cloud of sweet-smelling vapour.

She handed him the glasses. 'I think it's time I had a proper look at you,' she said. She stepped forward until her face was inches from his, placed a hand on his shoulder and made a show of examining him.

Turn this situation on its head, she thought desperately. Make him the subject. Refuse to be intimidated.

She circled him. No gun in the back of his waistband, she noticed, trailing a hand over his shoulder blades. Good. She finished her slow circle and returned to face him, taking a glass of champagne from his hand. 'I expect you like to enjoy yourself. Do you visit the jazz clubs?'

'I prefer entertainments that include a goal. A little risk and a payoff.' He loosened his cravat, his eyes locked on hers.

'Risk has its place,' she agreed. 'Alongside mystery and pleasure.' Divert him. *Beguile* him. It was frightening to hear him brag about his appetites. 'Shall I put on some music anyway? I won't force you to foxtrot. I have a new pressing from the United States.'

Xiao jutted his chin. 'You're wasting my time. Get undressed. Show me what I'm paying for.'

Violet smiled brightly, though inside she quailed. Too late to back out now. 'Of course.' She turned around. 'Unbutton me.'

His fingertips brushed the bare skin at the back of her neck, sending a tremor through her and raising gooseflesh down the length of her arms. Then, as he slowly unfastened the buttons of her dress, she felt her stomach tighten with dread. She reached to prevent the dress from slipping to the floor but he seized her arm, spinning her around roughly to face him.

'Stop. I'm paying to see you.'

The dress fell around her ankles.

'Wait.' She wrenched her arm away and clutched her clinging silk slip to her body. 'You don't have to force yourself on me. That's not how we do things here.'

He snatched her by the throat. 'We do things the way I want.' His palm crushed her windpipe.

She rose onto tiptoes and dug her nails into his fingers, prising them away from her neck. 'Let go of me, you animal,' she croaked.

The slap was so hard it sent her flying. She fell heavily against the table, bringing the ice bucket clattering to the floor with her. The room spun as she hit the carpet, feeling the impact crunch her back teeth. Before she had time to recover, he was reaching down to haul her to her feet by both arms.

The room lurched again.

He gripped her by the shoulders and drew her face close to his. 'Take off the rest of your clothes.'

She squirmed away. 'Please—Xiao.'

'Let go of her!'

Violet lifted her head to a blur of movement as the door burst open. As she gasped for breath, strong arms pulled her away from Xiao. It was Albert, pressing her to his side.

'You low dog,' spat Albert. 'I could—'

Madame pushed her way into the space between Albert and Xiao, arms outstretched. 'Xiao, you're no longer welcome here as a customer. You can follow me upstairs and check on your quarry, since that's the reason you're here, but Violet is no longer available. And you'll never pay for another girl here again.'

Xiao wiped his brow on the sleeve of his jacket. 'You're foolish amateurs,' he muttered. 'You'd do well to remember I represent a man who is more powerful than anyone you've ever known. He would enjoy destroying this pitiful dump. You wait—you'll pay for this.'

'You're wrong. You and I made a deal and I owe you nothing more.'

'Take me to the girl. She'd better be exactly as I left her, ready for collection tomorrow night.'

'Very well. Then I'll show you to the door.'

Violet sank to her knees, the room swirling. Her throat ached from the press of Xiao's hands.

'Vi! Are you alright?' Albert was beside her on the carpet, smoothing her hair from her face.

'I'm fine,' she whispered hoarsely. 'But, Albert, if he's not the worst of it, we've got a real problem.'

She now knew—knew, in some incontrovertible way—that Xiao would think nothing of taking their lives to pay for Shen's disappearance. Xiao would crush them as if they were so many dry leaves underfoot.

CHAPTER 15

THE MAN IN THE DARK SUIT and two-tone shoes strode to the sleek black car, wrenched open the door, got in and, slamming the door shut behind him, sped away.

Iris pressed herself into the shadows of the entrance to the workshop, unsure of what she'd just seen.

She replayed the series of events to herself. The car had arrived, lights low. The man had got out and strode up the stone steps to the grand front door. He moved as if he had an unwelcome task before him, unlike the other amblers and drunks who wobbled up the steps in search of gaiety.

Moments later, she had noticed Albert and another dark figure sneaking out of the laneway beside La Maison des Fleurs. They were followed soon after by none other than her sister Violet, teetering in her eye-popping heels, hissing for Albert to turn around and for them both to hurry back. The trio then disappeared back into the laneway.

After half an hour or so, Iris heard voices raised inside, then watched as the angry man returned to the car and drove off.

Now the street was quiet, but for the throb of jazz and the hum of voices from inside La Maison des Fleurs. She imagined her sister in there, stretching on a soft-bellied sofa and shedding those shoes, a drink in her hand.

Plates of food, more left to spoil than eaten. Trays of chocolates.

Iris's stomach lurched uneasily. All day she'd watched the house with nothing to keep her upright but the ragged bit of bacon and bread, hardly enough for a small child, that Albert had pressed into her hand that morning. The cold in her feet was making her ankles ache. Hunger gnawed in the pit of her belly. But that was nothing new: hunger was constant.

Well, she thought to herself, I've been punched and kicked and held down, but this hunger, this empty feeling, is the pain that defines me. What do you think of that, Violet Kelly?

She looked up at the grand facade of La Maison des Fleurs, her resentment giving way to a feeling she didn't like. Was it envy?

A faint disturbance across the road drew her attention: the two figures whom Violet had chased and retrieved earlier were creeping cautiously out of the laneway for a second time. Albert and his companion, whoever that was. They hurried up the road. Did she imagine Albert's backward glance in her direction?

She shuddered. It was time to move.

She pushed herself away from the shadow of the garage doorway and walked up the road in the other direction. She wouldn't go to the butcher's yard tonight. She'd had enough of the cold shed and the rank charnel smell.

She turned up towards Oxford Street and began to head east towards Centennial Park. The kids' camp would have a fire, perhaps a rabbit in a pot with a carrot or two swiped from the stable. She walked under the Moreton Bay figs, hunger driving her forward, then swung right into the parkland, followed the road to the posh houses, then joined a narrow path that ran alongside the sandstone wall of the stable.

Just a few minutes away now.

It wasn't much of a camp. To the untrained eye it was little more than a rag-and-bone pile. But now she longed for the comfort of that collection of shelters made of sackcloth and pilfered bits of tin, longed to sit by the fire on one of those tattered rugs or pieces of cardboard used to make a floor.

Some days the number of kids in the camp swelled until there were twenty or so, some barely old enough to speak. Who knew what horrors those babies were fleeing, dragged along by the dirty hands of older siblings?

These were children who should be tucked up in beds, in houses where they were loved. Where kindly adults laced their clean feet into pretty shoes. But Iris and the other kids weren't loved. They were used-up, second-hand kids. They fought each other and stole and looked out at the world with eyes narrowed by the meanness of their rotten luck.

It was better than facing the world alone, according to Tobias Grange, her boyfriend (if that's what you'd call him). But she wasn't always sure she agreed.

Ahead, she heard the voices of two older boys she knew: Sid and Eric Richards, the Aboriginal bare-knuckle boxers from Nowra, who toured up and down the coast with Jimmy Sharman and his troupe. The cool air carried the smell of charred meat. Her toes were icy now. She crunched along the path through the garden beds, the snapping twigs painful underfoot.

She paused in the shadows and wiped her nose on the sleeve of her threadbare coat. Summer was still months away. What do I need to do, she wondered, to get hold of a pair of shoes?

She thought of her sister once again, imagining a cupboard full of shoes and strings of pearls. A rabbit fur tippet and God knew what else. She puffed out her cheeks in frustration.

Oh, how satisfying the prank had seemed, that day when she had locked her sister up in the cupboard in St Michael's and walked out of the gate in Violet's place! How satisfying—and what a grave mistake.

She and her sister were so alike, they could exchange places without being detected. Only Albert could tell them apart and sometimes they even foxed him.

It was a trick they played to show off. Patrick Rose had double-jointed shoulders and Mabel Georgiou could turn a somersault.

But as they grew older it was Violet—sweet, charming Violet—who begged Iris to take her place to receive minor punishments or perform chores. Go on, Iris, oh please. You're a good egg, Iris.

Iris bit her lip and tucked her hands into her armpits, shivering.

Her ten-year-old self knew that even though they looked identical, it was her sister whom people liked. It was Violet who received the smiles, the favours. Violet who had her hair plaited by the sweet young novitiates, Violet who got the extra serve of jam on her bread-and-butter plate. Iris was the spare. The frowner, the shadow. The convenient stand-in who took the reprimands.

On the outside their identities were blurred. But they grew to be different people inside.

When a nice couple asked the Reverend Mother for a helpful and clever girl, around ten years old, to help with their baby, sweet Sister Philomena suggested Violet on account of her splendid bookwork and her recent spirited reading of *Just William*. Yet at the appointed hour, it was Iris who took pleasant Mrs Halliday's baby in her arms and stole away to Violet's new life in the shiny sedan, while Violet sobbed behind the locked door of the classroom stationery cupboard.

Iris walked out of that hellhole to take Violet's place on the cool leather seat in the Bentley with Mrs Halliday and her cooing baby.

Iris sniffed. Who could have expected such cruelty from people who spoke so well, who drove her home in that elegant car, with the lace-covered infant in her lap?

Mrs Halliday's baby was sweet and funny. He had gazed at her with large, chocolatey eyes and drooled on her cardigan all the way to the Hallidays' handsome home in Gladesville.

She still remembered clutching him to her thin chest in the dark of the bedroom while Mr Halliday kicked the other baby, the one Mrs Halliday was expecting, clean out of the woman's belly in the room next door.

Iris didn't really believe in God. But when she found herself out on the street, only a few months after leaving the orphanage, she wondered if it was some kind of divine punishment for deceiving her sister. There was no going back to St Michael's: not when all that awaited her were shame and recriminations. No, being outcast was her comeuppance and she was going to have to cop it sweet.

Oh, thought Iris, and I copped it, didn't it?

A hand landed heavily on her shoulder. 'Gotcha.'

Iris almost leaped out of her skin. 'Bloody hell, Tobias! You frightened me.' She sniffed. 'You been drinking?'

He rocked back on his heels. 'Where've you been? You said we were gunna trap rabbits over in Moore Park. Then you up and disappeared without sayin' why.'

'Sorry, Tobias. I've been about. Had to see someone.' It wasn't a lie. 'You've done okay, though. Smells like something's cooking.' She nodded in the direction of camp.

'Ducks from the lake,' said Tobias proudly. 'Got 'em with a slingshot. Come here.'

Out of the corner of her eye, she saw the flames of the campfire through the trees as Tobias pushed her down into the dirt.

—◆—

She rolled onto her side and pulled her dress down over her freezing legs.

Tobias had left her and returned to the camp. She could hear his voice rising loud and drunk above the others. She sat up and picked twigs from her hair.

If she didn't eat something soon, she was pretty sure she'd keel over.

Iris crept along, stepping quietly and keeping to the black shadow of the stable wall. The camp came into view. It wasn't much, but the sight of it still lifted her spirits.

She paused. The older boys had been busy in the time she'd been away, sleeping in the shed behind the butcher's. They'd rigged up new sackcloth roof to form a bigger canopy between the trees. In the centre, Iris saw new additions to the communal haul: some upturned wooden crates with *Kirk's Lemonade* printed on the side and some scavenged drawers from an old wooden dresser. These treasures had been dragged around the fire to form a circle of seats.

Iris counted the heads seated around the fire: seven kids of varying ages were sitting silently as Tobias, head crowned by thick, dark, firelit curls, turned two roasting birds over the fire on a contraption made of upturned tins and a long metal rod.

'Tobias,' Iris called hesitantly, walking into the circle of firelight.

The young man looked up, frowning. She knew the other girls thought he was handsome, had heard them say it. But she noticed odd and secret things about him. The curve of his neck where it met his collared shirt. The breadth of his back in his canvas army jacket.

But there was also his anger. The way he made her do things.

Iris moved cautiously to crouch by the fire opposite him, warming her hands. She longed to sit and thaw her feet. But you had to be careful with Tobias. His temper.

He lifted the metal rod from the fire and slid the roasted birds onto a sack laid in the dirt, shaking his scorched fingers. 'Ah, damn.'

Tobias gave her a long look and, after a moment, gave a quick tilt of his head, indicating the place next to him. Iris stood, wrapped her coat tight around her and hurried around the circle of kids to his side. She sat on a sack on the sandy soil and stretched her feet towards the fire. The relief was exquisite.

The tension in the group eased and Tobias started handing out piping portions of roast duck on the end of his knife.

He sliced her a generous wing, a recognition of her status beside him, and handed it to her. 'Me and Ollie get the legs, since we got the ducks and pulled all the farking feathers out.'

Ollie, a boy of about eleven who was sitting on Tobias's other side, gave a hoot.

'Too right.' Iris nodded. Her stomach cramped in anticipation as she took the oily portion and licked her dripping fingers.

Sid and Eric, the boxing brothers, appeared at the edge of the fire. Normally Iris liked them; she enjoyed their shifting, restless energy and their sense of fun. But today she would have preferred the quiet company of the smaller kids.

Tobias nodded to the brothers and they thumped down onto the sand on the other side of the fire. Tobias carved each of them a portion of the duck.

'Reckon I seen you up around Paddington this arvo, Iris.' It was Eric, the older of the two, wriggling closer to the fire. His hair was cropped close like his brother's and the muscles in his arms stood out under his shirt.

'That so?' she replied, eyes on the leaping flames. She knew what was coming.

'What's waiting for you in Paddo, eh? Pianola lessons?'

'Wouldn't you like to know, Eric Richards.'

'What's the big secret, Iris? Got a fancy man?' Tobias nudged her roughly.

She shook her head. 'None of anyone's business, is it?'

The chatter in the group stopped as everyone waited for Tobias to decide if this was an insult. Tobias licked his fingers.

'Who cares? Din't bring any food home, did she?'

The group fell quiet again as the kids ate with rapt solemnity. A small boy, sitting in the shadows with an older girl, finished his portion and started crying softly. His big sister gave him a shove, casting a furtive glance towards Tobias.

Tobias looked over at the boy. 'Snivelling shit! I'll give you something to cry for in a minute,' he snarled.

The boy fell silent, rubbed his eyes and hid his face behind his sister's sleeve.

Iris's belly clenched again, from anxiety this time. She looked at the dripping bones held in her fingertips.

Tobias held them all in a state of fear. Most of the kids, herself included, accepted his authority and tried to find a place in the pecking order, although it didn't always feel right. It was confusing. She felt heat rush to her cheeks. If Tobias was feeling generous, she was allowed to sit beside him, allowed to share his tent. Some of the time she was grateful to him; the rest of the time the uncertainty of her situation made her feel sick.

And she was so, so hungry. Overcoming her fear enough to take a bite, she ate ravenously, starvation taking over.

When she was done, she dropped the duck bones into the flames, let her hands fall in her lap, closed her eyes and felt the heat of the fire on her eyelids.

'Well, that's that.' Tobias's voice broke her reverie.

He handed the picked-over duck carcasses to Ollie to dispense. Emboldened, the younger children left their seats and clustered around Ollie. Tobias wiped his hands on his trousers and shoved Iris in the side with the tip of his boot. 'Carn then. I've got a job for ya.'

Iris froze. 'Not tonight, Tobias,' she begged. 'Please . . .' Foolish tears filled her eyes and she clenched her jaw to make them stop. Tobias had marched her down to South Dowling Street and found a man for her almost every night last week. He said the camp needed things they couldn't get without money. Oil for lamps. Candles. Flour. But she knew last week he had spent the money on bullets for his dead dad's gun from the Great War, and the glass flour jar on their meagre provisions shelf remained empty.

Tobias shook his head. 'Not that. Something else. Come on.' He kicked her side again, viciously this time.

Clutching her ribs, she scrambled to her feet and followed him away from the fire.

By the time she caught up with him, the warmth of the fire had left her body and the chill of the night made her clutch the coat to her chest once more. She fell into step with him. 'What is it, Tobias?'

He caught her arm and shoved her forward silently.

They reached the edge of the unkempt trees in which the camp lay hidden. In the semi-darkness, Iris saw they were at the place where the gravel road swept into the stable. Behind the iron gates, a single yellow light burned in the yard, casting a sulphurous glow.

'What're we doing? You know we can't keep nicking horse feed from the stable. The cops'll break up the camp.'

Sid and Eric emerged soundlessly from the copse behind them.

Tobias raised a fingertip to his lips. The boys nodded.

'We're not interested in nicking old carrots this time, Iris,' whispered Tobias.

Sid sniggered and received a sharp elbow in the ribs from his brother.

Iris folded her arms and scowled. It was bloody freezing. 'What then?'

Tobias grinned. 'My lads here spotted a car coming and going from here the last few days. Big car, imported. Real flash. Thought you might take a closer look for us.'

Iris shook her head. 'You pinch a car, Tobias Grange, and you'll get locked up or worse. You know it!'

Tobias grinned. 'That's why you're going to have a look for us.

If anyone catches you, you're just some girl looking for scraps. The police don't have anything on you.'

Eric stepped forward and, taking her by the arm, started steering her towards the wall in the deeper shadows. 'Come on, Iris. No need to worry, eh? Just take a quick look around the yard. Find the nice-looking car, test the doors, have a look inside and report back. We'll even give you a boost over the wall.' He gave her arm a squeeze.

Iris rolled her eyes. 'For God's sake, Eric. Do me a favour and stop speaking to me as if I came down in the last rain shower. Alright, let's get this over with.' It was simpler to do what they asked.

From behind, she felt Tobias pat her shoulder briefly. 'That's my girl,' he said, and she felt her belly flip, just for a moment.

They reached the wall. Iris supported herself against the cold sandstone with one hand and braced herself with the other on Eric's big shoulder. She stepped up into his clasped hands and was hoisted up roughly.

She winced as the palms of her hands scraped against the sandstone. She felt for the rounded top of the wall and swung her free leg over. It was easy enough; she and Tobias had scaled the wall plenty of times before.

She steadied herself on the top of the wall and looked out across the darkness of the park. In among the trees, she saw the orange of the fire and the thin plume of smoke that gave them away. The high cries of the younger kids carried across the park.

With a sudden and breathtaking realisation, she saw how obvious the camp was. Once the police noticed, the camp would be gone within hours.

There was no point in trying to tell Tobias and the others.

She took a slow breath, her chin against her chest. Tipping

forward so that her belly lay against the top of the wall, she swung her other leg up and over the top. She half-slipped and half-fell down the other side into the hay and muck of the stable yard, scraping her fingernails as she went.

CHAPTER 16

VIOLET PULLED THE SHEETS FROM the bed in Madame's guest-room, her mind racing.

Shen was gone: sweet, trusting Shen, saved from torture. Yet Violet now had to face what she had done to the rest of the household.

There was no choice, she reminded herself feverishly. Handing Shen over to be mutilated was not an option. The kiss with Shen replayed in her mind and the feelings of discomfort and despair returned. Shen seemed aware of just one way of living; she understood only the slavery to which she was accustomed.

Balling the sheets into a heap, Violet made a silent vow. She would help Shen to see herself differently. Shen would learn how to possess a kind of freedom that wasn't expressed in the release of manacles and chains: a freedom of self and a sense of choice.

Leaving Bunny to take the sheets to the laundry, Violet left Madame's guest bedroom and trudged downstairs to the first floor, entering the Rose Room with a heavy heart.

She closed the door behind her and switched on the light, then sank onto the bed and lay with her arms folded beneath her head.

Thoughts of Xiao returned to torment her. Without thinking, her hands flew to her throat as she remembered his quick-flare temper and the way he'd violently choked her. She had been a fool to underestimate the danger he represented.

She fought the rising sense of panic. Madame had seen it from the start: all of their lives were now in peril.

A soft knock sounded and then Bunny appeared in the doorway. 'Anybody in?'

Violet rubbed her eyes to dispel the anxious thoughts and patted the bed. Bunny came in and flopped down beside her, kicking off her shoes and wincing in pain.

'I reckon I'll be a cripple before I'm old,' Bunny said, massaging her cramped toes.

Violet frowned. 'Tell Madame to buy you some new shoes, Bunny. You work hard and she's got money, she can afford it. Not like some.' Her thoughts drifted to the man with the handcart she'd seen while standing outside the bakery—then, of course, to Iris.

Bunny yawned. 'Worried about Shen?'

'A bit.' Violet bit her lip.

'Me too. Hey, why don't we check on her at La Perouse? It's only old Doc's visit tomorrow morning and you don't need anything from him, do you?'

'No, I don't, thanks for asking! Yes, let's do that. Madame won't dare say no—not when Shen's life is on her conscience.'

'Okay,' came the sleepy response.

'We should go really early, though. Just in case Xiao decides to send his men to come looking. We don't want to lead them straight to Shen.'

'Mm-hmm.'

Violet's thoughts returned, slowly, to the problem of Iris. When should she tell Bunny the whole story? It must be before Iris turns up on the doorstep, she decided. Which, she thought with a tired sigh, could be any day now.

'Hey, Buns,' she began. 'I've got something to tell you.'

Bunny didn't reply.

Violet turned to see the girl was fast asleep, rolled onto her side with her hands tucked under her chin.

Wearily, Violet stood, pulled the covers over Bunny and turned to the dainty porcelain sink to brush her teeth. A stifled cough in the doorway startled her: Madame stood there tottering unsteadily in her brown brocade dressing-gown. She was weeping, a hand on the door frame for support.

Violet stepped into the hallway, pulling the door closed on the sleeping girl. 'Come on, Madame, it's alright. Shen's safe now.'

Madame shook her head. 'Shen might be, but what about the rest of us?' She gestured towards the bed, where her niece slept. 'When they come looking for Shen,' she whispered, 'they'll do whatever it takes to force us to give her back. And Xiao knows just what'll do it. It's Bunny they'll be after. Xiao told me as much himself.' She let out a sob. 'Oh God. What have we done?'

Violet felt her stomach constrict. *Bunny.* Could Madame be right?

She shook her head resolutely, heart thumping. 'It won't be

like that. They won't take Bunny from us. We'll offer them some-thing better. Go to bed, go on.'

She turned Madame in the direction of the stairs and watched her trudge up to her apartment. Then she slipped into the Rose Room, shut the door behind her and leaned against it, her breath coming in gasps.

Oh God. What *had* she done?

—

Dawn was warming the sky with gold as Violet and Bunny stepped out of the kitchen into the yard. Bunny shivered and wrapped her arms around her chest. Violet led the girl into the back laneway, rubbing her cold hands together.

'Don't be soft. Here, help me with this,' said Violet. She stopped at the wooden fence bordering the laneway that led to the house behind La Maison des Fleurs. She pulled at the palings. 'We need to throw anyone who's following off our trail, so let's get to the street behind.'

Together they yanked the paling free and, managing to loosen the adjoining one, slipped sideways into the yard of the house behind. A dog barked somewhere close by, and a flock of lorikeets lifted into the air from a neighbouring yard. Keeping to the shadows, they tiptoed past the house and out into the dimly lit street behind La Maison des Fleurs.

'Right, let's go,' said Violet, taking Bunny's hand.

They hurried to Five Ways, to the tram stop.

—

In La Perouse, they walked the path through the dunes to Ming's house as the morning sun rose over the ocean.

'Shen's this way,' said Eliza, joining them on the path.

She led them into the yard of a small wooden hut a hundred yards away. They approached the doorway and peered inside. The hut had an oiled wooden floor, a wooden bed covered in cosy-looking rugs and an iron stove with a piped chimney. Shen, covered completely in the high-collared white cotton shirt and navy pants of the gardeners, was bent over the stove, adding small pieces of wood to the fire. Her tattooed hands were covered with gloves and beneath the pants she wore long socks tucked into canvas slippers. Not a drop of ink was visible to the naked eye.

Shen turned and cried out with delight when she saw her visitors, then ran to embrace them, muttering in Chinese.

The little girl translated. 'She says it's wonderful to see you again. The dark bird she carried on her back has released her from its claws.'

Violet understood the metaphor completely. She clasped Shen's hands in her own and turned to Eliza.

'Can you tell Shen something important for me?' she asked.

The girl nodded. 'Of course.'

Violet looked for a place to sit, then drew Shen by the hand to perch on the edge of the bed. Eliza followed. Bunny sat in front of the stove, prodding the embers with sticks from Shen's pile.

Violet faced Shen. 'Shen, this place is only temporary. You're still in danger from the men who want to hurt you. We're going to get you far away from here. To a place where the dark bird won't find you.'

Eliza translated. Shen nodded, curiosity shining in her eyes. She spoke to Eliza briefly, and the girl turned to Violet.

'Shen says: will I be alone?'

Violet smiled. 'Shen will be alone but it will be different from before. She won't be lonely and afraid. She'll be able to choose her friends. She'll be free. She won't need to thank anyone for this or feel that she owes us. This is something we do because we hope others would try to do the same for us.'

Eliza repeated the words to Shen. The little girl smiled proudly when she reached the end and Shen drew her into a hug.

Violet continued. 'That thing on your neck, Shen, we have to get rid of it so that those searching for you can't identify it. Our friend Ruby is going to solve that problem for us.'

Again, Eliza translated. Shen's hands flew to the chain and lock at her neck, now concealed by the collar of her cotton jacket.

Eliza's face grew solemn. 'She says the chain still brings her pain. But it is different pain now. Now she knows the pain will end and she can bear it without tears.'

Then Shen stood. 'Thank you,' she said to Violet and Bunny in English.

Eliza jumped to her feet and clapped her hands. 'Let's go to the beach! Shen'—she began to mix up English and Chinese—'let's take your friends to collect pipis in the rockpool.'

Bunny stood and looked imploringly at Violet. 'I'd love a paddle—although I bet the water'll be Baltic!'

Violet turned to Eliza. 'Is it safe? How many people know Shen is here?'

Eliza seized Shen and Bunny by the hand and tugged them to the doorway. 'It's fine. Charlie Han brought her straight to Grandpa. To everyone else, she's a cousin come to work in the gardens.'

Violet hesitated as Eliza, Bunny and Shen made their way out of the dark cabin onto the sunny path outside. Shen cast an anxious look at Violet.

Bunny called over her shoulder: 'Close the door of the stove on your way past, Violet.'

Violet attended to the stove then followed the girls out of the cabin and into the sunlight. She walked behind them on the narrow path through the scrubby dune towards the beach.

Dressed as she was today in long pants, a shirt, cotton gloves and a wide-brimmed hat, Shen looked like just any other gardener, if a little overdressed. A curious observer might attribute her layers to vanity about the sun. According to Li Ling, Chinese girls prized pale skin and preferred to stay covered up. Violet turned these concerns over in her mind as she lagged behind the others. Shen's shack was comfortable but basic. It had no running water, no toilet. She would need to come and go; there would be no hiding her completely.

And there was the problem of the neck chain, of course, which bound her symbolically to the fate Xiao and the ghost-man would have forced on her.

Violet felt a surge of anxiety as she trudged along the sandy path after the other girls, her eyes screwed up against the glare. At the crest of the dune, before the final descent towards the sea, Shen turned to her again and beckoned for her to join them.

You *do* talk a good game, Violet scolded herself as she trudged forward to catch up. You've promised to keep Shen safe. Can you really keep that promise?

It was time to play her remaining card: Philip Chandler, the travelling diplomat and adventurer, who was leaving Sydney soon. He might be persuaded to take a vulnerable girl under his protection. He wouldn't be able to save the rest of the house from Xiao's searing anger, but by securing Shen's escape, he might make the whole gamble worthwhile.

I pleaded with Madame to let me find a way through this, one that allows all of us to survive, thought Violet. And I haven't found it yet, have I?

But Philip Chandler, she decided, was a good start.

Violet accepted Shen's outstretched hand and allowed herself to be pulled down the slope towards the beach.

CHAPTER 17

TOBIAS WAS GONE WHEN IRIS woke to the sound of a child crying just beyond her shelter. She lifted the canvas sheet and stuck her head out to see a small girl of around three years old sitting alone beside the cold ashes of the fire, her face creased in distress. Her woollen dress was grey from the camp dirt and her bare feet were filthy and scratched. Behind the girl, a large butcher bird was scratching in the dirt with its sharp beak, tearing sinews from a discarded duck bone.

Seeing Iris, the little girl lifted up her arms to be held. She was a pitiful sight, and Iris felt a familiar sadness tug at her throat.

Iris crawled out of Tobias's den and got to her feet. The wind shook the leaves above her head and the place felt chilly and abandoned. If older brothers and sisters had brought the crying toddler with them in the last day or so, they had now left her to fend for herself.

Iris bent and scooped up the infant, who buried her dirty face in Iris's shoulder, howling. The child's feet were freezing. Iris pulled her own coat around the girl.

After a while, the girl's weeping grew thinner and less frantic, so Iris hitched the child awkwardly onto her hip and carried her back into Tobias's den. Kneeling, she placed the child on the makeshift bed and wrapped her in Tobias's stolen army blankets. 'Hey, it's alright. You're gunna be fine. I'm here now.'

The child shuddered and hiccupped then, exhausted from crying, fell asleep.

Iris stroked the girl's matted hair. The canvas shelter let in a cool, green, filtered light that traced shifting patterns on the child's closed eyelids. Iris felt her own eyelids growing heavy.

She lay down beside the child and wrapped her arm around the fragile body. The girl gave a sleepy murmur and a sob. Iris pulled her close against her chest.

A few more minutes hiding from the world, she thought. That's all I want. She buried her face in the sweet, sweaty neck of the little girl and squeezed her eyes shut, avoiding a distressing truth: after the mission into the stable last night, she was faced with a dilemma.

—

She'd landed in the stable yard with such a thump, she'd worried the sound was loud enough to alert even the sleepiest stable-hand. She froze and waited for the lights, the shouts, but they never came. The yard remained in darkness. Outside the walls, a boobook owl hooted into the night and she heard an engine revving faintly in the distance. She imagined she heard the whispering of Tobias and the others. The stable was deserted, save for a couple of the horses kept for rich young ladies who lived along Darley Road. These expensive pets nickered sleepily in their bays.

She ventured out cautiously from the shadow of the wall, scuffing her feet on dry straw as she went. The long car was impossible to miss in the yellow light of the yard. It was a stark contrast to the filth of its surroundings, a powerful symbol of someone's wealth and influence.

She recognised it immediately as the car she had seen drive away from La Maison des Fleurs a few hours earlier.

A little awestruck, she padded over to the car on silent feet and drew a hand along its smooth, cold flank.

Her fingers reached the chrome of the door handle. She reached silently for the catch. It clicked open and she exhaled slowly. She crawled inside and breathed its expensive air, the dark leather cool and as soft as butter beneath her bare legs. She felt a sudden urge to lie down and sleep on those leather seats.

Then a sound in the yard had made her heart lurch in fear. A shadowy figure was unlocking the stable gates. Two men entered the yard on foot. The larger of the two walked with a faint tilt, dragging his leg slightly as if his hip was twisted. Iris flung herself down on the back seat and waited for the men to unlock and enter the building. The taller of the two men walked in an urgent, purposeful manner: she recognised him as the driver of the black car who had entered, then abruptly left, La Maison des Fleurs.

She saw the inside lights go on and heard the scraping of chairs against a flagstone floor. She slid from the seat of the car out through the door by which she had entered, landing in the dirt. She clicked the car door softly closed.

As she crossed the yard to return to the wall, she turned and caught sight of the two men through the stable house window.

One man—the man she identified as having the faintest limp—was holding a long, ornate sword. His hand travelled slowly along its blade. It was sinister and sensual; she imagined him talking as he stroked the blade, describing what it might do.

He sliced the air slowly. The gesture stopped her in her tracks.

As Iris's feet sank into the cold muck against the stable wall, a slow realisation dawned: these were the men threatening her sister and La Maison des Fleurs, a house full of silly girls. Violent men, threatening pampered, sheltered girls who were as helpless as kittens.

The way he wielded that sword: you could imagine him using it on a girl. Slicing the skin from her face.

Instead of leaving, as she'd intended, Iris watched and waited. Before long the men came out of the office, got into the car and left, closing the heavy wooden gate behind them.

She should have gone back to Tobias. The boys were just on the other side of the wall, waiting for her to return. She could hear Tobias's low whistle, his cuckoo call. But cold fear for her sister drove Iris to run across the yard and circle the stable building, looking for an unlocked window.

What she found inside the building had made her cry out and wish she'd never been so bold.

——

Now Iris sat up, pulling a musty, patched rabbit skin over the sleeping infant. Rooting around at the back of the den, she found a paper bag with a handful of stale monkey nuts. She placed these next to the child's balled fist and crawled out of the makeshift tent, blinking in the winter light.

There was nothing for it. Now she *had* to talk to her sister.

Otherwise, she'd have to live with knowing that she could have prevented a bloodbath, but didn't.

She stood and ran her fingers through her hair. Strapping a canvas bag across her chest, she turned to retrace her steps back to La Maison des Fleurs.

'Oi. Where d'ya think you're going?' shouted Tobias from behind her. 'There's four rabbits here need skinning.'

Iris's heart gave a leap. At the sound of Tobias's voice, the little girl gave a startled cry from inside the tent.

She turned around. 'It's fine,' said Iris, heart thumping. She dropped her bag. 'Take 'em over there so I can do it on the grass.' She pointed to a dull patch of yellow tufts a few feet from the camp.

Tobias trudged across the campsite and sat in the grass. One by one he untied the rabbits from his belt.

Iris slipped into the shelter. The child was awake, her big grey eyes round and pensive above the blankets. Putting a finger to her lips to silence the child, Iris lifted the little girl by her armpits and carried her out.

The child stared at Iris in mute confusion as Iris set her on her feet beside the fire pit.

'Go. Go on!' whispered Iris, pushing the little girl towards the trees.

The child blinked, frozen.

There was no point in risking Tobias's temper, Iris thought. You could never tell what would set him off, but a toddler in his bed was just the kind of thing that could earn her a clip around the ear.

'Go find your brothers and sisters. Go on, git!' Iris gave her a second gentle push.

The girl looked from Iris to the bag of monkey nuts clutched in her fist. Her little chin wobbled and her lips pursed as more tears collected in her eyes. Giving a sigh that shook her small shoulders, she turned and toddled off beyond the camp.

Iris gave a sigh of relief and turned towards Tobias, who sat waiting, watching, the sharpened skinning knife already in his hand.

CHAPTER 18

LI LING STOKED THE STOVE, rearranged a pan of cooling boiled eggs, then returned to sit at the scrubbed kitchen table where she had arranged squares of red paper into neat piles.

Madame, sitting opposite her, coughed and gave a shiver, then pulled the fox fur collar of her good winter coat more closely around her throat. 'Is it me or is it chilly? Roll on spring, I say. I could have sewn myself into my long johns this morning and I'd still be perishing.'

Li Ling tutted and looked up from the squares of paper in her hands. 'It's not weather, it's you. You need more breakfast. You look like an empty flour sack!'

Madame squinted crossly at the piece of folded paper in Li Ling's hands. 'I'll thank you to keep your insults up the Yellow River where they belong, my friend! What the devil are you doing anyway?'

They were interrupted by Charlie as he threw open the back door and stepped in, stomping his feet on the doormat.

'Close it, Charlie! That wind's straight from the Arctic.' Madame pinned her windblown hair behind her ear.

'Antarctic,' corrected Charlie. He slammed the back door, shucked his coat, hung it on the peg on the back of the door and then stood before the stove, rubbing his hands.

Li Ling nodded to her husband. 'She wants to know what I'm doing.'

He pointed at Li Ling's folded paper squares. As she tugged at one end of the folded paper it became a lotus shape. 'See? It's a lantern boat,' he said. 'Hungry Ghost festival on the fifteenth day of the seventh month, Chinese time. At the end, we make a boat for a candle to send the ancestors back to the afterlife. Not long now. The dead must be getting restless!'

Li Ling looked up at Madame serenely. 'You feed the spirits, maybe you won't feel so cold?' She smiled and reached across to pat Madame's hand before scooping up her paper squares and tucking them into the pocket of her apron. She stood, nodding her head at Charlie. 'We will send a message to Shen's people. Give her good fortune on her journey.'

Charlie hurried to open the back door for his wife. As Li Ling stepped out into the garden beyond, he turned back to Madame. 'Every year, I send gifts to my mother-in-law—to make sure she stays on the other side.' He winked then followed Li Ling into the garden.

Madame frowned.

There was so much to worry about. Xiao in her parlour last night. Shen spirited away. The hours ticking by before their subterfuge was discovered. *Bunny.* She closed her eyes.

Oh friends, my ghouls are very much alive, she thought. The dead ones will need to join the queue.

—

Doc Flanagan laced his thumbs into his leather braces and leaned back against the settee in her office. Madame noticed they strained rather against his gentlemanly midsection. Mrs Flanagan had always taken good care of the doctor; now that she was some years gone, Madame suspected he sampled the shortcrust of the Sail and Anchor's beef and Guinness pie a little too often.

'Of course,' he was saying, 'Charlie's quite right. When I was in the navy, we met a Chinese ship in New York. Flying the Yellow Dragon, it was. Those boys were mad for letting off bangers, the louder the better, all in the name of amusing the dead.'

Madame handed him a glass of brandy. 'Hungry ghosts? It gives me the creeps.'

Doc Flanagan laughed. 'Oh, come on. The dead can't be any worse than the staggering cretins you get in here any given Saturday.'

She sat on the settee under the window, their usual spot. 'You don't even know the half of it, Percy.'

With the brandy bottle somewhat emptied, Doc Flanagan rose and paced the small room, pinching the brow of his nose. 'Well? What now?'

Madame shook her head. 'We wait. Xiao will come tonight. Violet may have some plan. Cunning as a Swiss pocket watch, that one. Otherwise, I know what I need to do.'

Doc shook his head. 'I've met men like your Xiao. It's a priest you'll need after he's done with you, not a doctor.'

'He's a successful and respected businessman, Percy. I plan to bargain with him.'

'What do you have to offer him, Peg? I hate to break it to you, but he won't take you in place of that girl.'

'I know, I know. This old carcass is hardly a trade for a revered beauty like Shen, favourite of the deposed what's-his-name himself.'

'The emperor.'

'Exactly. No, I have a better idea. Xiao made it clear he'll take this place. Let him have it. It'll ruin us to leave, but at least we'll live.'

Oh, I'm tired, she thought. Let the jaws of the hungry ghosts open to swallow every one of us.

The doctor raised his glass in a solemn salute. 'What a fucking pity.'

'Indeed.'

She gazed out the window glumly. The sun was nearing its midday zenith. She felt her chest clench in a sudden wheeze and coughed painfully.

Doc Flanagan cleared his throat gently. 'Did you think about your options? For your lungs, I mean. I can see you're not feeling any better.'

Madame lowered her gaze to the carpet, clutching her sides. If the doctor could see she was suffering, it wouldn't be long before it was obvious to others. 'I wondered . . . well, I wondered if you'd talk to me about a different option entirely. The one where I take matters into my own hands.'

The silence lasted for long seconds. Eventually Doc nodded. 'I suppose we could talk about that, yes.'

Madame avoided his gaze. 'If I lose this place I'll be out on the streets, and I can't face that at my age. I take it there are times when a medical man feels he can be of a certain, er, help. Hastening things, as it were. Easing the suffering.'

Her friend hesitated. 'It's not much spoken about, of course.'

'Of course. Why don't you come and sit down over here, eh?' Madame patted the settee. 'Tell me about Mrs Flanagan. Those last days you spent together.'

'You're not suggesting I . . .?'

'I'm not suggesting, Perce. I know it to be true. You loved your wife and, like any good husband, good doctor, you couldn't bear to see her suffer. I hope you'll do me the same kindness when it's my turn.'

Doc Flanagan lowered himself onto the settee with a sigh. 'You know I will.'

'I hoped you would. Not the same thing.'

'Have you got your affairs in order?'

'Thank you, I have. You're a man of honour, Percy.'

He shook his head. 'I do find myself wondering, Peg. You go into doctoring for a good cause. Yet look at me now; I'm no credit to the profession. Hardly a day goes by where I'm not patching up one of the Kings Cross boys, giving them a lecture and a few stitches for nothing, only for them to come back the following week with something worse. And your girls—keeping them in their gilded cage.'

'Hey! I've got no prisoners here. Those girls are free to go.'

He laughed bitterly. 'Go to what? Husbands who beat them? Employers who chase them around the scullery wanting to take for nothing the very thing they're paid for here? Pimps who sell them for a shilling?'

'That's why we're crying over a house, Perce. It's been more than a roof over their heads.'

'True that, pet. True that.'

CHAPTER 19

VIOLET STOPPED IN THE HALLWAY and gave the Bushells tea tin a shake. The visit to La Perouse had strengthened her resolve. Mr Ming had taken five pounds, meaning there were five remaining—and she knew how she wanted to spend it.

I can set *something* right, she thought.

She stepped into the kitchen and surveyed the crowd around the table. Li Ling and Charlie, still wearing their coats, sat hunched in the wooden chairs closest to the back door, worry etched on their faces. Ruby was slouched in an armchair in the corner of the room, her white silk dressing-gown hanging open to reveal a brief pink nightie.

Behind Violet, Madame and Doc edged into the room, carrying with them a waft of brandy and cigars.

Five pairs of eyes turned in Violet's direction. Waiting to be told what to do, she supposed, when Xiao arrived. How many different ways could you beg for mercy, she wondered.

It was Ruby who spoke first. Or whistled, at least. 'Pheeeew,' said the redhead, leaning back in her armchair. 'Never fear, Violet is here.'

Violet cleared her throat, hiding the money tin behind her back. That part of her plan could wait.

'Well, Shen is safe at Ming's,' she said. 'We saw her. She's not going back to her old life. I have an idea how we can get her far away from here, which will involve asking a gent I know for a favour. In the meantime, the plan is . . . we don't get killed ourselves when Xiao comes calling. That's the plan.'

A long moment passed. They all stared at her. Once again, it was Ruby who broke the silence. 'Are you for real? That's all you've got?'

Doc Flanagan raised a hand. 'Now, now, let's not get impertinent.'

Ruby laughed. 'But you've got to be hecking kidding me, Doc! We'll be dead in our beds by midnight at this rate.'

Violet crossed the room and sank onto the arm of Ruby's chair, dropping the money tin to the floor and her head into her hands. She drew in a long breath and straightened up. 'Ruby's right, damn it. We can't just wait for trouble to turn up. Okay, what are our options?'

Li Ling crossed her arms. 'These are bad men. For bad men like this, what you have won't be enough.'

On the stove a kettle began to whistle.

Madam got to her feet and lifted the tin kettle from the heat by its wooden handle. 'Li Ling, make up a pot of Ceylon, would you, dear? Listen, all of you. This ghost, this man whom Xiao owes, is not going to accept another man, woman, child or beast in Shen's place. So I'll offer Xiao La Maison des Fleurs to settle his debt.'

'No!' Violet got to her feet. 'This is our home as much as yours. Where would we go?'

'That's not the point. It's better than dying.'

Violet's heart gave a lurch. *This* is the only life I wanted, she thought. This place, this life.

Doc Flanagan raised a hand. 'What if we try to pay him off, Peg—I mean Madame? What've you got squirrelled away?'

Madam sighed. 'Some. But even if I chuck in my pearls, I doubt it'd be enough.'

'What's the going rate for a girl's life?' Doc frowned and took the teapot from Li Ling. Delicious steam rose from the cups as he poured.

'Oh, come on, Percy, how should I know? We're working girls, not assassins.' Madame grasped Li Ling by the hand. 'Perhaps brandy as well. Pour a large one for yourself, pet.'

Li Ling nodded and turned to fetch the brandy bottle from the cabinet in the corner.

'How much more do we need?' asked Ruby, suddenly perking up. She unfolded her improbably long legs and sat up. 'My lock-picker mate who's on his way back from touring with Ashton's might be able to pick another lock or two for us as well as helping with Shen's chain? One of those nice little jewellery shops on Elizabeth Street, perhaps?'

'No!' Madame was on her feet again. 'Honestly, Ruby, you'll be in Long Bay soon enough without hastening your journey on my account.' She scanned the room. 'You've given me an idea, though. We could put on a show. Spread the word this after-noon, get as many men in the door as we can squeeze under the bloody rafters, bump up our cash reserves. We could offer that to

Xiao first. Then, if that doesn't cut the mustard, we still have the house to bargain with.'

'It might be our last hurrah,' Violet mused. 'At least we'd be going out with a bang. But what show?' It was hard to imagine getting onstage right now, let alone putting on a mustard-cutting performance.

Madame snapped her fingers. '"Raid on Cleopatra's Tomb", that always brings out the spenders. A full house might also make it harder for Xiao to throw his weight around.'

This sent a murmur around the room.

Violet studied her hands. It was a really *terrible* plan. As battle tactics went, performing a show was Napoleon invading Russia in winter all over again, except armed with French knickers instead of cannonballs—and we all know how that went, she thought.

Five minutes alone with Xiao had been enough to convince her he wouldn't be diverted from his purpose regarding Shen. But it was far too late now to give everyone a 'By the way, you're dead' talk.

For the sake of her friends, she summoned a smile. 'Safety in numbers, I like it.'

You can't regret saving Shen, she told herself. You can't regret saving a life. But as she stared at the those gathered around the table, her heart clenched. So many hopeful faces. So many tender dreams and plans waiting to be conjured into reality.

All this in Xiao's hands. You could collect their chances of success on the head of a pin.

Ruby clapped her hands and nudged Violet. 'Violet, the fellas go nuts for the Egypt costumes, you wait. And we get to bathe in ass's milk.'

'It's just normal milk, you nit.'

'Nevertheless.'

That was enough planning for Ruby, who stood, pecked Violet on the cheek and, pulling her robes tight around her, swept out of the room. 'I'd better go and start preparing myself,' she said over her shoulder.

A noise in the backyard made the rest of the room turn: suddenly Albert was bowling through the back door, face cut up and shirt covered in blood.

Doc Flanagan was on his feet in an instant, pushing Li Ling aside to reach him. 'Albert! I've told you a hundred times to stay away from the Cross.'

Charlie rose from his chair and Albert flung himself into it, wincing. 'It's not my blood. Well, not all of it, anyway. I'm alright—just got a shiner and a split in me eyebrow. But you have to go see young Arlo, Nico's brother. He'll be at Nico's shop, Doc. He's been sliced in the guts. Not real deep, but he's bleeding like a stuck pig.'

Doc grabbed his hat from the table and picked up his old leather bag from the corner of the room. He turned back to Albert. 'You'll get a talking-to about this later, young man,' he said, then pushed through the back door.

Madame called after him. 'You'll come back to look at Albert?'

'Peg, you can put a stitch in him yourself, if you like. Do me a favour and use your stoutest leather needle. Teach him a lesson he won't forget in a hurry.'

Violet passed Albert a tea towel and he winced again as he pressed it to his brow. He leaned over towards Violet. 'Got you some info about Xiao's shady crook pal, though, didn't I?'

Violet smacked him over the back of the head. 'You dickhead, Albert! Nearly getting yourself killed for that?

You're far more useful to us alive and in one piece. Remember that next time you think about swanning in here with a face like a dropped pie!'

He grinned. 'So, you don't want to hear it then?'

By now the rest of the kitchen had grown quiet. Li Ling stood by the table with the brandy in her hand, Charlie beside her. Madame was hunched in a chair by the stove.

Violet crossed her arms and nodded. 'Go on then.'

'Well,' Albert began, 'I went to see Arlo's girlfriend, Jeanie. She sings in a bar in the Cross, knows Tilly Devine's girls, knocked around with Big Jim herself a few years ago. Anyway, she hears the talk. So Jeanie tells me there's a bloke who fits our ghost-man's description. He's rich. Old Sydney money, she reckons. Some kind of backroom operator. Bloodthirsty. Wants the girls to do nasty stuff, so they won't go near him. Always in the shadows, always raising the stakes in other people's battles. Same as any gambler would, he takes a profit—but really, it sounds as if he just likes pushing situations until they get violent. Other people's lives are sport to him. They say he's got a war injury, something wrong with the way he walks. Maybe that's what turned him nasty. But I didn't catch what he's called. He's a ghost, right enough.'

Li Ling placed the brandy bottle on the table very quietly, then she turned and pushed her way out through the kitchen door.

Charlie shrugged and followed her out into the night.

Violet frowned. 'He's no ghost. The man we're after is very much alive and getting superstitious about him won't help anyone.' She threw a dark look at Madame, who was clutching the silver cross at her neck.

Madame drew herself up in her chair and poured herself a large slug of brandy. 'What's that look for? If you listen to the Irish, there are devils under every rock. But I believe I've never seen anything more frightening than men.' She rose to her feet. 'I'll go and see if Li Ling and Charlie are okay. Then I might go to the Carpenters Arms and start talking about the show. Get the word out.' She shuffled to the kitchen door in her slippers and left the room.

Violet bent over Albert's head and peered at the split in his brow. 'You didn't explain how you got cut.'

'The bar turned nasty and we just got in the way. We were trying to get out through the fighting. Doc's right—the Cross is edgy right now. Ticking like a dry paddock before a grass fire.'

'It's stopped bleeding. I can fetch Susan if you want some decent needlework, otherwise you can go without and you'll have another scar to remember us by.'

'I'll take my chances without Susan,' said Albert.

Violet regarded him. 'Would you help out with one last thing, Albert?' She'd made her mind up about a couple of things. She took a crumpled note and some coins from the tea tin and dropped them on the table. 'I was hoping you'd go shopping for me.'

'Jeez, you don't ask for much, do you, Violet Kelly?' He shook his head.

Violet patted his cheek and rolled one of the coins along the table. 'In for a penny, in for a pound, Albert McAllister.' She sat down and pulled a pencil and paper from her cardigan pocket. 'You'd better take this down.'

She knew a couple of things for certain. First, Xiao had

a personal score to settle with her now. She might not get a chance to spend her money after tonight. And looking around the room at her friends, she had become resolved: with no better solution, she would offer herself to Xiao for the ghost-man's private pleasure.

CHAPTER 20

GOD'S HANDS SHAPE TOMORROW, *so ours are free to work today.* That was one of Sister Bernadette's pithy sayings. A girl should be content to piously polish the parquet, trusting in the Lord's plan.

What a load of bunk, Violet mused. If you were to add God's hands into the mix, it seemed there were altogether too many menfolk trying to meddle in the future of La Maison des Fleurs, which had been going along quite nicely, thank you very much, without their interference.

Still, getting on with the evening's preparations, while trying not to think about the near future, was not altogether bad advice so, after seeing Albert off, she threw herself into the business of preparing for the show.

From her position on tiptoes on the marble washstand with both arms raised above her head, she now gave a cry of desperation.

'Damn it! Bloody thing's stuck fast, Bunny. Jesus, I think I've lost all feeling in my arms!' The entrance to the attic, a small square hole in the bathroom ceiling, refused to yield to charm, persuasion or brute force.

Bunny, waiting below, raised a finger. 'Wait!' She turned and ran out of the room.

Violet heard the door to the broom closet in the hallway open and close. She lowered her arms and shook them to make the sensation return.

Bunny reappeared, brow creased with concern, and handed Violet a broomstick. 'Here. But use the soft end, please. Madame'll kill you for putting marks in the ceiling paintwork.'

With a shout of exertion, Violet pushed open the manhole and was rewarded with a shower of dust to the face. She sneezed, causing the washstand to wobble precariously.

She steadied herself and wiped the dust from her eyes. 'No-one told me that to raid Cleopatra's tomb we'd have to break the ancient seal on the attic first.'

Violet reached into the darkness above and, after feeling around in the dusty cavity, pulled a curiously short and somewhat spindly folding wooden ladder down. It was attached to a braced beam in the cavity and unfolded in segments.

She gave it a peremptory jiggle, testing its stability. 'You've heard of the curse on the explorers who opened King Tut's tomb? I can see how this might end with me being cursed with a broken neck. Alright, come here by the washstand and hold the ladder. And throw yourself under me if I look like I'm going to fall.'

'Right you are.' Bunny skidded into place beside the washstand.

Violet hitched up her dressing-gown. Really, she thought,

in a moment of practical self-castigation, culottes would have been a smarter choice.

Violet stepped onto the rickety-looking ladder and began the ungainly climb. She reached the top rung and hoisted herself onto the bare, dusty boards next to the opening. It was gloomy in the attic but not as dark as she had expected: sunlight fell in beams through air vents in the roof and, unexpectedly, she could hear the sounds of the street outside.

A small area of flooring had been laid to accommodate Madame's spare clothes, costumes and household items. A broken fringed lampshade stood crookedly off to one side. Behind it, Violet could see the costume trunk. She wriggled over beside it and opened the lid. With a flush of relief, she saw the skimpy gold-sequined Egyptian outfits were on the top of the pile.

She called down to Bunny. 'We're in luck, for once! The costumes are right here.'

'Thank goodness, I was getting a cramp,' Bunny called up through the manhole, gripping the foot of the ladder.

'I'm going to start chucking things down, okay?'

Violet leaned towards the manhole and dropped the first handful of rather racy smalls onto Bunny's head.

—◆—

With the essentials for 'The Raid of Cleopatra's Tomb' released from the attic, Violet sent Bunny to go from room to room, raising the girls from their various leisure-time pursuits— napping, reading, listening to the wireless, playing backgammon, trying out hairstyles—and telling them all to assemble in the parlour. Violet laid out costumes on the armchairs and settees with Ruby's help. Dido and Aeneas chirped in the background as Violet sifted through the spoils.

As well as the dainty sequined items, there was a perplexing two-person camel outfit and some rather tired-looking props, including a painted tomb entrance made from cardboard, complete with rather suggestive hieroglyphics, some moth-eaten paper palm fronds and a mangy stuffed cat.

Bunny held up the cat to show Ruby and frowned. 'Do you think this was one of Madame's pets?'

'Of course!' Ruby seized the mottled creature and planted a kiss on its musty nose. 'Beloved Twinkles.'

'You're having me on.'

'I am. But listen, if you can find someone, anyone, in this life who loves you so much they want to stuff you and keep you in the attic, then think yourself lucky!'

Bunny grimaced. 'I'd be happy with two lines in the death notices and an urn on the mantelpiece, thank you very much.'

The other girls straggled into the room. Violet appraised them. They were subdued and bleary-eyed, collected in their nighties and hair curlers.

After some discussion, it was agreed that Theodora (*not* Dora, she insisted), a small, olive-skinned Greek girl, would play Cleopatra on account of the fact that her straight, black Louise Brooks hair was so perfectly suited to the role. Also, Bunny confided to Violet, in Madame's version of the raid, Cleopatra didn't really do much except walk around discarding her clothes. Any lunk could do it.

The girls' enthusiasm grew as they eyed the piles of costumes. The possibilities of the night ahead becoming clear, they descended upon the outfits with a vigour that even Violet found surprising.

Madame appeared at Violet's side and began coughing violently, her eyes filling with tears of pain. Violet turned to her with concern.

Madame nodded to Violet, wiping her eyes. 'That means you have to be the head slave, Violet. The one that seduces the tomb raiders and leads all the slave spirits to freedom.'

'Marvellous. I'm all for female emancipation.'

'Just make sure you do it in your tallest heels and your tiniest panties.'

'Remind me not to put you in charge of the revolution.'

They both chuckled. Bunny handed Violet a costume that, as far as she could tell, was merely a few wisps of silk chiffon and a half-dozen fake pearls.

Ruby wolf-whistled over Violet's shoulder as they examined the diminutive outfit. 'Goodness, that leaves nothing to the imagination! I hope Madame casts me as a lonely, helpless tomb raider.'

Madame pinched Ruby's peachy cheek and handed her a tight-fitting olive-green body suit adorned with paste diamonds. 'Oh, no, dear. I've got something different in mind for you. You're doing the enchanted snake dance.'

Ruby threw her red curls back and laughed. 'If Albert can rig up my contortion table, you've got a deal.'

'You leave that to me,' said Madame, a little of her usual hauteur returning.

Violet hid her smile then checked herself. It was too early to smile, too soon to let down her guard.

Bunny nudged Violet, the girl's eyes searching her face. 'Hey, it's going to be fine! We'll make a pile of money and buy Shen's life and she'll live happily ever after. You'll see.'

Violet squeezed Bunny's hand. 'Of course.' How little she knew.

Bunny added, 'Anyway, the other girls will start to wonder what's up if you get around with a face like a wet Wednesday. They'll want to know why. They look to you, you know.'

Violet blanched and turned away, folding clothes into piles. 'I know they do, Buns.'

The girls dispersed with their costumes and the promise of an excellent late lunch, courtesy of Li Ling.

Violet and Bunny were left to pack away the remaining items and plan how to move the furniture to erect a small stage. Li Ling bustled in carrying a steaming pot of tea and a plate of shortbread, then returned to the kitchen, leaving them to it.

Violet saw she would have Bunny to herself for a moment. It was time to tell her about Iris. 'Listen, Bunny,' she said cautiously, 'I gotta tell you something. Something important.'

Bunny brightened. 'Oooh! Don't tell me you've met a fella? Is he rich? Is he taking you somewhere nice?'

Unbidden, the image of Philip Chandler appeared in Violet's mind. 'No! Anyway, I don't want to go somewhere nice. Here is nice.'

'What then?'

'There's something I haven't told you. Madame was right. I have been looking for someone. And I seem to have found her.'

'Your sister.' The familiar Irish-French brogue at the door made her turn. Madame leaned against the doorframe, her eyes misty. 'You thought we didn't know, pet?'

Violet gasped. She looked from Bunny to Madame. 'You knew about Iris this whole time?'

'Folks in this part of Sydney'll trade gossip as easily as drawing breath. Bunny was just too sweet to tell you we knew.'

Bunny winced. 'Sorry about the whole charade with the newspapers and everything. I just wanted you to find her—and now you have.'

Violet rubbed her forehead. 'Yep, well, that's the gist of it.'

At that moment the door was flung open and Albert shouldered his way in with a box in his hands, bellowing a greeting.

Frowning at the interruption, Violet wondered anew at Albert's gift for suddenly and wholly filling a room.

Red-faced and puffing, he came to a halt beside them. 'Well, well, well, what's in this box, I wonder? Is it something for our Bunny here?'

Bunny turned and squealed, delighted. 'Albert! Is it a present?'

Violet grasped Bunny's thin arm, exasperated. 'Albert, shut up for a minute. I'm trying to tell Bunny and Madame about Iris.'

'Oh. Oops.'

'Listen to me!' The words came out in a rush. 'Iris has found me, she's mad as a snake and she could turn up here any minute.'

Albert, stupefied, opened his mouth then promptly clamped it shut. He placed the box on a side table. His hands found their way into his pockets and he rocked on his heels.

Bunny wheeled back to Albert. 'Is it true?'

Albert nodded and shrugged. ''Fraid so. As if larks weren't weird enough right now.'

This was too much for Bunny, who sank into one of the chairs and reached for her cup of tea. A quizzical look crossed her face as she turned to Violet. 'But you've found each other, so it's good, right?'

Violet and Albert exchanged a look. Violet cleared her throat. 'Sure. Sure, it's good.'

'And you can be sisters again. Make amends.'

Madame gave a strangled cough, which Violet took to mean she understood the complications between Violet and Iris a little better than Bunny.

'Of course. I mean, it's probably going to end well. By the way, Albert, what *is* in that box?'

Albert, recovering his senses, took the cue from Violet in the flawless manner of an old comrade. He sank to the carpet on his knees next to Bunny's chair and pulled the box onto his lap. He lifted the cardboard lid to reveal a beautiful pair of kid leather boots in dark red, with delicate tooling and scalloped edges. Bunny reached into the box. She lifted one of the boots out and held it aloft.

'Oh, they're lovely, Violet,' Bunny breathed. 'They look like they're made for a Russian princess! For dancing in the snow. Don't you think, Aunty?'

Madame gave a wan smile. 'You're a lucky girl. Just make sure you can still carry a full basket of washing without tripping over, eh?' She turned and left the room for her office.

'Well, Bunny, they're for you,' said Violet. 'We can't have you hobbling around in shoes that're too small.'

'Oh! You didn't have to.'

'Stop that, you deserve to have something nice.'

Bunny stood and threw her arms around Violet's neck. 'You're the nicest person ever, Violet. I love you, I really do.'

Violet smiled and squeezed Bunny before releasing her. 'You run along now. I've got a show to plan and you're expected in the kitchen to help with lunch.'

'Yes! I'm going to put them on. With my best skirt.' Bunny gathered up her boots and the box and hurried out of the room.

Violet flopped into the chair Bunny had vacated and let out a sigh. Albert, still seated on the floor, leaned his head against her knee and she tousled his hair. 'Thanks, Albert. Did you get the other pair?'

Albert saluted her. 'Yes, ma'am, just like you asked. They're on the kitchen bench. Li Ling said she'd find you some socks from her darning basket to go with them. I'd better be getting back to the shop. Mr Cavendish'll be wondering what I've been up to.'

'You're a good man. I'll make sure Li Ling gets her roast from Mr Cavendish this weekend.' And let's hope we're still alive to enjoy it, thought Violet.

'Good-o, I'll put in the order myself.'

He got to his feet and gave Violet a kiss on the cheek. 'See you later. I hear there's going to be an ex-trava-ganza.' He twitched his eyebrows and gave a little jiggle.

Violet cuffed him on the shoulder. 'Don't get any fancy ideas about being in the show. Unless you want to be the back end of a camel.'

'I'd consider it,' he offered mildly. He straightened up and smoothed his shirt. 'Right-o, then.'

'Go on, get back to the shop. We'll see you in your front-of-house wear at seven.' Violet waved him away and he left, whistling, through the front door.

Violet surveyed the remaining piles of props and costumes. She might need to call on Susan and the others to spruce up the dispirited tableau pieces. Susan was deft with a set of watercolours.

She left the parlour and went into the kitchen. There, on the table, stood a second pair of shoes. These ones were plain brown lace-ups with stitched seams and a sturdy sole. They were practical shoes but not altogether ugly; Violet could never have chosen something wholly unattractive. But these would suit her purpose. Something to last all the way through to next winter and beyond, she thought.

Li Ling handed her a darned pair of socks and Violet placed one in each of the shoes. Li Ling smiled across at her, her hands tucked into her apron.

Violet folded her arms. 'I think Iris watches us at night-time, Li Ling. So, we'll wait until it gets dark, then we'll leave the shoes across the road in the garage doorway.'

—◆—

The Waste Land by T.S. Eliot lay open on Violet's bed in the Rose Room. As she'd hoped, Philip Chandler had tucked a business card inside, bearing the telephone number of his office.

Violet looked at the clock on the wall: it was just past 3 pm. Madame would typically retire to her rooms before the evening to take a draught of Doctor Flanagan's cough medicine and read the news.

She stood and picked up the book. Hearing Bunny in the hallway, she called out to her. 'Bunny, love, has Madame gone upstairs?'

Bunny's red-booted foot appeared around the corner of the Rose Room door, waggling rakishly. 'Indeed, she has,' said the boot.

Violet threw a pillow and hit the boot on its red shiny ankle. Bunny's grinning face appeared around the door. 'What's up? Need me to help you practise getting into that little bit of nothing from the costume box?'

'No. I'm going to the telephone box to make a call.'

—◆—

The phone trilled at the other end of the line and at last Philip Chandler picked up.

Violet cleared her throat, then read from *The Waste Lands*, in her very best reading-serious-poetry-aloud voice.

After a beat of stunned silence, Philip Chandler gave a hoot of laughter. 'Violet Kelly, you're quoting Eliot to me. In my office.'

'I am. Is it a good time to intrude?'

'I should say so! My time is paid for by the King himself and I'm sure even *he* knows better than to refuse an interruption from a famed lady of La Maison des Fleurs. Especially one with poetry on her mind.'

This made her smile. 'We famed ladies don't like to be denied, it's true.'

'Only a fool would try. How can I help?'

'First, please tell me when you're booked to leave?' It was so very hard to keep the tremor out of her voice at the thought of never seeing him again. She swallowed hard.

'Oh. I'm booked on the P and O to London in three days. A stateroom beside the officer's deck. They don't like agents of the Crown to mix with the rabble, in case we get drunk at dinner and expose state secrets. Or ourselves, I suppose.'

Perfect, thought Violet sadly. Almost made to measure for hiding a fleeing girl on board. 'I—I have a rather important instruction and a very unusual request.'

'Please give me my orders, captain.'

'Philip, you mustn't come tonight. It's not safe.'

'But how will I say goodbye?'

'I'll find you, I promise.' She hoped this wouldn't turn out to be a lie. But with Xiao's arrival drawing near, the future had acquired a new uncertainty.

'Alright. You'd better explain, and then tell me what you need me to do.'

—

By 8 pm, all the visitors were seated at last. At Madame's cue, the electric lights were extinguished. Over the murmuring of the crowd came the swift rasp of a single match being struck.

A flickering candle illuminated the kohl-smudged faces of Susan and Anne, in the centre of the room, wearing pith helmets, unbuttoned khaki shirts and black lace suspenders. In Madame's retelling, archaeologists eschewed trousers.

'Behold,' boomed Susan, pushing aside the fronds of the parlour's indoor palms and stepping between the pots. 'At last! We have found Cleopatra's tomb!'

At that moment, low house lights lit a small stage in the back corner of the room, where the painted plyboard front of the pyramid, cunningly retouched by Susan and Doris, stood rather shakily on its struts.

Anne followed Susan through the palms and stepped up onto the stage. With an expression of anguish, she dropped to her pretty knees and gasped aloud. 'But how will we get inside? The door is sealed tight.'

An approving titter rustled through the crowd.

Susan bounded over to Anne, vaulting onto the stage with a convincing vigour. She helped Anne to her feet. 'Kiss me and we will destroy the curse!'

'I will kiss you!'

'Kiss me where the sun don't shine!'

'But I don't have the train fare to get us to Melbourne.'

At this the audience erupted in laughter.

'Just kiss me, you fool!'

The room was filled with whistles and claps as Susan and Anne locked lips. Anne emitted a satisfying moan and softened in the arms of strapping Susan.

At that moment, the door to Cleopatra's tomb wobbled open. A low ramp covered in velvet was wheeled onto the stage, and along this ramp slid Ruby, in her jewelled one-piece snakeskin. Balancing on her forearms in a sort of handstand, she lowered her legs forward and arched her back improbably until her toes came to meet beneath her chin. She paused there, a snake turned in on itself, and winked. The audience roared. Then she inched her feet towards the ground and the rest of her followed, rolling forward in a spectacular moving contortion of knees, hips and ribs, until her weight came to rest on her forearms once more.

'Aha! The charm has worked!' declared Anne in her stage voice. 'Look, it's the guardian of the tomb . . . Cleopatra's snake.'

There was a ribald whistle from the gentlemen as Ruby, only a little ahead of schedule, placed her feet on the ground, drew herself up to her full height and began shedding her clinging skin.

CHAPTER 21

IRIS STOOD STARING AT THE fine pair of brown leather shoes tucked into the dark recess of the door of the workshop opposite La Maison des Fleurs.

She bent down to peer at them more closely. They had socks tucked inside! She reached in and pulled one of the woollen socks out. It was repaired at the heel.

Curious.

She sat immediately in the gutter, brushed the sand from the soles of her feet and put the shoes on. By some further miracle, they fitted perfectly.

A sound from the pleasure house across the road made her shuffle sideways into the shadows. Still sitting on the concrete kerb, she listened hard. A ground-floor window was being unlatched and thrown open. The sound of applause drifted into the street. Men's applause, clapping and hooting.

Cigar smoke and tinkling, foreign-sounding music wafted into the evening air.

Goodness only knows what they're up to inside, she thought. Drinking champagne and cocktails. She rubbed the smart leather toes of the shoes thoughtfully.

A second sound in the street made her turn abruptly. It was the long black car, travelling slowly up the road towards her with its headlights turned off. She recognised it immediately.

From her position seated in the gutter, she scrambled backwards into a low crouch, withdrawing into the deepest shadow.

The car purred to a halt outside La Maison des Fleurs. Iris supressed a gasp. The street fell silent, but for the sounds from the downstairs window. Whatever the motive of the people in the car, for the moment were content to sit and watch.

She bit her lip. This felt ominous.

Her gaze traced the sinuous contours of the car's outline. A dark car belonging to dangerous men, an empty street . . . If Tobias were here, he would tell her to run like a hare avoiding the beam of a flashlight.

But she didn't. Couldn't, in fact: the sound of her new shoes on the paved footpath would surely give her away. She had no choice but to linger in the shadows and wait.

She fancied for a moment she saw movement inside the car: a pooling of darkness that must be figures inside. Two, three. She couldn't be sure.

Now she heard the car doors open softly and saw four men emerge silently onto the street. They walked briskly to the front door of La Maison des Fleurs.

Iris saw them draw guns from beneath their coats and clamped her hand over her mouth. Breaking the silence of the street with a sound that seemed to explode inside her head, the man at the front of the group shot away the door lock with a silenced pistol. They pushed inside.

Iris darted across the street and threw herself onto the ground under the jacaranda in the house's postage-stamp front yard. She strained to hear the scene unfold from the open window above her head, fighting the urge to climb in over the sill to get a better look.

The music stopped abruptly, with muffled objections from the crowd. Then a woman's voice rose above the rest, offering reassurance and calling for calm. Iris listened as men's voices barked instructions. Then she heard footsteps thudding up the stairs inside.

In the floors of the house above, she heard doors opening and closing. Shouting. The men were looking for something—or someone.

Suddenly an outraged voice called down from an upper floor. The front door was thrown open and gentlemen guests began spilling onto the pavement, startled, fleeing in pairs or alone down the empty street.

Long minutes passed as Iris listened to the ongoing exchange in the parlour: a woman begging and consoling. A man's voice shouting angry demands.

Iris now heard the woman's voice rise above the others, pleading. Then came a single, terrified scream, issued from near the top of the house. It was a scream of such terror it made Iris sink low into the shadows of the jacaranda and wish that she had run when she had the chance. This was a bad business—bad enough to make a girl scream in a way that told you she was staring her own death in the face.

Iris turned as more figures fled through La Maison des Fleurs' front door. Footsteps echoed on the tiled front steps as two of the men from the black car emerged into the street with a whimpering girl, a jacket thrown over her head to conceal her face. They shoved her into the back seat of the car. From below the window, Iris heard the shattering of glass somewhere inside and heard the faint *whoomph* of kerosene catching alight.

Within minutes, orange flames were visible. Black smoke began to pour out of the downstairs window and Iris shrank back in terror.

The two remaining intruders now emerged from the house and hurried to the car. With a screech of tyres, it sped away.

Iris scrambled over a low railing and charged up the tiled steps to the open front door of the house. There, out cold in the hallway, lay Albert. A huge red mark was already blooming on his forehead. More screams and smoke issued from inside and Iris felt panic rising inside her. In her head she could hear Tobias's voice: *Run, just run.*

Iris put her own fear aside, squatted beside Albert and tucked her hands under his armpits. With great effort, she half-dragged, half-rolled him out the door and down the front steps, away from the smoke and flames. A group of young women in bejewelled costumes staggered into the street after her, coughing and spluttering.

As she crouched on the pavement, panting over Albert's unconscious body, a tall figure in a long gold dress, her face a mask of distress, loomed in the doorway. Iris recognised the woman who ran La Maison des Fleurs. 'Help us!' she cried. 'Go get the fire brigade and the police. Oh, my Bunny! My poor, poor Bunny.' The woman sagged against the doorframe.

Iris stood, her face suddenly illuminated by the shaft of light from the open door, and the woman in the doorway drew in an astonished breath.

'Saints preserve us, if it isn't the lost twin. For heaven's sake, girl, you'd better move quickly. Violet's hidden herself somewhere in this house and not even God knows where.'

Then the woman staggered out past Iris into the street. 'Bunny!' she wailed.

Iris didn't hesitate a second longer; she turned and pelted down the street in the direction of the Darlinghurst fire station.

CHAPTER 22

VIOLET OPENED ONE EYE. The pain was almost enough to cause her to sink into darkness again. She lifted her head slightly. The second-floor bathroom resolved into focus just as dizzying nausea gripped her and her body convulsed in retching.

The retching stopped and Violet became aware of her body pressed against the cold tiles. A bruised shoulder and hip. An angry lump on her head. She blinked. With a return to consciousness came a flood of panic.

Bunny.

Xiao had refused to take her in Shen's place, no matter how she had begged. It was Shen they wanted—and Bunny was the key to persuading Madame to give Shen up.

Tears came in a horrified rush, streaking her face and pooling on the bathroom floor under her cheek. She curled into a ball. The tiles were freezing, as if the chill of night had waited in them, ready to leech into her bare skin. The blow Xiao had dealt her had been strong enough to lift her off her feet. The side of her face and her temple throbbed from where she had hit the doorframe, then the bathtub, then the floor.

She closed her eyes and a sob tore from her chest.

After a few seconds, or minutes, or hours—she wasn't sure—she struggled to a sitting position, her back against the enamel bath. The pain in her side seemed worse. More tears came as unfamiliar sounds reached her from the lower parts of the house.

Above the shouting drifted a new sound: a sweet, sinister rustling. *Shhhhhhh.*

This new sound was comforting.

Sister Bernadette was right, she thought. Girls like me amount to nothing in the end. We arrive and we disappear so fast, we barely leave a trace.

She found, to her surprise, that she could accept her own insignificance.

She sank back, eyes closing and darkness descending once more. With the new sound in her mind, she imagined a wide lake, the wind whipping the water's surface into gentle waves. Then she saw a great wind stirring the tops of trees, causing old branches to peel away from the trunks and tumble to the ground.

She slumped to the floor as the first curl of smoke crept into the bathroom from the hallway. In the fading world beyond, she heard the clanging of a bell.

CHAPTER 23

IRIS RAN BEHIND THE FIRE ENGINE, her mind racing.

The truck accelerated down the street, disappearing around a bend. Iris's lungs and throat burned from the effort of running, and her thoughts were jumbled.

She considered the small, scared figure hidden under the intruder's jacket and thrust into the back of the long black car.

It could be the girl with the bung lip, the one she'd seen talking to the scarred man who had asked for matches. Small. A sparrow compared to the other girls, the ones Violet's age and older. It could be her.

Then she thought of the scream coming from the top of the house. That terrified, bloodcurdling scream. It might have come from the small girl, seeing her captors approach, feeling their hands on her body. Or it might have been Violet.

So, thought Iris, feet pounding and lungs on fire. So.

The scream had come from one of the upper floors of the house. Iris would go there first.

She ran, her arms pumping and her heart hammering in her chest. Her new shoes smacked against the tarmac. Protected as they were, her feet felt invincible, armoured and sure.

Firemen were unwinding an enormous rubber hose in front of the grand terrace when she arrived. She grabbed the leather coat of one man and tried to make herself understood, her hair flying and her words coming out in breathless gasps. A cry from the street announced the hose had been connected to the hydrant and a torrent burst from the hose in the direction of the flames on the ground floor. The fireman turned away.

Exasperated, Iris slipped past him and ran up the steps into the smoke-filled house.

There was no time to consider whether the stairs would hold her. Iris could see there were only a few places where the treads hadn't yet burned through, so she tried to be light and quick on her feet, feeling more than one crack and split as she scrambled upwards. Once she reached the top of the grand staircase, she was beyond the reach of the blaze, but the smoke had filled the upper levels and in places she saw that the floor might start to give out from the flames below.

Up and up she went, her lungs screaming.

Violet's body lay more or less where Iris expected: on the second floor, close to the front of the building, the very spot from which the scream had seemed to come. Her sister was huddled on the tiles of the bathroom, her head bloody, completely unconscious, and wearing a costume so skimpy that Iris initially thought she was naked.

Iris threw open the window and shouted down at the street. A single, beady-eyed fireman looked up at the sound.

As smoke poured into the room and a loud crash announced the complete collapse of the grand staircase, Iris bundled Violet's limp body over the window ledge and launched her, bare arms flailing, into the void. She landed in a blanket held out to catch her.

Iris followed, her tatty coat flying up around her ears and her leather shoes smouldering magnificently.

CHAPTER 24

FIRM HANDS TRAVELLED VIOLET'S BODY, taking in the length of her. He was slower this time. More thoughtful, considered.

This time, they walked the stairs of La Maison des Fleurs side by side, the treads falling away beneath urgent feet. He waited as she bent to unlatch the Rose Room door. Violet led him inside and pressed him against the closed door, the starched folds of his ridiculous shirt in her fists.

In the dream, as she kissed Philip Chandler, Violet envisioned the mahogany and brass of the stateroom in the majestic vessel that would transport them. She savoured, for a moment, the thought of the consort's title Mr Philip Chandler, Esquire would invent for her. *Secretary. Associate.*

She gave herself over to the pleasure. His fingers tugged her tousled hair away from her mouth, drew the clothes away from her flesh. She drove her body against his. The Rose Room had never before witnessed such passion.

—◆—

Now she woke like a shipwrecked person thrown to shore: coughing, retching and feeling so wretched she almost wished she were dead. With the arrival of consciousness came a stark realisation. She was in a narrow bed in a small room on the ground floor—in an apartment, perhaps—with the smell of cigars in her nose and the taste of morphia on her tongue.

A face appeared in front of her: a face that was unmistakably her own.

'Well, bugger me,' said the person with Violet's face. 'The princess awakes.'

Iris.

But it was a different Iris who peered down at her now: Iris had washed, she had brushed her hair. She had been given a set of clothes which Violet recognised as Madame's old things. A faded blue blouse; a dark, patched cardigan.

'You're here?' Violet croaked.

'Surprise.' Iris shrugged, showing just the hint of a smile.

The room swam a little as Violet took this in. Morning sun was shining through the square window of the little bedroom, lighting the side of her twin's face.

It was too much to comprehend.

Another face came into focus beside Iris: it was a bruised but grinning Albert.

'Dang. You win sixpence, Iris,' he said. 'I had money on you being out for another twelve hours at least, Violet. But here you are.'

'Where? And how long have I been here?'

Somewhere on the vast continent of the counterpane Albert found her hand and squeezed it. 'We're at Doc's place, so you're still in Paddington and you've just been here the night. Not long.'

This made Violet smile, although she felt far away, as if the distance between her and Iris and Albert might be measured in fathoms or hours, rather than inches or seconds.

A third face arrived in her field of vision: it was Doctor Flanagan, scowling and leaning over her to adjust a bandage on the side of her head. She touched fingertips to the tender spot and blinked back the pain.

She cleared her throat. 'Well, Doc, how did I do?'

He frowned. 'I didn't see the other chap, so it's hard to say.'

'What about the state of me?'

'A C-plus to your assailant. Must try harder. You'll be in rude health in no time.'

'Ha! At school I never had a mark lower than a B.' She gave him a wan smile.

He chuckled. 'Quite so. You get a A-plus for coming out of your concussion with your wits about you.'

'Living up to signs of early promise,' Violet rasped. She sat up gingerly, the pain in her side making her wince.

Doc nodded, reaching down to put an arm around her shoulders to help her. 'Oh, yes, that'll be the cracked ribs. Should heal up nicely but they'll hurt for a bit. Nothing wrong with your lungs, though, luckily.'

'Feels like I've had a kick in the chest from back legs of a donkey.'

He shifted the pillow behind her head. 'There now, that's as far as you're going today, young lady.' He handed her two pills and a glass of water.

She swallowed the tablets then blinked up at him groggily. 'But if we're all here at your place, who's out rescuing Bunny? Not Madame?'

The room fell silent for a moment.

'No, love, not Madame.'

Iris cleared her throat and exchanged a furtive glance with Albert, who sighed. 'Madame's taken to bed herself,' he explained. 'Went on a roaring drunk and had to be put out by something from the doctor's kit. She's swearing death to anyone who comes near her.'

'Well, actually, she's snoring like a pussycat right now,' said Doc. 'But she's not likely to be any use until she's calmed down.'

Violet nodded. 'But Bunny?' It hurt even to ask.

'Bunny's still at large, I'm afraid. I'll go check on Madame.' Doc Flanagan left the room hurriedly, swiping at the corner of his eyes.

Oh God.

Albert sat down on the edge of the bed. 'Iris is helping. She saved you, you know. And she thinks she knows where to start looking for Bunny.'

Violet shifted against the pillow. Her eyes were gritty and her lungs felt scalded. She had a sudden sensation of falling through clouds of billowing smoke. Her heart lurched. She remembered heat and the wailing of sirens.

The fragments came together. 'Oh, Albert—La Maison?'

He squeezed her hand again. 'Easy, now. The ground-floor parlour is burned out, but the rest of it don't seem too bad.'

'No!'

'Hey, now. It's alright. Nico's got some mates keeping an eye on the place until we can get in there, retrieve some of your stuff and clean up.'

Violet allowed her chin to sink to her chest. She felt the sadness closing in: Bunny, Madame, the house she adored. Hot tears welled in her eyes and she fought against them. Not in front of Iris, she told herself sternly.

Iris patted her arm. 'Hey, didn't you hear what Albert said? We have a clue. I recognised the car that took your friend away. We're going to take a look to see if it's where I think it'll be.'

Violet straightened up. 'I'll come too.'

'Oh, no, you don't.' It was Doc Flanagan re-entering the room. 'You're in no fit state. And besides, I have another task for you. Ruby's lock-picking gentleman friend has arrived in town, which means I'm off to collect Shen and bring her back here, so he can remove that cursed thing around her neck.'

Violet thought about the locked chain and jade owl around Shen's neck. A lock picker could remove the object, but would she be truly free? 'When Shen finds out about Bunny, she'll want to give herself up. She'll go in a heartbeat.'

The room grew quiet again, then Doc Flanagan nodded. 'Ruby and Albert said the same. Which is where you come in.'

'How?' Violet's head was swimming.

Albert cut in impatiently. 'She'll listen to you, so you're the one who's going to have to stop her. Convince her to lay low, go back to Ming's. Just for now.'

'Alright.' Her voice wavered and she glanced in turn at the faces staring down at her.

'They're not asking you to be her jailer.' Iris folded her arms across her chest. 'Just remember: you didn't risk everything to free her only to have her give that freedom up like it meant nothing.'

Violet blinked. In her addled state, her mind was travelling backwards, via pathways of confusing association, to Shen's kiss.

Doc Flanagan hauled his Gladstone bag onto the foot of Violet's bed and snapped the clasp shut with an air of finality. 'Iris is quite right. You should persuade Shen to stay in hiding. Unless we all agree that a trade—Shen for Bunny—is an acceptable solution?'

'What?' Violet gasped.

Doc nodded. 'I didn't think so. Good, that's decided.' Percy Flanagan drew himself up to his full height and stiffened his naval bearing. 'Come on, Albert, Iris. I'll drive you to the top of the road so you can investigate Iris's leads. Madame's out cold and I have the keys to the van.'

Iris snapped a salute in the doctor's direction as he strode out the door. Albert leaned across and kissed Violet on the cheek.

She swatted him away. 'Don't get soppy.'

'I'm not. I just know how much you hate being left out of the action.'

'Just come back as soon as you know anything about Bunny. And don't do anything stupid.'

Iris gave her a thoughtful look as she waved goodbye.

What a way to reunite with your long-lost sister, thought Violet. With the others gone, she sank back into the warmth of the bed. In her painkiller haze, the appearance of Iris with Albert began to seem impossible. Had her twin really saved her? Iris the cheat?

The doctor's pills were making her tired, and her mind felt both light and heavy at the same time. She thought of Bunny, alone and afraid, and felt sick with anguish. But soon the feelings began to fade. Ideas seemed to evaporate into mist. She closed her eyes and wished for Philip Chandler to return to her dreams but instead she drifted into sleep thinking about Madame, who would eventually wake and need to be faced. What would Madame have said in response to Doctor Flanagan's question about trading Shen for Bunny? Violet knew, and it made her shudder.

There were patches of the night that remained a haze in her memory, but Xiao's arrival and his pursuit of Bunny were inked indelibly in her mind.

It had happened so fast. From the moment Xiao had entered the parlour with his men, Violet knew that her fears had been well founded. After his altercation with Violet and Madame the night before, he had anticipated a fight and had come prepared.

Madame, seeing Xiao and his men from her position in the show's audience, had sent Violet an urgent glance before shouting across the room to end the show.

Violet knew immediately that she had to find Bunny and get the girl to safety. From her position in the makeshift wings to the side of the stage, Violet whispered to Ruby to collect the other girls and lead them to safety through the front door. Then Violet dropped to her hands and knees and crawled silently around the seated audience rows, out of sight of Xiao.

The customers rose around her, confused by the interruption to the show. Major Davidson, upon seeing her crawl past, had hissed, 'What on earth's going on?'

Violet shook her head. 'Get out now, Major, sir. Tactical withdrawal. Show's over for tonight.'

He had nodded, winked and got to his feet, dragging his companion in the seat next to him upright. 'I say, this seems like a dratted shame! But we'll come back for the ending another night, Madame.'

Around him, the men grumbled and shuffled to their feet, allowing Violet to stand and slip out the kitchen door. Shouting followed.

Bunny was found shivering, wide-eyed and terrified, in the shadow behind the door. Behind her, Charlie and Li Ling were throwing on coats.

Violet nodded to them urgently. 'Go. Make sure Shen is safe and can't be found.'

They hurried quietly out into the backyard but the immediate sounds of a scuffle told Violet that Xiao's men were blocking the exit. A new wave of panic surged through her.

Violet nudged Bunny in the direction of the servants' stairs but the girl pulled back. 'Wouldn't we be safer hiding in the scullery?' she said.

Violet shook her head. 'There's nowhere secret but the attic space above the second-floor bathroom. And we live in a brothel, remember. That bathroom is the only room in the whole place that locks from the inside.'

'Why don't we try to get through the parlour to the front door?'

'God, no. The parlour's full of Xiao's men. We have to hide you, Bunny.'

It was painful to recall how Bunny had turned solemn brown eyes to her, not comprehending. 'What? Why?' It was heart-breaking to recall it.

She had held Bunny by the arms. 'You can't be seen. They'll take you to make Madame give Shen up.'

The girl had cried out. 'Oh God. *Help me.*'

So, Bunny and Violet had raced up the narrow back stairs, the sounds of the argument in the parlour gathering volume.

Violet pushed Bunny onwards, tiptoeing on her bare feet past the tiny landing that opened onto the first floor. She paused. Artemis, the only weapon in the house, lay in a drawer in her room, just a few paces away. But she could hear the heavy footsteps of Xiao's men running up the grand parlour stairs.

There was no way to retrieve it without risking being seen. Locking Bunny away was the only priority now.

She heard outraged shouts from above. The men who had come with Xiao were in Madame's private rooms, at that moment discovering Shen's absence. She heard them calling for Xiao.

Pushing Bunny along, Violet wound carefully up the back stairs to the second floor, wincing as Bunny's smart red boots tapped on the wooden treads.

Suddenly, the door to the first-floor landing below them opened. A man's voice called out. Violet pushed Bunny through the door and into the bright hallway on the second floor, closing the door swiftly behind her. She grabbed Bunny by the hand.

'Run to the bathroom, now!'

But they were too late. Xiao stepped into the hallway from the grand stairs at the very moment they reached the bathroom door, his broad shoulders heaving as he recovered his breath.

He put his hands on his hips and laughed aloud. 'Ho! Little flowers! Where do you think you're going?'

Violet stepped between Bunny and Xiao, shoving the girl behind her. 'Let us be. Shen is gone. You can't hurt her now.'

Xiao laughed again, closing the distance between them with powerful strides. 'How poorly you understand the seriousness of your situation,' he said calmly. 'Your Madame should have explained the gravity of this mistake. Shen is one of a kind. She must be recovered.'

'I know what your ghost-man wants,' Violet said, her voice quavering. 'Take me instead.'

'Oh, don't worry, you'll pay for your part in this fiasco. But tender as it is, your flesh won't offer my employer the same satisfaction as Shen's will.'

'Then fight me—I'm not afraid.'

'In that case, you're not as clever as I thought.'

At that, Violet launched herself at him, only to collide with his giant sweeping fist. She tumbled sideways towards the bathroom, her head hitting the doorframe then the bathtub, each of which caused explosions of pain.

It took hardly more than seconds, she thought. Seconds to be completely overpowered.

Blackness closed in. Then a single piercing shriek shook the night.

From the floor, Violet opened her eyes through dizzying pain to see Xiao grasp Bunny by the hair and draw her close.

Looming over Violet, Xiao landed the tip of his boot in her side. She cried out in pain. A second kick cracked a rib.

Clutching the sobbing Bunny close, Xiao bent over Violet. 'I'm not a fool. It's the niece we need, not you.' He nudged Violet with his toe. 'Nothing to say?'

Violet coughed and felt blood pool in her mouth.

Xiao laughed. 'Your Madame won't come for *you*, slut. But she'll come for her niece, with Shen following sweetly behind. Nobody is coming for you. In this universe, you are nothing more than a *speck*.'

Now, lying in bed in Doc Flanagan's little ground floor apartment, with Xiao's condemnation ringing in her ears, Violet closed her eyes and willed the universe to swallow her once more.

CHAPTER 25

IRIS REGARDED ALBERT FROM HER position opposite him on the hard wooden bench in the back of Doc Flanagan's van. He looked the same as she remembered: the squashed nose of a fighter, the big shoulders of a lad who was expected to lift and carry.

And he was still as loyal as a hound, following Violet around, his care for her clear in every gesture and every word. It broke Iris's heart to see it. Violet was utterly blind.

But Iris felt an undeserved, unaccustomed happiness, sitting there being thrown about in the van, the bones of her arse absorbing the shocks. She liked Violet's people. They had accepted her without question. It was confusing. What prepared a person to see the world as one full of friends rather than enemies?

She wanted to learn the trick of it.

From the driver's seat, old Doc Flanagan was holding forth. 'We're outmanned and outgunned, so we need to use the element of surprise against Xiao. That's how we'll get the better of him.'

Albert leaned over from the bench in the back and shouted over the clatter of the engine. 'Xiao'll send us a message, won't he? Try to force us to give up Shen for Bunny?'

Doc Flanagan nodded. 'I reckon. But even if we could meet his terms, which we probably can't, you couldn't trust him to keep his word. We'd just as likely all die in a flaming shootout.'

'Fark,' said Albert.

'Quite so.'

Albert folded his arms and frowned. 'Can you shoot, Doc?'

'Me? Only if you mean billiards,' came Doc's shout from the front.

Albert paused thoughtfully. 'I could get a gun. Whaddya think, Iris?'

Before Iris had a chance to reply, Doc swore loudly. 'Saints alive, Albert. You with a gun you've never fired before? You'd be about as useful as nuts on a dairy cow.'

Iris braced herself as Doc took the corner into Oxford Street a little wide. Her stomach lurched as the tyres on her side of the car lifted off the road.

'So it comes back to finding Bunny first,' said Iris, leaning in. 'Or we could go to the police, I suppose.' When Albert looked over in surprise, she shrugged. 'What? It's what some people would do.'

Doc Flanagan slowed down enough for the engine noise to drop back to a rheumatic rattle. He glanced over his shoulder at them both. 'I've been treating the Kings Cross boys long enough to know that the cops won't act against anyone if it cuts into their kickbacks.'

Albert considered this. 'Forget the cops. Let's focus on finding Bunny ourselves. We'll try the stable first. If she's not there, I've got another idea: Arlo's girl Jeanie said Xiao and his lot used the docks for bringing stuff in. I reckon they'll have a warehouse there.'

Doc Flanagan nodded. 'Alright, see what you can find at the stable. If there's no sign of Bunny there, we'll reconvene back at my place and then turn our attention to the docks.' He pulled over to the kerb.

Iris shuffled to the back of the van, recalling with a jolt the terrifying sight she'd seen in the stable. Albert opened the van's back doors and he and Iris stumbled out into the street.

—

Iris beckoned for Albert to follow her through the copse of casuarinas along the side of the stable wall. The winter sun was high in the sky now: they would need to be careful not to be seen.

'Just a bit further,' she said. 'Then there's a fig tree we can climb to see over the wall.'

The trees opened out and she let out a cry of surprise, halting suddenly and causing Albert to crash into her. She walked slowly into the camp clearing, her hands covering her mouth.

The kids' camp was gone. The clearing was strewn with the leftover trash of human settlement. Stepping over a broken wooden crate, she crouched by the pile of ash and cinders where the fire had been.

A sob tore her throat as she picked out a few tiny, blackened bones. What had happened to them all? Where was the little girl she had soothed?

She sank into the dirt, sifting the ash through her fingers and allowing the tiny bones to fall back into the firepit. She wiped her hands on her coat and sniffed.

After a moment, she stood and walked around the edge of the fire. Her toes dislodged a small stuffed doll from the dirt and she-oak needles, its face made of an old brown stocking and both of its button eyes missing. The tears came freely.

'Struth, Iris,' said Albert, his butcher's bravado gone.

''S okay,' she managed. 'It's nothing.' She turned her face into the sleeve of her jacket.

It wasn't that she wanted the kids in the camp back: she was well shot of Tobias and she knew it. She felt no urge to run around looking for him. But this was the closest thing she'd had to a home.

I sent that toddler off by herself, she thought. I'm an animal.

Albert cleared his throat. 'Jesus. Well, the orphanage was no Shangri-la, but I'm guessing the Hallidays didn't work out so well in the end.'

'I don't want to talk about it.' Iris shook her hair back from her face. 'It's fine. Let's go.'

She *did* want to talk about it. But not with Albert; with Violet. When the time was right. Now she could name the feelings she'd had when she stared up at the front of La Maison des Fleurs, when she looked at her sister and saw Violet's expression of hurt and betrayal.

She felt regret. And shame.

She used the toe of her shoe to cover the doll with sand then led Albert silently back to the wall. Her hands were shaking as she shoved them into the pockets of her coat.

'Come on.'

'Wait,' said Albert, who was marching behind her. He stopped. 'I know you don't care what I think, but I don't think you have changed at all. Either of you. You're still both the smartest, nicest people I've ever known.'

Iris stopped and turned to face him. '*Both* of us?'

'Yes, you dill.'

She sucked in a breath. How hard she'd let herself become. Harder than stone or iron. As dense as the very centre of the earth. 'Thanks, Albert.' She sniffed again.

'Don't mention it.'

She trudged on, the she-oak needles snapping under the heels of her blackened leather shoes.

At last, they neared the stable wall and she stopped at the base of an ancient fig with branches sweeping low to the ground. Without waiting for Albert, she hoisted herself up and climbed it nimbly, hands and feet seeking familiar bumps and hollows.

Albert followed more cautiously, until his footing was sure enough to allow him to stand in the crook of the tree's spreading branches beside Iris and peer over the wall.

'Ah, fark, we're too late—the car's gone,' she said, bitter disappointment in her voice. 'Damn and blast it.'

Albert took a small pair of binoculars from his shirt pocket and scanned the stable yard. 'There isn't even a horse left in the stalls,' he said.

Iris grabbed the binoculars and peered into the yard. It was empty; it looked almost as abandoned as the kids' camp. Even the stable doors were open. 'I reckon we should go over the wall. It's possible they've left Bunny tied up in one of the stalls.'

Albert shifted uneasily on the branch. 'No-one said anything about trespass, Iris. I'm an apprentice. I'd lose my position!'

Iris wriggled past him. 'Don't come then. Wait for me here. But there's something in there so wild it'll make your hair fall clean out.' And she jumped down from the tree in a single leap.

Albert gave a resigned sigh then half-jumped, half-fell after her. 'Ah, damn it . . . Wait up, Iris!'

Iris slid her knife along the bottom edge of the stable's kitchen window, catching the simple turning lock and nudging it to the horizontal position. Using the blade as a lever, she slowly jemmied the window up until there was a crack through which Albert could slip his fingers and hoist it open fully.

'The trick is doing it slow,' said Iris, accepting a leg up onto the windowsill from Albert. 'Real slow. These old windows never fit quite the way they should. Easy enough to open once you know how. Plus, this lot never got around to putting bolts on theirs.' She swung her legs over the sill and landed softly on the kitchen floor.

Albert lifted himself up onto the sill easily and dropped to the floor beside her.

Iris looked around. They were in a simple flagstone kitchen at the rear of the stable block. Empty benches lined each side of the room and a blackened wood stove hunkered in the centre of the back wall. The room was cold and smelled of old ash.

They walked silently into the dim room beyond. A large window was cloaked by curtains that blocked the daylight. It was the same window through which Iris had glimpsed the men from the stable yard. A big wooden table had been pushed under the window against the heavy drapes.

She saw what she was looking for: the two wooden packing crates.

She turned to him. 'We'll do a quick check of the place first, make sure Bunny isn't here. Then I need to show you what's in those.' She pointed at the crates.

He nodded.

They walked silently through to an adjoining room and made a circuit. The room was cold enough to make her shiver. Unbidden, her heart leaped to think of the little girl Bunny, tied up and terrified in a dark and cold place such as this.

The room was empty.

'We should look for the entrance to a cellar or something.'

Albert nodded again. 'Sure.'

They walked back into the kitchen and Albert nudged the flagstones on the floor. There was no sign of a cavity beneath or a trapdoor. He sighed. 'Nope, nothing.'

'Come on then,' said Iris, 'and I'll show you what's in the crates.'

They walked back into the main room. Albert crouched beside her alongside one of the big wooden boxes and watched as she slipped the blade of her knife below the lid and carefully lifted one of the plain pine boards.

She saw his face register astonishment.

'Tell me I'm not flipping dreaming,' she said. 'There's enough guns here to tear the whole of Kings Cross in two, right?'

'Sweet Jesus,' said Albert, his eyes glued to the sight. 'There's enough here to take out half of Sydney, let alone Kings Cross.'

He took the knife from Iris and with the utmost care he used the hilt to squeeze the panel back into place, pressing the lifted nail gently back to its original position.

'I reckon they'll be back soon,' he said. 'They wouldn't clear out and leave a hoard like this here for long.'

A screech in the stable yard made Albert scramble to his feet.

Iris giggled. 'Just white cockatoos. They love this place—lots of grain from the horses. Come on, let's go.'

Albert shook his head. 'Wait. Look!'

She turned and saw what he was pointing at. On the side of the crate was a merchant's address: *Wharf 4, Hickson Road.*

Iris whistled softly between her teeth. 'Good job, Albert! There's your warehouse. Now let's get the hell out of here!'

When they got to the kitchen, Iris went over the window ledge first and Albert followed, landing softly in the dirt beside her.

They stood blinking in the noonday glare. Iris turned and placed her hands flat against the glass of the window and lowered it back into place. 'Easy does it.'

'Iris, you're a genius bringing us here. Right-o, let's make tracks.' Albert turned to go.

'Wait.' She wasn't even sure why she wanted to kiss him—out of gratitude, excitement or relief—but she kissed him hard, her cold hands holding his face and her lips soft against his.

Then she pulled away. Her pulse was beating in her eardrums. 'That's because.'

'Because why?' A crimson flush had raced up his neck and reached his ears.

'Because I'm glad I found you again. And because she'll never kiss you.' It came tumbling out before she could stop it.

'What do you mean?'

Iris saw Albert's face fall. She punched him softly on the shoulder. 'Hey. Don't be a goose. I see the way you look at Violet. You've probably been looking at her that way for so long she doesn't even notice it.'

He sagged against the stable wall. Then he straightened. 'Would you kiss me again? As Iris?'

She laughed. 'Jesus, Albert! Don't be such an egg! Lives are at stake here. And pick up your feet: it's a long way to Hickson Road.'

With that she turned and strode back into the stable yard, keeping to the shadow of the wall.

Albert stumbled after her. 'Aren't we going back to Doc's first?'

'Nope. We're going to see for ourselves if Bunny's at the wharf. We'll need to stay out of sight, so the fewer of us, the better. Plus, I doubt we'll be strolling through the front door. I can't see your Doc shimmying up a drainpipe, can you?'

—

As they sat in the tram heading north to the harbour, Iris felt her impatience growing. Albert was tapping his foot restlessly against the floorboards, his brow creased with anxiety. A troubling thought occurred to her: if they were to discover Bunny, would Albert blunder in without any thought for his own safety, or hers?

This was the problem with boys: they were ruled by something unpredictable that overpowered judgement and sense. They were as thoughtless as rams half the time.

She looked out the window at the passing buildings. She would have to keep Albert close, to make sure he didn't do anything rash. The last thing Violet needed now was two more people requiring rescue.

Half an hour later, they stood facing the warehouse on Hickson Road, half hidden by a large fig tree. 'You ready?' asked Iris.

Albert nodded.

She pointed to the metal fire stairs that crisscrossed the side of the building. 'That looks like the easiest way to get to a good vantage point. You're not afraid of heights are you?'

'Why do you ask?'

'Because if we can find a skylight on the roof, there's no better way to take a look inside.' She caught Albert's alarmed look. 'It'll be fine. There's hardly a roof in Sydney that I haven't scaled. There's not much you won't do when you're hungry.'

He nodded. 'I'm impressed.'

She shrugged. 'Don't be. Come on, let's do this before you lose your nerve.'

They crossed the road and crouched beside the fire escape. Giving Albert the 'all clear' signal, Iris raced up the stairs with him close behind.

At the top of the fire escape they pulled up short at a locked door. Iris tutted. 'Pity, that might have saved you a climb. Can't win 'em all I suppose,' she said.

'So?' asked Albert.

Iris pointed to the roof. 'To the roof. Give me a boost, will you?'

—

It happened so fast. After just a few minutes of looking down into the warehouse, Iris was able to make out the approximate layout of the building's interior. They heard Bunny before they saw her when, in a quiet moment during which Xiao's men left the building, they heard soft crying. Iris noticed the play of light on a wall, describing a human silhouette. Bound to a chair, head hanging. After shifting her position on the roof, Iris saw Bunny: face bloodied, her little red boots dragging in the sawdust.

Then, as Iris had predicted, Albert reacted, issuing a shout that brought the men running from outside.

Iris seized a fistful of Albert's jacket and, with all the strength she could summon, she pulled him back from the edge of the skylight and out of sight. Albert's flailing arm caught her on the side of the head, causing her vision to fill with stars. Then he fell back, his arm thrown over his face.

She choked back a cough. They were so close to being seen! At any moment, Xiao's men might appear on this side of the building, looking for the source of the noise. She pressed herself flat to the roof, hoping Albert had the sense to do the same.

Voices carried from below. Iris closed her eyes, heart pounding.

Ten minutes later, after hearing their voices grow faint, Iris sat up and peered over the edge. The yard at the side of the building was empty, at last. She slid silently back down the sloping tin roof to the empty fire escape below, landing softly. Above her, Albert swore under his breath then followed.

As Albert straightened up, she pressed a finger to her lips and padded silently down the fire escape stairs.

At the bottom of the metal staircase, she darted along beside the building and out into Hickson Road, dodging the oncoming cars and carts. She didn't stop running until they reached the top of the hill on Pottinger Street, overlooking the wharves below.

There, on the pavement, she turned to Albert angrily. 'You nearly got us both killed.'

'Sorry. I just couldn't bear to see Bunny like that.'

'Well,' she said, 'it's your turn to run for help.' She sank into the gutter, panting.

Albert looked at her blankly. She ran her hand through her hair in exasperation. 'Albert, go to the doctor's! Get help!'

CHAPTER 26

VIOLET AWOKE TO THE FARAWAY screeching of rosellas beyond the bedroom window. The ghost scent of smoke lingered in her nostrils. In her woozy state, it was enough to lie there and blink at the light.

She rolled onto her side, exquisite pain shooting through her ribs and chest. The crisp cotton pillowcase was cool against her cheek. Get up, she urged herself. Get out. *Find Bunny.* She swung her legs over the side of the bed and planted her toes on the chilly floorboards.

With great effort, she rose to her feet.

Violet moved slowly through the apartment, using the wall for support, past the glass-windowed front door, past the doorway to the master bedroom and into the small living room. There she took in the ephemera of Doctor Flanagan's life. The bookshelf crammed with paperbacks. The framed maps, the service medals on the wall. Unexpectedly, a shapely wooden leg, with leather straps for attaching the contraption at the knee.

On the couch lay a neat pile of blankets and sheets. So, Iris must be sleeping here. Of course.

She considered this information. Incongruously, it placed Madame in Doc Flanagan's bed. My, that pair of sly dogs, she thought. Good for them.

Clutching her side, Violet shuffled slowly into the neat kitchen beyond, which opened onto a paved courtyard. She fumbled with the back door latch, then opened it and breathed deeply. New trailing jasmine plants, trained against the dark brick wall, showed rounded buds. A shabby pigeon fluttered down from the top of the wall to peck at seeds left out in a chipped saucer.

Turning back to the neat kitchen, she noticed the dusty tea set, the two rinsed tumblers on the draining board.

A cough behind her made her spin around. Madame loomed in the living room doorway, a man's dark red robe drawn tight around her. Her eyes were glazed with the intensity of a drinker's two-day binge. 'You!'

Violet raised her hands to reach for her mentor. 'Madame—'

Madame drew back with a wild toss of her head. '*You* brought this curse down on our heads,' she rasped.

'Only a monster would have handed Shen over to those men,' Violet protested. 'You wouldn't have gone through with it.'

Madame shook her head. 'No! It was you who set us along this path, not me. And now I've lost everything.'

Violet's breath stopped in her throat as she watched Madame lurch back down the hallway with uneven strides and slam the master bedroom door behind her.

Violet sat down on the couch, drew a blanket around her and curled up to the sound of the wretched pigeon cooing in the yard.

Moments later, her anguish was swallowed once more by dark, drugged sleep.

—

It was Eliza's tinkling laugh that brought her around properly, at last, on her makeshift bed on the couch. Ruby, Shen and Eliza sat on the carpeted floor beside her, and a handsome young man sat on the edge of a threadbare Victorian easy chair, his elegant hands clasped in his lap.

Violet took in his immaculate fawn waistcoat; the shiny tan boots that shifted restlessly on the carpet.

Ruby, laughing, launched herself to her feet with athletic ease, her navy crepe pants falling in elegant folds. 'Blimey, Violet, you really snore! We thought the coal train from Newcastle was passing, didn't we, Doc?'

Doctor Flanagan leaned in from the kitchen doorway. He was wearing an apron and drying a cup with a tea towel. 'Indeed we did. You ought to lay off the Cuban cigars, Violet, they're playing havoc with your pipes.'

The well-dressed young man stood and thrust out his hand. 'Well, for God's sake. If these jokers aren't going to introduce me, I'll have to do it myself. Johnny.' His accent suggested a comfortable home and a private education, and his hands were cool and dry.

'He's actually Slippery Jack to the circus crowds,' said Ruby. 'Johnny can get himself out of just about anything. Chains, safes, straightjackets: you name it, he's shucked it.'

'That's encouraging.' Violet stole a glance at Shen, who sat observing her pensively.

Johnny grinned at the room, rubbing his hands together. 'Well, I reckon we can get that lock off Shen's neck rather easily.'

His careful enunciation reminded her of the St Michael's classroom, where very good diction was considered next to godliness itself.

'That *is* good news. I feel better already.' Violet was fully awake now. She eased herself upright on the couch. 'Let's do it.'

'That's the spirit!' Eliza patted Violet's leg. 'Grandpa says lying about is a waste of heartbeats.'

'Quite right.' Doc Flanagan came in with a tray of steaming teacups and Violet took one gratefully. 'What else does this grandpa of yours say?'

Eliza clapped her hands together. 'Oh, I nearly forgot! Grandpa has a message for Li Ling. He said to tell her that the fireworks for the Hungry Ghost Festival should be here by now. He said it was very important that I tell her.'

Doc Flanagan frowned. 'Is that so? How interesting. Thank you, Eliza dear. We'll pass the message on.'

Johnny declined a cup of tea from the doctor and rubbed his hands together. 'Shall we begin?'

From her place sitting cross-legged on the carpet, Shen smiled cautiously at Violet and shuffled closer to take her hand. Then she nodded to Johnny, who hoisted himself from the chair and kneeled beside her. He drew a flat leather pouch and a magnifying glass from his jacket pocket.

'Now you just stay nice and still, my dear, alright? I'll have this off you quicker than the Saturday sprint at the Randwick Racecourse.'

They watched as Johnny turned the jade owl pendant over in his hand, examining it. 'This bird's creepy, I'll give you that,' he said. Then he turned the padlock over in his fingertips, scrutinising it for long minutes with the magnifying glass.

Shen winced as the chain bit into the skin of her neck.

'Easy now.' Johnny paused and placed his hands on Shen's shoulders. 'Deep breath, then we'll proceed.'

With great care, Johnny placed the magnifier on the carpet, unbuttoned the leather pouch and opened it flat. It was full of gleaming silver tools. He drew out a long instrument no thicker than a lady's hatpin. He turned back to Shen, who nodded at him. He inserted the pin into the lock at an angle and, after some jiggling, the mechanism sprang open in his hands with a pleasing click. 'There. Even easier than I expected,' he said.

The jade owl pendant tumbled to the floor, pulling with it the bruising chain.

Shen gasped, her hands flying to her neck to touch the tender skin. Ruby let out a cheer and gathered Shen into an exuberant hug.

A powerful curse disarmed by a hatpin, thought Violet. Perhaps there's room for hope after all. 'Where on earth did you learn that, Johnny?' she asked.

He smiled. 'Boarding school. Plenty of locked doors to practise on.'

Ruby leaned forward and planted a kiss on Johnny's cheek. 'Johnny had the living crap beaten out of him for being queer, didn't you, sweetheart? But now look at you! A sought-after artiste with a flock of boyfriends.'

'I wouldn't say a flock. A modest cabal at most.' He winked at Violet.

'They should count themselves very lucky,' she said.

Eliza gave a low whistle and took the cursed jade object in her hands. The magic of the gesture brought the room to silence. She ran her fingertips over the carvings in the jade ever so slowly. She lifted it close to peer at it the bird-omen's obtuse expression. Then she put it back on the floor thoughtfully.

'I say, Doctor Flanagan,' she said. 'Do you have a very big hammer?'

—◆—

They assembled in the courtyard to watch the ceremonial crushing of the jade owl. The bird shattered into sparkling green fragments on the courtyard pavers. The threadbare pigeon tottered over to peck lazily at the specks, while Johnny was sent to find a dustpan and brush from the neighbours.

Eliza wiped her hands on her cotton smock and beamed at Shen. 'See? No more owl, no more curse,' she said. She shook her dark hair and went back into the kitchen.

Violet followed her inside and pulled up short at the sight of Nico entering the living room, followed by the doctor. Nico pulled out a chair and sat, looking grim. 'I bring a message.'

Violet's insides turned over. 'Go on.'

'Xiao came to Madame's 'ouse. He tell my men this: you must bring the tattooed girl to the Hyde Park fountain at midnight or they will kill the little one.'

Violet steadied herself against the table, as Doc Flanagan sank into a kitchen chair.

'Well,' he said. 'Now we know.'

Ruby appeared at the back door, clutching Shen by the arm. Shen caught Violet's eye and, sensing the news was bad, let out a low cry of despair.

Nico got to his feet and pulled a cloth-covered package from inside his jacket and put it on the table. 'Your friend Albert got a message to me. 'E asked me to find this and bring it to you. Now I bid you goodbye.' He buttoned his jacket and left the kitchen via the courtyard, the garden gate swinging closed behind him.

Holding her breath, Violet stepped forward and unwrapped the package on the table. There lay Artemis, her Beretta, cleaned, oiled and ready to use.

Doc Flanagan gave a startled cough. Ruby drew Shen into the kitchen and all three girls stared down at the gun.

'Holy heck. How long have you had that?' Ruby asked.

'A few days.'

'Wow, Violet.' Ruby shook her head in disbelief.

Eliza nudged her way into the group. She whistled through her teeth at the sight of the gun. 'You know what my Grandpa says? He says once you've cut the loaf, you may as well go ahead and make the sandwich.'

Ruby looked up, brows furrowed. 'Make a sandwich? That doesn't sound very Chinese.'

Eliza nodded earnestly. 'I *know*. That's what I thought!'

Violet picked up the gun. It was warm from being held against Nico's chest, as if it had already begun to take on a pulsing life of its own. 'Your Grandpa's right, Eliza. He means if you go so far as to buy a gun, then in some place in your heart you intend to shoot it. And you need to face up to it. Nico once told me as much himself.'

Johnny appeared at the back door, a dustpan full of jade fragments in one hand. At the sight of the gun he stopped short. 'I surrender! I didn't have you pegged for a gangster, Violet.'

Violet shrugged. 'You and me both.'

Johnny placed the dustpan by the back door. 'Okay. Time to scram.'

Violet led them through the apartment to the front door, Shen's hand in her own. She wondered how much the girl had understood of the message Nico had delivered. After hastily fare-welling Ruby and Johnny, Violet stopped in the hallway and took

Shen's other hand in her own, hoping her pain and discomfort weren't noticeable behind her encouraging smile.

'You must hide again.'

Eliza squeezed between them and tapped Shen on the shoulder. 'Your gift for Violet, remember?'

Shen gave a little cry and patted her pockets. She drew something out and pressed it into Violet's hand, closing Violet's fingertips over the cool, smooth object then leaning close to kiss her. Shen was crying silently, salty tears collecting on her lips.

Violet pulled away, eyes closed. With a final squeeze of her hand, Shen turned and followed Eliza out the door.

Violet opened her palm to see a twinned shell: on one side, it bore the raised swirls of two conjoined helixes. On the other, it was flattened into a perfect figure eight.

Doc Flanagan appeared beside her in the hallway and put his finger to his lips, gesturing that Madame was behind the door to the master bedroom. 'Come back to the kitchen. Don't wake the dragon. By the way, where do you think a person would choose to store Chinese fireworks imported for a festival?'

Violet followed him down the hall, considering this. 'You think Mr Ming was trying to help us?'

'It's a theory.'

'Right. Well, I'd say a person would store fireworks in some kind of warehouse.'

'What if the fireworks were going to be set off on the harbour?'

'Then I'd look for a barge of some sort. That's what they use for Chinese New Year.'

Doc Flanagan scratched his chin. 'And where would you moor a barge?'

'A wharf?'

They turned at the sound of the back door being thrown

open. Albert ran into the kitchen. He bent double over the table to catch his breath. 'Get the car, Doc,' he panted. 'They've got Bunny at Hickson Road.'

Doc Flanagan took Violet's hand and squeezed it. 'You see? Old Ming's a crafty bugger.'

Along the hallway, the door to the doctor's bedroom opened and Madame stepped into view. She was fully dressed and buttoning her coat. 'Let's go.'

—

Charlie was fetched with haste from Chinatown and told, in rather a rush by the doctor, that he had a special part to play in the heist. Then Albert, sitting in the back of the van with Violet and Charlie, directed Madame to the Millers Point corner where Iris would be waiting.

Violet held her breath and gripped the wooden bench under her thighs, wincing in pain with every bump in the road.

As promised, Iris was standing on the street corner, attempting to blend in with her surroundings. She stood, hands in her coat pockets, looking up at the sky. With the approach of the green van, she looked over coolly, spat into the gutter and walked to meet them with unhurried ease.

She stuck her head in the passenger-side window and nodded. 'Good, that was fast. I've found a place down on Hickson Road where you can leave the car—it's close but far away enough not to be seen. I'll get in the back and show you.'

'Right you are,' said Doc Flanagan.

Iris climbed into the back of the van and joined Albert on the bench opposite Violet. She looked around at Violet, Albert and Charlie hunched in the cramped confines. 'Hang on,' she said. 'Is this it? This is Bunny's rescue army? I've seen tougher church choirs.'

Violet saw Albert's look of irritation. 'That's not fair,' he said crossly. 'Anyway, what did you expect?'

Iris shrugged. 'At least a few men who can fight.'

Violet leaned forward, bringing her face close to Iris's. Her sister had a point. We may as well give ourselves up to the ghostman, she thought, *and* skin ourselves to save him the trouble. But there was no sense in destroying everyone's hope. 'Get on with the directions, or leave us to deal with this ourselves.'

'Have it your way,' said Iris. She turned to the doctor and directed him to drive the van down the hill.

Violet bit back the urge to have the last word. The pain in her side was sharp and pulsing. Her head wound throbbed and the drugs had left her feeling weak. She shoved her hand into the pocket of her coat and felt the dense weight of the gun.

That's our only weapon right there, she thought, and we're walking into a vipers nest. We must be raving mad.

As she felt the van slow to a stop she nudged Albert. 'Right. Albert, get out. Iris, you're staying here.'

'What?' Iris looked at her, stunned, and shot a frantic glance at Albert.

'I mean it. You're going to stay put. Doc and Charlie will go to the waterside and see if Old Ming's information is any use. God knows how, but at least it will keep them out of trouble. Albert and I will go find Bunny and bring her back here. You have no part in this fight and you don't need to get mixed up in it, so stay here and keep Madame from doing anything stupid.'

Violet waited as Doc Flanagan opened the van doors and

quietly helped Charlie out. Albert scrambled past Violet into the fading daylight to join the others.

Iris shook her head and thrust out an arm to stop Violet from shutting the van door behind her. 'No way! I'm better at this stuff than you are. I know how to fight. You need my help.'

'No, I don't.'

Iris shook her head, incredulous. 'Who the hell do you think you are?'

The question hung between them: I could ask you the same, thought Violet. We don't know each other at all.

'Save your own life, Iris. Please. Look at us. You're right: we're amateurs. We have no idea how to get Bunny to safety. Stay here. Stay alive.'

Without waiting to hear Iris's reply, Violet slammed the van door and turned to face Albert. Doc Flanagan and Charlie disappeared into the busy wharves.

As Albert and Violet turned to go, Madame rounded the corner of the van to stand in their path.

Violet looked up into Madame's face and saw the same uncompromising expression she recognised from their confrontation at Doc Flanagan's earlier. Madame's will was a rod of iron.

'Madame, don't be a fool!' Violet hissed. 'You can barely stand upright. You'll just make everything harder.'

'I need to be there every step of the way until Bunny is safe,' said Madame.

'Please, Madame! Let us go by ourselves!'

'No, I will not.'

Albert shook his head. 'Well, we're fucked.' He sighed. 'Come on, then—this way.'

CHAPTER 27

VIOLET CROUCHED BEHIND ALBERT in the shadow of one of the adjacent warehouse buildings, looking across at the metal fire escape attached to the main warehouse building of Wharf 4. If Albert's skylight spying was to be trusted, Bunny was behind that wall directly in front of them, hidden by ironbark and steel.

Two men, wearing rough donkey jackets and caps pulled low, were stationed at the large wooden doors that opened into the loading space between the wharves. Guards or sentinels, thought Violet. Of course, Xiao would naturally seek to protect whatever else he had in the warehouse besides Bunny.

Violet cast a hurried glance behind her. Madame was crouched between two parked cars and was covering her face with her hands in an attempt to smother her racking cough.

Albert looked back at Madame then at Violet and shook

his head. 'This is crazy. With that racket going on we won't even get close enough to see Bunny, let alone find a way to get her out.'

'Let's just you and I go a bit closer.' Violet turned to Madame and signalled for her to stay put. Madame shook her head furiously.

Violet's heart was beating hard in her chest. Albert darted across the short distance between the buildings at a stooped run, choosing the moment the guards were distracted by seagulls squabbling over by the water to dart into the open expanse. Violet followed close behind him. Every step was a risk. These men would shoot first, ask questions later, and give a nosy parker a swim with the fishes wrapped in a long chain, just to be sure.

They huddled against the walls of the warehouse. Behind them, in the shadow of Wharf 5, Madame had struggled forward and appeared to be watching the men, waiting for an opportunity to dart across and join Violet and Albert.

Pressed into the shadows, Violet felt a bolt of pure terror as she looked around at the open paved expanse of the yard. They were trapped. A single error in judgement from Madame would expose all three of them and there were no alleys on this side to vanish into, no cars to hide behind.

Suddenly Albert held up a hand. 'Did you hear that?' he whispered.

Violet shook her head and concentrated. A faint cry carried through the walls. It was Bunny's pleading voice, followed by the voice of a man, perhaps Xiao, rebuking her. Violet caught her breath and Albert pressed his fingertips to her lips.

Bunny really was here, behind the wall. Crying.

Violet felt hot tears rush to blur her vision. She blinked them away and turned to see a colourful barge drift into view at the end of Wharf 4.

At the same moment, the idle guards seemed to notice the barge too. Violet watched as their heads drew together, discussing this seemingly unexpected turn of events. Then, overcome with curiosity, they stepped from the open doorway into the yard and craned to look at it, heads still drawn together in conference.

A man appeared at the prow of the barge and Violet recognised him immediately. It was Charlie Han, one foot on an open wooden crate, smoking a cigarette with the appearance of a man at his leisure. In his other hand he held up a small object, perhaps a cigarette lighter. Behind him were stacks of boxes and crates, which appeared to have been torn open. Curiously, the front of the barge was littered with the small items, presumably the contents of the boxes, and dusted with dark powder.

The guards hesitated, apparently unsure how to respond to the stranger and the unexpected delivery. But the barge's appearance was odd and its trajectory was irrevocable: in less than a minute it would collide with the wharf. After another muttered exchange, the guards left their post and hurried towards the oncoming boat, reaching into their jackets and retrieving handguns.

With an elegant flourish, as if he had planned his actions to the precise second, Charlie flipped the open lighter into the pile of boxes beside him then dived swiftly into the water.

With a sizzling crack, the first of the fireworks ignited; the boat collided with the wharf and, just as Xiao's men reached the barge, the incendiary hoard began to catch fire.

It was only a matter of seconds before there was a loud explosion. A fantastical shower of sparks shot into the sky while, on the dock, an enormous cloud of smoke engulfed Xiao's men. Their cries carried over the expanse of the yard.

Violet, momentarily dazzled, felt Albert seize the front of her coat and drag her in the direction of the open warehouse doors. Her ears were ringing.

He continued to pull her along until they were well inside the doorway. Outside, the fireworks continued to explode in a deafening cacophony.

As smoke billowed into the warehouse, they plunged onwards, keeping to the wooden walls as Albert led them unerringly to the corner, just visible from the skylight, where Bunny was captive.

Violet stopped in shock and seized Albert's wrist, pulling him to an abrupt stop. Bunny was there alright—but she was no longer tied to the chair. She was standing on it, a rough noose around her neck, the rope's other end tied around the warehouse's ironbark rafters. She was whimpering softly, shaking her head.

From the corner came a voice Violet recognised.

'Violet Kelly. Less a flower, more a tenacious weed.' Xiao stepped forward. 'My business partner was already angered by you and your Madame, and now you pull this childish stunt.' He waved in the direction of the water, where the shrieks and whistles of the conflagration could still be heard.

Bunny let out a hoarse cry. She stood on the toes of her boots, swaying, with the rope tight around her neck. 'Violet! Help me!'

Violet coughed as the smoke drifting in from the wharf filled her lungs. 'You don't need to kill an innocent girl.' She drew out her gun, Artemis, and pointed it waveringly at Xiao.

Xiao drew a larger handgun from his jacket and levelled it at her in turn. 'Go ahead, shoot me with that toy. You won't stand a chance. Shall we count to three?'

A sound behind Violet made Xiao shift his gaze. The clouds of smoke parted and Madame appeared. She walked quickly and deliberately, head high, towards her niece.

Xiao shook his head and laughed bitterly. 'Now this is just a circus!'

Madame shook her head. 'Take me to your partner, your ghost-man, whoever he is. Tell him we can come to terms. Let the girl go. Let all of them go.'

Xiao gave a careless laugh. 'These kitchen sink melodramatics do you no credit, Peggy O'Sheehan. I will find Shen without your help.'

Madame ran at him. Xiao turned the gun towards Madame and fired it once, twice into her chest. She staggered forward, gasping, and fell to her knees beside Bunny's chair. The girl screamed.

'No!' Violet shrieked, steadying the gun in front of her once more. The scene seemed to swim before her, and Xiao became a moving target.

The man threw her a look of callous contempt. 'You fools. My men and I have cargo to move before the authorities arrive.' Turning abruptly, he kicked the chair out from under Bunny's feet. Albert lurched to grab her, reaching her just in time to stop the deadly rope from snapping taut. Bunny clawed frantically at her throat.

In that second, Iris sprinted out of the smoke and, with a bloodcurdling cry, cracked Xiao over the back of the head with a metal chair.

He dropped his gun and Violet saw her chance. The howl of rage came from deep within: she fired Artemis once, twice and a third time before Xiao let out a startled grunt and, clutching his arm, sank to the floor.

Albert's terrified voice carried to her from the corner. 'Violet! Hurry. We need to help Bunny.'

Violet ran to him. He was managing to support Bunny's

weight, but the noose had tightened around her neck and her face was turning pink.

Violet went through Albert's pockets frantically. Where was the Swiss army knife he had carried since they were kids?

She found it and flipped it open with trembling hands.

Iris appeared at Violet's side. She picked up the kicked-over chair and helped Violet on to it, holding the chair steady as Violet sawed through the rope. Bunny toppled into Albert's arms just as his strength gave way. They both fell to the ground into a crumpled heap, their landing softened by Madame's body, which lay prone at their feet. From Bunny's gasp, Violet knew they had saved her.

The relief caused Violet's knees to give way, and she toppled off the chair and onto the concrete, her shoulder smacking against the floor. For an instant she was back on the bathroom floor of La Maison des Fleurs, the wind rushing at her face and her world collapsing into blackness.

A slap across the cheek brought her around. Iris pulled her to her feet. 'We have to go, *now*, while it's still chaos out there.'

'Wait!' Violet got to her feet then crouched and pressed her fingers to Madame's neck. There was no pulse.

Iris shook her head. 'We're too late. *Please*, Violet, let's go!'

It was this exhortation from Iris, this 'please', that brought Violet undone. Albert and Iris hoisted Madame's body between them and carried her into the smoke. Violet, summoning all her strength, lifted Bunny to her feet and dragged her out into the clamour and noise, her heart breaking.

CHAPTER 28

IT WAS FIVE HUNDRED AND forty-seven steps from the gate of St Michael's Orphanage to the front door of La Maison des Fleurs. Violet had counted them as she walked in the weak March sunshine, on that first day, her cardboard case in her hand and her chin held high.

Only five hundred and forty-seven steps to change my life, she had thought happily, reaching her destination and placing her case on the steps of the grand and beautiful house. She wiped her sweaty palms on her hand-me-down skirt and caught her breath. The imposing front of the imposing terrace loomed before her.

A surge of excitement had propelled her from the gate of the church, quickening her pace and lightening her stride. But at around two hundred steps, as she'd rounded the corner and passed the grocer's, Violet's resolve had begun to crumble unexpectedly.

Perhaps she was unprepared for her new life. Perhaps she was wrong to have been so sure about her path. Were the nuns right after all? How her sandals pinched her toes. How dowdy her clothes seemed, now she was a part of the real world and free from the orphanage squalor.

She'd bit her lip and paused, shivering, on the footpath. Sister Bernadette had refused her a new pair of sandals, calling it a flagrant waste of shoe leather. The parish owed Violet nothing more than the objects she held in her battered case and, besides, Violet would soon be someone else's problem entirely. In this same vicious spirit, the Reverend Mother had also refused Violet a coat from the parish donations box.

These punishments were visited on Violet because she had declined the nuns' advice. With Violet's skills and education, she was told, she might aspire to eventually be a rural trainee teacher, or perhaps to dream of a position as under-tutor in a middle-class house. Naturally, her bad start in life and her regrettable wilful streak would place limits on her advancement. Nevertheless, from such a role, a modest and purposeful life might unfold: a small house, a working husband, children to be raised in dignified and noble near-poverty. There was just such a position waiting to be filled at a worthy but challenging Wagga Wagga girls' day school, where Violet might be joined to God's plan for bringing civilisation to the ungrateful native children. Sister Philomena was happy to recommend Violet. Shoes and coat could be thrown in.

But Violet had other ideas about how her attributes might be put to use. It hadn't escaped her notice that the sight of her in her gym slip made the young visiting male postulants stutter in panic. The local deacon had whispered a scandalous invitation for her to sample the communion wine in the comfort of his rooms—an offer she'd tactfully declined. Even Sister Philomena blushed upon encountering Violet doing high kicks in her bloomers for eurythmy and physical culture. Violet was determined to set her sights higher than a rat hole in the regions with a woeful clutch of brats. If exploiting her natural advantages was the way to escape the dizzying banality of the life for which the nuns had prepared her, then so be it.

Here she was, legs and all.

That day, calling on those reserves of resolve, she seized the rope and rang the brass doorbell. It swung heavily and issued a luxuriant baritone clang, filling Violet with hope about the opulence that awaited within. She'd heard the rumours. Who hadn't?

Unexpectedly, the door was opened by a young girl of around twelve. She was dressed in a childish pale blue woollen dress with smocking across the front. Violet glimpsed the deformed upper lip. The girl caught the look and inched backwards into the shadows, clasping her hand over her mouth.

Before Violet could say hello, a voice called from the hallway within. 'Who the devil is it, Bunny?'

Footsteps sounded behind the girl, who ducked her head and slipped away.

A tall thin woman stepped into the open doorway. Appraising Violet and her suitcase with a bemused frown, she said, 'Yes?'

Violet took in the woman's elegant dress. Her auburn hair, with roots that hinted at a more pedestrian brown. Her bony chest and arms. Violet shifted from one foot to the other, clumsily knocking the suitcase flat with her aching toe. 'I've come to work here.'

A faint smile crossed the tall woman's face. 'Is that so?'

Violet took in the faint European tinge: *Is zat so?* 'Yes. I think I'll be good at it.'

'You what?'

'I think I'd be good at it. Ma'am.' Violet blushed, then rallied. 'I've got references. Would you like to see them?'

The woman laughed, a great hoot that rang out into the street. 'You do know what we do here?'

'Yes.'

'And who on earth gives a girl references to work in a place like this?'

Violet cleared her throat. 'Nuns do. Well, they gave me a reference to take to my next employer, so . . .' She tapered off, her sense of control over the conversation rapidly slipping away.

This sent the woman into fresh torrents of laughter. She shook her head. 'Well then, pet, you'd better come in and show me these references. If the nuns say so.'

Violet reached for her suitcase and followed the tall woman up the steps and into the dark hallway, her heart beating fast. She had to trot to keep up with the woman as she disappeared into the gloom.

'Push the door shut after you! It's perishing cold out there. Cold enough to snap a woman's bones.'

'Yes, ma'am.'

'Actually, it's *Madarme*. Like alarm. Or farm. The French way. Not madame like ham.'

'Ah, *oui. Bien sûr.*'

Madame cast a heavy-lidded glance over her shoulder. 'Don't get fancy.'

'Right you are.' Violet was smiling so hard her face hurt.

—

Of course, Madame told her later, *I took one look at you and thought you were some kind of a trap. I thought some spook was trying to get*

a mole inside my place. Girls like you don't just fall out of the sky.
I mean, look *at you. But then you started on about the nuns and I*
nearly lost my dignity, right there on the doorstep.

But I did fall out of the sky, thought Violet. The St Canice's
church choristers began their hymn. I fell out of the sky and
landed in the best place on earth.

She placed a hand on the varnished coffin in front of her, the
thin sound of the organ wheezing from the altar beyond. Her tears
fell onto the wooden surface. She dug a nail into the glossy edge,
obeying a black urge to leave a mark on this strange, incongru-
ous box that held Madame's body. Her knuckles whitened. She
wanted to shout.

A faint cough made her turn. Doc Flanagan, waiting behind
her, placed a steadying hand on her arm and drew her away from
the coffin. The sweet, cloying scent of the jasmine piled on the
coffin lid caught in her throat.

She pulled away from his hand and managed the walk, head
down, to her place in the pews.

Violet felt an almost physical longing to have Bunny by her
side. It wasn't right that Bunny couldn't be here but the doctor
had been adamant. Bunny, now wearing a neck brace, needed to
rest and heal. Her vertebrae had been stretched apart, her throat
all but crushed. Her neck was a pitiful ring of welts. She could
barely speak, her voice little more than a whisper. The blood
vessels in her eyes had burst and she had bitten her tongue. She
was lucky to be alive.

The choir embarked on the second verse. Violet shifted on
the hard wooden pew, conscious that all eyes in the half-filled
church were inspecting her and the other Maison girls for signs
of sin. Violet scowled at a woman who was staring at her from
across the aisle. Only the ingrained habits of orphanage worship

stopped her from crossing the aisle and stamping on the toe of the woman's battered ankle boots.

Doc Flanagan slid into the pew beside her. 'Had enough?'

The choir launched into another verse of their dispiriting hymn.

'Hell, yes!'

Violet got to her feet and led the way down the aisle, meeting the hard gazes of the parish women head on.

Ruby slipped out of her pew near the back and fell into step with them. She linked her arm through Violet's and, at the final pew, turned and stuck two fingers up at the organist, who gasped aloud.

They spilled out into the sunshine and stood for a moment under the pointed sandstone arches of the church front.

'Oh, the torture!' Ruby said. 'Did Madame really believe any of that stuff?'

'I think she did,' said Doc Flanagan. 'Some things you can't unlearn. She found some comfort in it, I suppose.'

'Well, fat lot of good it did her. I mean, can you see those women getting on their knees and praying for her immortal soul?'

'Not likely,' Violet said. She raised her face, eyes closed, to the morning sun. 'I reckon they're praising God for smiting her.'

'Smiting? You made that word up.'

'I did not. God likes to smite. Although He doesn't smite enough vicious busybodies for my taste.'

'Quite,' said Doc Flanagan. 'Shall we get the tram to Mortuary station, ladies? The Rookwood train leaves in fifty-five minutes and Madame has already paid her fare.'

Ruby turned to face them, her face anguished. 'I can't, I'm afraid.'

'You're not coming to the burial?' Violet took Ruby's hands in her own.

Ruby blushed, her awkwardness clear. 'Oh, Vi, don't hate me, but I've got to go and pack. Ashton's Circus said they'll take me and Johnny back if we meet them in Bathurst. Our train leaves this afternoon.'

Violet drew in a breath. It wasn't fair to make Ruby feel any worse than she already did. Besides, with La Maison des Fleurs still in disrepair, what could Violet say to make her stay? 'Of course. You should go. That's—that's wonderful news.'

She drew Ruby into a hug and held on tight.

Ruby squeezed her hard. 'Don't be a prig, it doesn't suit you. It's not wonderful—it's horrid that I can't be here with you and Bunny and Albert and Shen. But I can't sleep on Johnny's floor forever and, besides, I'd like to renew my acquaintance with a certain dashing knife thrower.'

Violet pulled away and smiled. Ruby had mentioned Diego the knife thrower. He satisfied Ruby's taste for danger and, according to her, had certain intimate talents she remembered fondly.

'Just until things settle down,' said Ruby.

'Just until then,' Violet echoed. 'Goodbye, Ruby.'

Ruby kissed her on the cheek. 'Don't forget me.'

'How could I?'

Ruby turned and hurried away. Violet was grateful for the short farewell. She took Doc Flanagan's arm. 'Shall we?'

'Let's.'

They walked down the street, in the direction of the city. The doctor patted the hand held in the crook of his elbow. 'You're not to blame, you know.'

They walked together in silence for a moment while Violet

took this in. The sky was a dazzling blue: a hint of the spring to come. 'I got Madame killed,' she said at last. 'Let's not pretend any different, Doc.'

They came to a halt on the pavement and he turned to face her.

'No, you saved her. When Shen turned up she was afraid, more afraid than I've ever known her. But if she'd let Shen go with those men, she wouldn't have been able to live with herself.'

'Do you mean that?'

'Of course I do. Peggy O'Sheehan was a Catholic right down to the marrow. Condemning that poor girl to death would have sent her to her grave. She couldn't have shouldered the wretched guilt.'

Violet's thoughts swam. 'No. I forced her to help me save Shen. And look where it got us.'

'Shen is safe. That's where it got us. When do she and Philip Chandler sail?'

'The day after tomorrow.' The thought made her heart sink.

'You couldn't have known what was to come, Violet.'

'I *should* have known.'

Doctor Flanagan folded his arms and shook his head. 'Well, if you're so determined to take the blame, don't let me stand in your way. But here's something for nothing: Madame was dying anyway. She just chose her way.'

'What?'

'Madame's lungs were going to finish her. Now, if I have my facts straight, she died just a little ahead of schedule, but you got Bunny out. I reckon that's as she would have designed it. Shall we get this tram?'

He gestured at the tram waiting at the stop before them, its engine rattling into life.

Violet nodded. Doc Flanagan stepped up onto the wooden boards and pulled Violet up behind him. The tram car lurched and started downhill towards the city.

'See? Things beyond your ken, Violet Kelly.'

'I see.'

'Besides, I have a surprise for you. For all of you: Bunny, Iris, Albert, Charlie and Li Ling too.'

'Really? What's that?'

'Well, you haven't asked about Madame's wake. You know it's traditional to share a drink and a meal with friends in honour of the departed?'

'Yes. I just assumed—'

'There you go again. Assuming. Don't for one minute imagine you had the measure of your Madame. You'll never guess where her undertakers have booked us for this evening.'

—◆—

The taxi pulled into the driveway in front of the thick pink marble pillars of the Australia Hotel and Doc Flanagan opened the door. 'Here we are then.'

Violet, in tall heels, stepped out behind him gingerly, scooping up the skirt of her beaded pink satin dress. Albert, in borrowed tails, scrambled out behind her. They took in the grand entrance of the building and Violet laughed out loud. Albert shook his head at her, eyes wide at the sight of the impressive hotel front.

'You've got to be heckin' kidding me, Doc!' he said.

'I hecking assure you I am not, young man. Now where's that bathchair?' Doc Flanagan strode off in the direction of the hotel porters.

Violet looked around at her companions. She was still exhausted from their ordeal and it felt ever so good to be following someone's else's lead—in this case, the doctor's—today. She longed to feel normal again. The burial had been a depressing affair, just Doc Flanagan, Violet and the parish priest at the crudely prepared graveside. The ancient words of the graveside committal seemed out of place in the newly cleared corner of Rookwood Cemetery. Instead of evoking ceremony, the necropolis reminded Violet of the pictures she'd seen of the new housing subdivisions springing up for returned soldiers in Sydney's suburbs. This was the new estate of the dead: sandy graves and unused paths disappearing into knotty stands of bush littered with chocolate wrappers.

She had returned to the doctor's apartment in low spirits, anxious to figure out a way forward. She needed to see La Maison des Fleurs, to know the extent of its damage. But first, they must conduct a grand wake: Doc Flanagan was most insistent.

Li Ling, dressed in a beautiful, embroidered satin jacket and matching flowing pants, climbed out of the taxi and clutched her purse to her chest nervously. Behind her, Charlie was paying and tipping the cab driver.

Overawed by their surroundings, they stood together beside the marble pillar, straightening one another's clothes.

A second cab pulled up and Violet saw the rapt faces of Iris and the invalid Bunny inside. Doc Flanagan approached, pushing a wicker chair on wheels. He brought it to the door of the second taxi and reached in to lift Bunny out.

Doc Flanagan had told them to dig out their finest clothes and be ready to mix with the very best of Sydney society. This had meant sending Charlie and Albert on a trip into the hunched and blackened hulk of La Maison des Fleurs to retrieve dresses and shoes.

Yet despite Violet and Iris's attempts to spruce her up for the evening, Bunny looked frail and crumpled in Doc Flanagan's arms.

The doctor placed her carefully in the chair and fastened the brace around her neck. 'There,' he said. 'You look like a princess.'

His kindness caused Violet to feel a surge of sadness.

She joined him at Bunny's side. 'So, the Australia Hotel, opened by Sarah Bernhardt herself. This is how Madame wanted us to send her off?'

Doc Flanagan beamed. 'It was all paid up in advance. A private room and a banquet. I imagine she knew you'd want to stick one in the eye of the St Canice's crowd. What better way?'

Violet took the handles of Bunny's bathchair from Doc Flanagan and pushed her towards the grand entrance. Through the door she could see more pink, veined marble and a dark mahogany staircase. Soft light shone from the elegant crystal chandelier. 'I believe we're being asked to enjoy ourselves magnificently. I don't know about the rest of you, but I think I can manage it—for Madame's sake.'

The liveried doormen stepped forward and Violet pushed Bunny through the leadlight doors.

They were led to a room off the main ballroom, set with sparkling crystal and silver. Bottles of champagne rested in chrome ice buckets at either end of the oval table. At each setting was a single pink rose and a tiny glass of pink aperitif. Large silver urns, filled with pink roses, were placed at either end of the linen-covered table.

In the background, a waiter discreetly wound up a gramophone. Duke Ellington, Madame's favourite, filled the room.

Doc Flanagan fussed around, indicating to Charlie and Li Ling where they should sit. He placed Iris on one side of Violet while Bunny, in her bathchair, was on the other.

Taking a seat at one end of the table, Albert said, 'I could get used to this, Doc.'

Doc Flanagan settled himself into a chair at the opposite end. 'A young man like you should have ambition. So, here's a taste of what wealth and class can bring you, Albert McAllister. Enjoy it while you can.'

'I intend to!'

Violet picked up the tiny glass before her and took a sip. 'Rose-flavoured. Delicious.' She handed Bunny a matching tiny glass.

Bunny tutted. 'I'm only thirteen, Violet,' she croaked.

Violet downed the rest of her own drink in a single swallow. The liqueur was sublime. 'You're thirteen and you've just become an orphan—for the second time. I'd say the world owes you a drink.'

Iris leaned across and raised her glass. 'You know, it pains me to say it, but Violet's right. Come on, girl, let's start as we mean to carry on.'

Bunny rolled her eyes and, acquiescing, sipped the liquid. 'Oh! That's heavenly,' she whispered.

'Exactly.' Violet and Iris grinned at one another.

Bunny took a second sip and Albert called across the table, 'Wait a minute. Did I just hear Violet and Iris agree on something?'

Iris shot Violet a conspiratorial smile. 'Don't be silly. Whatever gave you that idea?'

Silently, and as if instructed by a whisper from beyond the grave, waiters appeared and began to place tiny pots of pâté with orange glaze in front of each person. Elegant baskets of French bread followed. Linen napkins were whisked off the table and placed onto laps.

There were cries of delight as Albert and Charlie tasted the appetisers. The waiters filled their glasses with champagne topped with floating pink petals.

Iris took a sip from her glass and leaned towards Violet. 'I was thinking we could call a truce, you and me.'

Violet's eyebrows registered her shock. 'What, put the past in the past, you mean?'

'Yes.' Iris nibbled the corner of her bread speculatively.

Violet considered this. 'Well, I suppose you did save my life.'

'Twice, actually.'

'Quite. Though the second time was just showing off.' Violet hid her smirk.

Iris shrugged. 'Let's say you owe me one.'

Violet laughed. 'You can't be serious.'

Iris lifted her glass towards her sister's with a wicked smile. 'Can't I?'

Violet touched the rim of her glass to her sister's. 'Alright— truce.'

'Truce.'

Iris turned back to the table and raised her voice above the noise. 'What is this champagne? It's delicious.'

Violet studied her twin. Iris was wearing a blue silk shantung gown that Ruby had left behind. Bunny had instructed Li Ling on the process of setting their hair and now Iris's was swept back from her face in an elegant roll. She wore two paste diamond hairpins from Madame's own jewellery box.

The girl beside her was a very different creature to the one Albert had plucked off the street. Iris had thrived in the company of Violet's friends. She was beautiful and she was enjoying herself.

A nudge in the ribs from Bunny caught Violet off guard.

'Ow! You nasty little thug.' She went to pinch Bunny affectionately on her hollow cheek but the girl's instinctive flinch caused Violet to pull back. 'Hey, I'm just kidding.'

Bunny smiled sadly and leaned in close. 'Oh, Vi, Madame's gone. How will I ever get used to it?'

'It'll take time, Bunny. But you've got me.'

'Really? Even now that Iris is back?'

Violet put an arm around Bunny's narrow shoulders. 'Oh, heavens, don't worry about Iris. She can look after herself. She won't need my help. So we can stick together, you and me.'

Bunny gave a wan smile and rested her head against Violet's shoulder, her dark eyes closing.

Charlie Han reached across the table and prodded her other arm. 'Look, artichokes! Li Ling says they cool liver fire.'

Violet straightened up in her chair. The waiters had placed before each of them a single elegant globe artichoke floating in a dish of melted butter. They were as pretty as camellias. Beside each plate was a strip of rolled paper.

The head waiter cleared his throat. 'The message is from the person who invited you here.'

Doc Flanagan clapped his hands together. 'How marvellous. Madame has prepared a message, to be shared from beyond the grave! What does she have to say for herself?' He reached for his glasses.

Violet took the strip of paper from her place setting and unfurled it. The message was written in fine gold lettering. *Enjoy, dear flowers. Until we meet again.*

Violet folded the slip of paper, looking around the room. Something didn't feel right. But Albert was already on his feet, champagne glass raised to propose a toast. 'To the flowers!' he shouted.

The skin on the back of Violet's neck prickled.

As the others lifted their drinks rowdily, she remained frozen, the paper clenched in her hand, a chilling sense of dread breaking the surface of her calm. Xiao was injured; perhaps he was dead. But his superior, the so-called ghost-man, was still out there. Unidentified, hidden from view. For all Violet knew, he could be watching them now . . .

As if sensing her thoughts, Iris turned to Violet, her face as white as her sister's. 'The message isn't from Madame, is it?' she hissed.

Violet, unable to speak, shook her head. She pushed herself back from the table, her head swimming already from the strong drink. She felt dizzy, unsteady on her feet.

She had to shout to be heard above the noise. 'Listen to me! We have to get out of here. *Now!*'

Her words were met with silence. Albert, still standing, gaped at her. 'What are you on about?'

Violet felt the colour draining from her face. 'This isn't safe. We should go.'

Doc Flanagan shook his head. 'You're wrong, Violet. This is Madame's farewell gift to us all. The undertaker told me.'

'What did he actually say?' asked Iris.

Confusion crossed the doctor's face. 'He said . . . he said it was all paid for. That's all.'

Charlie and Li Ling exchanged looks. Li Ling slowly placed her fork down on the tablecloth.

Albert shook his head. 'No. You're going crazy, Violet. There's nothing to worry about here.'

'Am I crazy?' Violet turned to Iris. 'Are we?'

Iris pressed her hands to her cheeks, shaking her head. 'I really don't know.'

Bunny tapped Violet's arm, and Violet turned to her. The girl's face was white. 'Take me home, Violet. I don't want to be here.'

Violet stood and threw her crumpled napkin on the table.

Iris rose too, draining the champagne from her glass. 'Pity to waste that. It's divine.'

Violet pulled on the handles of Bunny's bathchair. 'Iris, that could be poisoned!'

'I may not live to taste champagne again, so I consider it worth the risk,' her sister said. 'Come on, you lot. And quit grumbling.'

Behind them, the others rose to their feet.

'Well, now we know,' said Violet sombrely. 'The ghost-man won't leave us alone. As long as we have Shen, we're in danger. We can't afford to relax, even for a minute.'

CHAPTER 29

ALBERT AND VIOLET LEFT DOC FLANAGAN'S at sunrise and hurried through the quiet streets to La Maison des Fleurs.

From the street, the state of the place was heartbreaking. Violet held Albert's hand as they entered the house to inspect the damage and look for the strongbox, in which Madame kept her papers.

As the morning light poured through the gaping ground-floor windows, Violet took stock of the parlour. The flames had caught the drapes and couches first, tearing across the carpets and quickly engulfing the tiny stage. Nothing remained of Cleopatra's tomb, and most of the furniture was reduced to ash. Where the fire had burned hottest, the ceiling plaster had fallen to the floor in great blackened chunks. The cast-iron frame was all that remained of Madame's Beale piano.

But the quick actions of the fire brigade had stopped the fire from spreading beyond the ground floor. The stone kitchen and scullery were sooty but usable. The scene was grim—but not entirely hopeless.

Indeed, Albert was upbeat. As Violet watched, he kicked at the charred wooden treads at the bottom of the house's grand staircase. 'It looks bad, but we can replace these. And underneath, the stringers are fine.' He showed Violet the undamaged stair supports. 'Reckon they're made from turpentine. You can't burn that for quids.'

He continued his examination, calling, 'Violet, come have a look at this.'

Violet joined him to inspect the parlour wall, her foot colliding with something that gave a wiry clang. Recognising the domed shape, she reached down and picked up the empty cage of Dido and Aeneas. There was no sign of the birds—alive or dead.

Albert was peeling back the smoke-stained wallpaper. 'See? Underneath the paper, the plaster is fine, just a bit cracked. I swear to you, Violet, we could fix this place.'

She turned and took in what remained of the parlour. In her mind's eye, she saw the drapes, the palms, the settees, the light fittings, the rugs, the elegant paintings that had been the realisation of Madame's vision. She sneezed loudly, doubling over from the pain and causing a pile of ash to lift and drift back to the floor at her feet.

She straightened up and rubbed her nose. 'I see what you mean. It's not a complete wreck. But putting this back together will cost a fortune. Where would we find that kind of money? Besides, for all we know the bank'll want to take the place to settle Madame's debts.'

Albert pulled a bent silver tray from the detritus at his feet and studied it. 'We'd better go find the strongbox, then. Put this to one side, Vi; we might need to pawn it later.'

Violet took the tray and carried it into the hallway, where she placed it beside the charred bottom stair. Albert climbed the stairs, taking care to tread on the unburned sections. 'Watch your step. It gets better the higher we go.'

Violet followed.

On the first floor, she saw the hallway wallpaper was stained a greasy brown from the smoke. They made a short detour to the Rose Room, where Violet hurriedly packed a few essentials into an ancient musty carpet bag. Violet was tempted to linger, but Albert tugged her out by the arm.

'No time for moping. We've still got to get Shen out of La Perouse without those crooks realising. Let's find the papers and go.'

They left the bag on the landing, to collect on the way down, and climbed the grand staircase to the second, then third floor. Violet couldn't help but recall Xiao and his men running up and down the stairs. Dragging Bunny away. Frightening the girls, lighting the flames that had wrought so much damage.

She felt a twinge in her side as she remembered the kicking she'd received.

At the entrance to Madame's rooms, Albert produced the key Doc Flanagan had given him. They stepped into the cold sitting room and looked around. Madame's things lay as she had left them: a book was face down on the floor beside her chaise as if she'd dozed off mid-sentence, and clean stockings were lined up on a wire rack in front of a small stove. In her kitchenette, a single fly buzzed around a dirty cup and saucer. The evidence of her life was everywhere: the opium pipe on its stand by the window; the newspaper folded by the grate, ready to be kindled; the fine brandy she kept for best on the top of the kitchen cupboard; the backgammon set on the side table.

Albert whistled and shoved his hands in the pockets of his pants. 'Jeez. It sure drives the truth home, doesn't it?'

Violet shook herself out of her reverie. 'Come on, let's get some fresh air in here.'

She went to the sash window and unlocked it, then flung it open. It was another glorious late winter day. The lazy fly, drawn to the crisp gusts from the window, left its place on the draining board and made its escape.

Turning back, Violet brushed dust off her fingers. 'Right. Bunny says we're looking for a metal cashbox about the size of a woman's handbag. You make a start on her bureau and I'll do the wardrobe in her bedroom. Look for hiding places. Don't forget we're looking for a key too.'

'Aye, aye, captain.' Albert turned to the bureau in the corner.

Madame's bedroom was the same tableau of a life paused. Her ivory silk dressing-gown was thrown over the end of the bed and a chair by the door was piled with clothes. Violet opened the wardrobe door and inhaled the ghost scent of Madame's Shalimar perfume. She reached in to run her fingertips along the surface of the opulent fabrics. The silks and fur rustled sensuously under her touch. It seemed impossible that the world of La Maison des Fleurs was completely lost. She lifted Madame's rich fox fur stole from its hanger and nuzzled the reddish pelt. If only I could bring it back, she thought.

Turning to face the room once more, she cast a critical glance around. She would start with the wardrobe then shift the rugs. The place was riddled with loose floorboards: perhaps Madame had hidden her strongbox under her feet.

But after just ten minutes of moving items and examining

their contents, the back panel of the wardrobe yielded to her prodding fingers, sliding sideways to reveal a second panel and a dark cavity in between. Sure enough, her groping hand closed around the metal corner of the strongbox.

Albert appeared beside her as she hauled it out and placed it on the bed.

Albert shook the clasp. 'Locked. So where would a person hide a key?'

They looked around the room. Albert scratched his chin. He walked to the wooden window frame and reached up, running his fingers along the top.

Violet emptied the pots on Madame's dresser, rummaging through beads, hairpins, brooches and buttons.

Albert continued his sweep along the wooden doorframe until eventually something dislodged and clanged onto the floorboards. He bent and picked up the object then showed the squat brass key in his palm to Violet. 'Bingo.'

Violet applauded. 'Good work!' She took the key and tried it in the lock. It was a perfect fit. She placed it in her pocket. 'Right, let's not stick around here. It's bad for the soul. You can bring the box.'

'You don't want to open the box?'

'Nope. Doc Flanagan needs to hand it over to the lawyer. But let's do a quick tidy before we get out of here. I couldn't bring Bunny back when it looks as if her aunt just popped out to buy a pint of milk and a pack of Woodbines.'

They swiftly cleaned up Madame's apartment, replacing the book she had been reading on the shelf and washing the dirty dishes. Then they picked their way down the stairs, collecting Violet's bag on the way.

Nico and his younger brother Arlo were sitting on the front

step when they walked out of the house and into the sun. Violet took deep breaths of the fresh air, trying to purge the smoky taint from her lungs.

Albert clapped his old friend on the back. 'Arlo, you on the mend?'

Arlo flashed a quick smile. 'Doc Flanagan patched me up. It was only a flesh wound. Seven stiches—just enough to impress the girls.'

Nico stood and lifted his cap to Violet. 'Miss Violet. My condolences.'

Violet sighed. 'Thank you. We're grateful for your help with the house. I don't know what we'd do without you here to keep an eye on things.'

Arlo snapped his fingers. 'Eh! My Jeanie told me something last night. She said the cops found a dead Chinaman in the Hyde Park fountain. Had 'is throat cut from ear to ear. He'd been shot in the shoulder too, apparently.'

Violet cast an alarmed look at Albert. 'Did she say anything else?'

Arlo shrugged. 'She says the gangs in the Cross are so keen for a fight that you could cut the air with a switchblade.'

This information was concerning. Violet remembered what Jeanie had told Albert about the shady crook they were calling the 'ghost-man': that he seemed like the kind of person who liked to light fires. The kind of man who would arm two sides of a fight just to see it escalate. That crate of guns could set the whole place ablaze.

Violet looked from Albert to Nico to Arlo, then into the street beyond. It was quiet, save for the clanging from the workshop opposite. In the gutter several yards away, a pair of kids were tying a small dog to a lamppost with a skipping rope. Their laughter carried across the dirt.

Violet frowned. With the sunlight glancing off the tiled roofs of the terraces opposite, it was hard to imagine malign forces at work. As she watched, a pair of squabbling pigeons descended between the dusty painted gateposts marking the entrance to La Maison des Fleurs.

She smiled, then caught her breath.

There, on the footpath at the bottom of the steps, lay a single pink rose.

The men grew quiet as Violet broke away from the group, walked slowly down the stairs and stooped to pick up the flower.

She turned back, holding the rose by its stem. 'Albert, do you still think I'm crazy?'

'Oh, shit.' He hurried down the stairs, struggling with the carpet bag and the strongbox.

'He's watching us. Just like I knew he would. We have to move fast if we're going to keep Shen safe.'

Violet threw the flower into the gutter, reached into her pocket and took out the strongbox key. She tucked it into Albert's shirt pocket. 'Give the box and key to Doc Flanagan, no-one else. Then get a message to Eliza: tell her that Shen needs to be brought to this address as soon as it's safe to do so.'

Violet dug in her handbag and pulled out a tattered business card, then rummaged for a pencil. She scribbled the name of Philip Chandler's hotel on it, then handed it to Albert. 'Here.'

Albert studied the card. 'You want to move Shen today? Are you sure?'

'Dead sure. Tell Ming and Eliza to make sure they're not being followed. Philip Chandler is the one person the ghost-man doesn't know about.'

Philip Chandler answered the door to his hotel suite in a mono-grammed bathrobe with hair damp and freshly washed, holding a glass of amber liquor and looking every bit a suave man of the world. From beyond the door, Violet caught the drifting strains of a Chopin piano prelude.

She felt a surge of panic. Had she happened upon a seduction scene? 'Oh God, I'm terribly sorry, I—'

Philip swept Violet into his arms and into the room. 'Don't be silly! Good grief, are you alright? I've been worried sick.'

The door closed behind them. Violet, still in his arms, held on tight. She pressed her face into Philip's chest, where the fine hairs were still dewy from bathing.

'I suppose you could say I'm technically alright,' she mumbled into his robe. 'But you should stay exactly where you are just in case.' It was very soothing to be held.

'Can't hear a word, so I'll assume you're desperate.' His hands responded, drawing her into a tighter clinch.

At length, she pulled away and looked at him. 'You must have heard about La Maison. I've come to tell you that we need to bring Shen to you now. We're in deep trouble, otherwise I wouldn't invade.'

'This isn't an invasion. It's more a peaceful coup. Consider me willingly co-opted. Tell me everything. I heard about the fire and it's driven me mad not knowing where to find you.'

Everything: the fire, Xiao, the guns, Bunny's rescue, Madame dying: where should she begin? 'I think I need to just sit down for a minute. Is that okay?'

He led her across the room and she flopped onto one of the gracious lounges. 'Philip, we're being watched. At La Maison, and probably at Doc Flanagan's. Shen must come here tonight and very secretly if we want to be sure you both get away safely tomorrow. I made sure I wasn't followed, before you ask.'

He perched on the arm of the lounge, eyes twinkling. 'Goodness me, I *wasn't* going to ask. That could explain why the diplomatic corps gave me a desk job and not one in the field.'

'You have to take this seriously.'

He smiled. 'Of course I'm taking it seriously. I'm about to spirit a young woman away from a gang of murderous thugs. Don't assume I haven't thought this through.'

She reached up to touch his hand. 'I keep hearing that.'

'Which bit?' He laced his fingers through hers.

'The "don't assume" bit.'

'Well, my love, perhaps it's a sign you need to trust in the capabilities of others.'

'Did you just call me your love?'

He leaned down and kissed her. 'I did. Can't a tipsy man say reckless things?'

She pulled away, laughing. 'You can. But only because I'm ever so grateful that you're prepared to risk so much to help a young woman you don't even know.'

He tilted his head to one side philosophically. 'Shen deserves it. What sort of brutes would we be if we let such a cry for help go unanswered?'

'Indeed.' He had echoed her thoughts precisely.

He straightened up, then got to his feet and strode across the room to a sideboard and returned with two generous glasses of whisky from a bottle on the coffee table. Violet took a sip. The whisky was a burst of heavenly warmth. After a moment, she felt the muscles in her neck relax.

'Can Shen get here safely, without being seen? The Hotel

Royale has its charms but I doubt that a personal security detail is among them.'

'I think so. Between Albert, Charlie and the Ming clan, I believe they know how to manage that. But I expect they won't try to deliver her here until much later, when it's dark.'

'Well,' said Philip, draining his glass, 'seems that we'll have to find a way to occupy ourselves until then.'

'Seems that way.'

'Would it be rude to enjoy ourselves while we wait?'

Violet felt the flush reach her cheeks. 'It would be rude not to.'

With that, Philip refilled Violet's glass, unbuttoned her shoes and left the room with the air of a man on an important errand. He returned with a small suitcase of gramophone records.

Violet smiled as she watched him. The whisky had entered her soul, making her feel languorous, almost sleepy. He, on the other hand, was graceful and decisive. Disarmingly attractive.

She rested her glass on the table and tucked her feet underneath her on the sofa. 'It must be strange to be going home.'

By the gramophone, Philip paused, an unsleeved record in his hands. 'Stranger than I can say.'

'Does Mary prefer it when you're away?'

At the mention of Philip's wife, the air in the room seemed to stir then grow still.

Philip busied himself winding the gramophone. 'Naturally, Mary's happiest when I'm not there. But I have my uses, so she tolerates my return visits.'

'I hope it isn't too awful.'

'I hope so too. Needs must. Appearances et cetera.' He placed the needle on the record, filling the room with Debussy. 'She'll want children soon, so I expect my home duties may change somewhat.'

'She'll want you to stay and raise a family?'

He turned to Violet, shaking his head. 'Oh, sweet Violet. No. Mary will need a hand *making* the babies. She and Eleanor can't accomplish that alone.'

'Ah, quite. Well at least you'll be playing to your strengths.'

'I suppose.'

'All those years of practice won't be wasted.'

'You're enjoying this far too much.'

'Not at all. I speak for all your past lovers when I say it's a role you were born to.'

'Yes. About that . . .' He crossed the room and joined her on the sofa, then, taking hold of her feet, drew her legs across his lap. She rolled onto her back and stretched her arms over her head luxuriantly. Slowly, his hands travelled the length of her legs. 'Come here.'

Violet closed her eyes. The whisky had dulled her pain just enough to make pleasure a possibility. 'Oh, say that again.'

His hands were under her skirt, his thumbs pressing the insides of her thighs. She arched her back.

'Come here,' he repeated.

—◆—

The hotel bed was as soft as a cloud. Hiding a wince as pain stabbed at her ribs, Violet untangled her feet from the sheets and lay beside Philip, her neck and face beaded with sweat. They stared up at the wooden ceiling fan making lazy circles above them. His hand found hers.

'So tonight I have a beautiful girl in my bed, and tomorrow I smuggle a fugitive to safety. Don't I sound exciting?'

'Positively dashing. I won't tell anyone you're really just a soft-handed pen pusher.'

He laughed and rolled to face her, an arm tucked under his head. 'What's next for Violet Kelly?'

She admired the smooth muscles of his arm, his neck. She traced his jawline with a fingertip. 'People to save, things to do.'

'You're being evasive.'

'No, I'm not.'

'If that's the truth, then tell me: what are you living *for*? What do you want?'

She tucked her hand under her cheek and frowned. 'I want to eat lobster in a bubble bath.'

He leaned forward and kissed her softly. 'Bubble baths are nice. But I think you're built for a life of greater influence.'

She shook her head. Why were people always insisting they knew what was best for her? Plus, it was jarring to be reminded of Sister Bernadette while she was naked, sleek and sated. 'Sweet of you to say. *You* can afford to believe whatever you like.'

He sat up and scratched his head then stretched. 'If you say so. But when I come back to Sydney, I hope you have a different answer.' He swung his legs over the side of the bed, shrugged his shoulders into the silk bathrobe and padded across the carpet in the direction of the bathroom.

Violet sat up carefully. She heard the crash of water in the bathtub as he turned on the taps. What did he mean by *when I come back to Sydney*? She stood and followed Philip to the bathroom.

He tested the temperature of the bathwater, then turned to face her. 'No bubbles, I'm afraid. But we can check the menu for lobster.'

She wrapped her arms around his waist and rested her cheek against his silky shoulder. 'I'd settle for a bucket of eels! I'm famished.'

He turned off the taps. 'In you get, then.'

Violet slipped into the delicious hot water. A knock on the door startled them both.

Philip motioned for her to stay put. 'I'll see who it is.'

A moment later, two figures in black loomed in the bathroom doorway. It was Father Eddie with Shen, who was dressed as a nun. Violet gave a shout of relief as Shen drew back her veil.

Violet launched herself out of the bath and across the tiles to embrace her. 'What a cunning disguise!'

Father Eddie covered his eyes as Violet streaked past. 'Crikey! I'm a man of the cloth, you know. Are you trying to get me struck down?'

Violet released Shen from her soapy embrace and tiptoed back across the tiles, stepped back into the bath and arranged herself with as much modesty as her impressive nudity allowed. 'Better look away, Father. I can't leave this bath; it's too heavenly.'

Violet saw that Shen was gaunt and pale. Her eyes were dark hollows. She seemed to sway on her feet, the black robes swinging about her.

Father Eddie turned and shook Philip's hand. 'I've got to be on my way. No offence, but the man upstairs is taking years off my life for every minute I spend with you lot.'

Philip slapped him on the shoulder. 'Go well. Thank you.'

'No, you're the one who ought to be thanked. You're righting something wrong.' Father Eddie touched Shen gently on the arm then turned to Violet. 'Shen hasn't slept a wink for days, Eliza said. She's been terrified, poor mite.'

Philip showed Eddie out and returned to find Shen sagging against the doorframe.

'She's out on her feet. Let's give her the bed, Philip,' said Violet.

From the bath, she watched as Philip led Shen to the bed. The girl sank into it and murmured protests as Philip took off her shoes and drew the bedclothes over her. He lowered the light from the lamp beside the bed. His tenderness was reassuring: Shen rolled onto her side and fell asleep almost immediately.

He came back and appraised Violet from the doorway, with a softness in his eyes she hadn't noticed before. It gave Violet a melting sensation in her stomach, to be looked at like that.

She bunched her knees up under her chin and beckoned. 'I think you'll have to join me. Since the bed's taken.'

He dropped his robe in the doorway and stepped into the bath.

The room was silent but for a slow drip from the sink. The steam from the bath rose around them.

Philip was gazing at her. He reached for her face and held it in his hands, studying her. She took his hands in hers, fingers seeking fingers.

When he finally spoke, it was barely more than a murmur. 'I forgot the lobster.'

It was almost painful to hold his gaze. Violet felt a strange nakedness, as if he had found out a secret she wasn't aware she was keeping. She became aware, suddenly, of her own sharp longing. He would be gone before dawn: the realisation tore a sob from her throat. 'Lobster doesn't matter,' she whispered.

—

The next morning, when she awoke in a nest of blankets on the sofa, she was quite alone. She allowed the tears when they appeared.

When she felt emptied of grief, she rose and drifted naked around the suite in confusion, like a person caught between life and dreams. She drew her fingertips along the cherry wood sideboard, where no sign of Philip's gramophone and records remained.

Eventually, she stopped. Of Shen there was no trace at all. She had left as she arrived: a mere shadow.

Conversely, the envelope stuffed full of banknotes on the hallstand was Philip's very worldly way of saying goodbye.

CHAPTER 30

IRIS NUDGED VIOLET OUT OF the way and took the handle of Bunny's bathchair. The solicitor's office was only a short walk from Doc Flanagan's so the girls had set out for the reading of the will with time to dawdle and enjoy the sunshine. The narrow terrace fronts on Doc Flanagan's street were sooty and in need of paint, but even they seemed cheerful in the spring light.

Iris was regaling them with facts about the doctor. 'It's God's honest truth!' she squealed. 'He really *does* use the wooden leg!'

'No!' Violet gave her twin's shoulder a hard push. 'You're fibbing.' Her guts were sore from laughing.

'I'm not! He says that he lost the real one when his troop ship got torpedoed in Egypt. The only real question is: did he amputate the broken bit himself?'

Bunny snorted with laughter. 'That's disgusting.'

They rounded the corner to the intersection where Violet had first seen Iris, outside Averil's mother's bakery. Iris showed no sign of recognition. Instead, she threw her head back and laughed again. 'Ugh! You know what *is* disgusting? His medical books.'

Violet shook her head in disbelief. 'You've been reading Doc's medical books?'

Iris nodded eagerly. 'They're actually really interesting. He says he can help me study if I want. Nursing or something.'

Bunny turned her head stiffly, mischief in her smile. 'That's great, Iris. You'll make a terrific nurse. Bedpans and enemas and the like.'

'Oh, buzz off,' replied Iris.

Across the road, the front door of the bakery opened and out came Averil, a metal bucket and mop in her hands. She peered over at the group, then raised an arm in a tentative wave.

Violet, remembering her last ambivalent encounter with Averil, gave a wave in return. A show of friendship? That was unexpected.

A shabby, unkempt young man stepped into their path from the shadows of the boarded-up hotel. He stopped in front of Iris, fists clenched.

Iris gave a shout of alarm. 'Jesus, Tobias! You half-killed me with fright. What are you doing here?'

'Come to get you, Iris.'

He was dark-haired and muscular, eyes narrowed into hard lines. He's just the kind of thug Albert would turn away at the door of La Maison des Fleurs, Violet thought.

Iris shook her head, casting a frantic look in Violet's direction. 'No. Nope.'

'Carn, Iris. We're a team, aren't we?' He seized Iris by the arm, then registered Violet with astonishment. 'Sweet flippin' Jesus. *This* is what you've been hiding?'

Iris ducked away from him, wrenching her arm free. 'Leave me be, Tobias. Violet, get Bunny out of here.'

Violet backed away, pulling Bunny's wheelchair to a safe distance.

Tobias shook his head and seized Iris roughly. 'You're mine, remember?' Tobias shouted. 'Or does your memory need jogging?'

Bunny gave a yelp of fear. Violet seized the girl's hand.

As Violet watched in horror, the man dragged Iris by the throat and threw her against the wall of the pub, her head making a painful thud as it made contact with the bricks. Iris fell, dazed. He picked her up and threw her again, her shoulder thumping the wall. This time she slumped at his feet, looking up at him. Violet attempted to cry out but was too shocked to speak.

'Leave me alone,' Iris pleaded, clutching the side of her head. 'I don't owe you anything.'

Violet found her voice at last. 'Get away from her, you monster!'

Tobias leant down and grabbed a fistful of her Iris' hair, pulling her to her feet. 'You're coming with me. You can pay me back for every meal I ever got for—ow, fark!'

A clattering of footsteps made Violet turn in time to see Averil hurling herself at Tobias. She brought her metal bucket down swiftly across the side of his head, the heavy bottom making contact with his temple. He gave a single panicked look then crumpled to the ground, out cold.

Iris clutched her scalp, sobbing. Averil helped her to her feet. 'Come on.'

Violet steadied herself on the handles of Bunny's wheelchair and blinked at Averil. 'Crikey.'

The girl shrugged, and helped Iris to Violet's side. 'Can't abide a bully. Anyway, my mam says we should look out for you two, now you're back together.'

The neighbourhood *knows* about us, thought Violet. Madame was right about the gossip.

Averil picked up her bucket. 'You'd better scram. His mates'll be somewhere close by.' She looked from Violet to Iris, then turned and crossed the road back to the shop.

Violet, squinting, spotted a round face in the window of the shop, and saw the baker's faint nod.

Turning to Iris, she pulled her sister into a frantic hug. 'Are you alright?'

Iris brushed away tears. 'I'll have a lump on my head the size of a fig by bedtime. But other than that, I'm fine.' She spat at Tobias's prone body. 'Let's go.' She turned to Bunny and dropped to her knees before the girl, clasping her hands. 'Sorry you had to see that. Let's shake a leg. I don't want to be here when Sleeping Beauty awakes.'

On the ground, the young man was already stirring, clutching the side of his head.

Violet and Iris each took hold of one of Bunny's wheelchair handles and propelled her down the street at a jog. Iris winced at every step.

Once they were a safe distance away and out of sight, Violet turned to Iris.

'Wait up. Was that your boyfriend?'

'Sort of. Time was.' They were both breathless from the run.

'He's a bastard. Did he hurt you very often?'

'Not very often. Sometimes.'

Violet shook her head, her hands propped on her knees, panting. When she could breathe freely again, she turned Bunny's chair to face her. 'Listen, both of you. You *never* have to let a man treat you like that. Do you hear me?'

Iris's face fell. She wiped away defiant tears. 'Are you preaching to me, Violet? For Pete's sake.'

'I'm not preaching!'

'You are. You've had choices I didn't have, Miss Lah-di-dah.'

'That's not fair. I'm just saying you don't have to put up with an animal like that.'

'You don't know *what* I've had to put up with.'

The surge of rage and irritation took Violet by surprise. 'Iris, you can't be angry at *me* for how things turned out for you.'

Iris clenched her hands into fists. 'They put me out on the street, Violet! I was just a kid!'

Violet shook her head in confusion. 'What do you mean?'

'Mr and Mrs Halliday. She was so beaten up herself, she couldn't stop him. They put me out on the street.'

Violet took a sharp breath. She felt dizzy, as if the past was rushing towards them. The words raced up and tumbled out before Violet could stop them. 'You brought it upon yourself. You tricked everyone!'

Bunny was on her feet quick as a flash. Violet heard the girl's gasp. 'Violet! How could you?'

Violet felt Bunny's stinging slap and recoiled in shock.

'You take that back, Violet Kelly!' Bunny's face was red with rage. 'No child deserves to be mistreated like Iris was.' She stumbled back into her wheelchair, her hands gripping the armrests.

Violet covered her face with her hands. 'Iris, I didn't mean it. But you left me.'

The shame closed in, bringing startling clarity. *You left me.* This was the kernel of her hate for Iris: it was the abject sadness at being abandoned, the pain and loneliness of losing the only person who counted.

Violet felt her twin's hand rest gently on her arm. She dropped her own hands from her face. Iris sighed. 'Ah, fuck. It's true. I tricked you and I left you. I'm sorry.'

A tram rattled by, blowing newspaper around their feet as they stood staring at one another.

Violet closed her eyes. She was tired. She felt Iris's thin arms encircle her. She drew her sister closer and a little of the anger melted away. 'I've hated you all this time.'

Iris chuckled. 'Oh, believe me, I know. We're still identical twins. I feel things, even when you're not around.'

'Right, so you have special powers now?'

'Ha. Better believe it.'

Violet sniffed. 'Well, I don't think I hate you anymore.'

'Let's not get ahead of ourselves.'

Violet pulled away and gave her twin a lidded look. 'You're right.'

'See? Knew it.' Iris took charge of the wheelchair and started pushing it ahead, chin lifted.

Violet fell into step beside her and raised a quizzical eyebrow. Her sister was getting awfully good at besting her in an argument. That was going to have to change. 'Are you being *smug*?'

'Are you being thick?'

Bunny, with unexpected dexterity, twisted in her chair and landed a hard punch on Violet's thigh and a second on Iris's. 'Are you both being flipping ridiculous? Have you forgotten we've got somewhere to be? Let's get a move on!'

They turned into Oxford Street, where the sight of Madame's green van, parked outside the solicitor's, caused them all to fall silent.

—

The solicitor's office was a first-floor tenancy on Oxford Street in the smart new corner buildings facing Centennial Park. Bunny would not be carried but consented to letting the sisters take an arm each and help her up the stairs. A semicircle of smart leather chesterfield chairs had been arranged in the large boardroom, and a young assistant ushered them briskly to their seats. It was clear the reading was about to commence.

The solicitor entered the room with Doc Flanagan in tow. The solicitor was thin and stooped and his moustache trailed in dignified points below his chin.

'Let us begin. It shan't take long as there are only three items.' He spoke with the brisk clarity of a man accustomed to being listened to. *Only. Three. Items.*

Doc Flanagan gave Violet a solemn nod from across the room.

The solicitor continued, peering over his half-moon spectacles at the papers in front of him. 'I read from the will of Margaret Orla O'Sheehan, recently deceased. Let's see . . . *This is the last will and testimony, etcetera* . . . You get the drift. Right. *To Doctor Percival Flanagan, Esquire, I leave the sum required to finalise the purchase of one green Holden van. This sum is to be drawn from my estate.'* The solicitor looked over at Doc Flanagan and nodded. *'And far may he roam,* she says. Next: *The sum of one hundred and twenty-eight pounds and all my jewellery, I leave to Beatrice Emmeline Dunstable, known to all as Bunny.'* The solicitor looked over his spectacles at Bunny, who sniffled and reached into her sleeve for a handkerchief. 'There, there, dear. That's a tidy amount and should help you on your way. Now: *Lastly, the house at 47 Glenmore Road, Paddington is left to Beatrice Emmeline Dunstable and Violet June Kelly in equal measure.'*

Violet gasped and clapped her hand over her mouth. She looked around the room as everyone turned to face her.

The solicitor looked up, eyes merry. 'That's what it says. The house is to be held in a trust administered by Doctor Percy Flanagan until you girls come of age.'

Bunny grasped her hand, her pretty brown eyes shining. 'It's alright, Violet. She's left it to you and me together!'

Violet shook her head and turned to Doc Flanagan. 'But I never thought . . .'

Doc Flanagan winked at her. 'Don't assume, my dear. Madame knows what she's doing.' He looked up at the ceiling. 'Don't you, Peg?'

―

The Dawes Point ferry wharf was dark and quiet but the lights of the nightwatchmen, perched on the span of the new bridge above, blinked into the night.

Violet inhaled a lungful of the briny air and stared up at the enormous iron hulk of the bridge cutting across the night sky. The girders of the arch would join across the harbour any day now. Violet felt a rush of affection for Albert, remembering their childhood conversations about the bridge. He loved it so.

Her attention returned to Li Ling, Bunny and Iris, who were crouched beside her on the sandstone steps leading into the water where the wharf met the seawall, the high tide lapping at their bare feet.

Li Ling showed the three girls how to place the little red paper boats in the water and light the stub of the candle propped inside with toothpicks. One by one, they released the spindly lantern boats in silence.

Apparently satisfied that her own ghosts were appeased and farewelled, Li Ling stood and stretched her back, a hand on either side of her spine. Then she pulled her pipe and tobacco from her top pocket and packed the bowl. In the distance, a night ferry tooted in the darkness, the sound echoing across the water.

Li Ling lit the pipe and exhaled with obvious satisfaction. 'My mother always said the ghosts will follow the flame. At hungry ghost time they come. We feed them, we burn money for them. Now we send them back.'

Bunny got to her feet too. 'You don't think Madame's in hell, do you?'

Violet splashed Bunny's toes. 'Are you kidding? She's in an enormous feather bed with seven insatiable young men, all named Adonis, with some lissom young ladies thrown in for good measure. There's free opium and a brandy fountain. She eats bacon sandwiches for every meal. When she gets tired of all the pleasure, she goes riding in sunny fields on a tall chestnut horse called Percy. She's having a hoot. Anyway, you should take it easy, Buns. That's enough exertion for you for one day.'

Li Ling sat on the sandstone step and patted the place beside her. 'Come. Sit.'

Bunny sat and Li Ling put a companionable arm around the girl.

'Tell me what else you did for the hungry ghosts,' said Bunny.

Li Ling smiled and sent a jet of dragon smoke from her nostrils. 'You have to fold your clothes. Put them away in a drawer, not hang them up. The ghosts like to get inside them and run around.'

The girls laughed at this.

'God help us if the ghosts ever get a taste for Doc Flanagan's long johns. Those things have got stains on their stains.' That was Iris, stirred from contemplation. 'What else?'

'You put an extra chair at the dinner table. If the ghost is hungry and there's no place set for dinner, you get trouble.'

Bunny giggled. 'That's creepy.'

'They do that in other countries too: a place for the silent guest.' Violet chewed on a hangnail. 'It *is* pretty creepy.'

Li Ling shrugged. She nudged Violet on the step below with the tip of her toe. 'You make your peace?'

Violet turned back to the dark harbour. Very carefully, she launched her little paper boat, the candle stub flaring. She sent with it her hopes for Shen, her longing for Philip and her grief for Madame. She conjured in her mind the image of La Maison des Fleurs repaired and thriving; she sent that wish with the boat too. It seemed like such a flimsy vessel to hold so much of her heart. It wobbled on the surface of the water then drifted into the darkness. After a moment, the wind caught it sidewards and the candle began to gutter. Violet watched the flame extinguish. She felt a final tug of sorrow.

Drying her hands on her skirt, she stood up. It was time to move on. 'I'm finished. Shall we go?'

Iris extended her hand. 'Pull me up, would you? I think my arse has gone to sleep.'

Violet hauled Iris to her feet. 'I know, let's get a fish pie and a bottle of beer in the Fortune of War. My treat. That's a send-off Madame would approve of.'

Li Ling stood and nodded. 'Okay. No more ghosts. No more bad luck.' She turned and climbed the stairs to the jetty.

Iris and Violet each took one of Bunny's arms and helped her to climb the stone steps to the jetty above.

'Bad luck,' ruminated Bunny. 'Do you think that's what happened, just a run of bad luck?'

Iris tutted. 'Perhaps. But I think there was some good luck too.'

Violet smiled. 'Yes, there was.'

But her stomach knotted and she fell behind, watching as the other three women walked, shoes in hand, up the dark street to the Fortune of War hotel.

Would their lives from now be determined by luck? The future seemed full of promise and danger in equal measure. She had inherited Madame's house, true. But were she and the others still burdened with Madame's enemies too?

So far, there had been no more roses on the doorstep of La Maison des Fleurs. No more cryptic gifts or notes. Not yet. But who could be certain their 'ghost-man' wasn't still watching?

I would have lit a hundred candles and sent them off in boats into the harbour to lure away our enemy, she thought, if I only believed that would be enough to keep us safe.

She walked on, her footsteps a metronome, marking the rhythm of her thoughts. Perhaps it'll be okay, she mused. Perhaps he'll leave us alone now. The angry screech of a bat, lifting into the air from a fig tree beside the bridge pylon, seemed a shrill answer to her question. She hurried to catch the others, her heart racing in her chest.

She fell into step with Iris, who turned towards her, eyes flashing with mischief. 'Bunny was just sharing her ideas for redecorating the downstairs parlour at La Maison des Fleurs.'

Bunny gave Iris a shove. 'You're so mean! All I said was that we could think about toning it down a bit.'

Iris hooted. 'You said we could get a nice brown carpet. You said you thought chintz was *tasteful*!'

'Well, it is!'

Violet laughed. 'Good grief, Bunny! Did your aunt teach you nothing? The last thing our gentleman visitors want is a place that reminds them of home.'

Li Ling laughed. 'They want the movies!'

Iris took Li Ling's arm. 'Yes! They want velvet.'

'They want tigers!'

'And chandeliers!'

They arrived at the front of the pub and stood in the pool of light by the door. Violet linked her arm through Bunny's and led her up the steps. 'I was thinking we should make it just like it was. Only more so!'

Iris let out a cheer. 'Brilliant! Can we get a tiger?'

CHAPTER 31

THEODORA SCOWLED, WRINKLING HER diminutive nose. 'One minute I'm Cleopatra, the next I'm running from a burning building. Now look at me: a hunchback. Wearing sackcloth!'

She twitched the sacking outfit in the mirror and gave a haughty sigh. Bunny, standing behind her, sniggered, earning her a level look from Violet.

'It's only one scene. And Dracula's castle needs a hunchback. It simply wouldn't do *not* to have one. Honestly, you're going to bring the house down,' said Violet. Frankly, pretty little Theodora (never Dora) still managed to look alluring, even as she stood pouting while they stuffed a feather pillow into the back of the costume.

'Go to La Maison des Fleurs, they said. Get treated like a princess, they said,' muttered Theodora.

This triggered fresh giggles from Bunny. 'That sour expression is just right for your character. Have you been practising?'

Theodora poked out her tongue at Bunny in response.

Violet gave the girl an encouraging pat on the shoulder and crossed the Rose Room to open a window. With all of La Maison's girls using the room to dress, the air was beginning to feel a little close.

She threw open the latch and hoisted up the sash window. The fresh air was an immediate tonic. In the street below a small group of men had already begun to gather in the twilight, awaiting permission to come inside.

Violet gave them a wave and received a cheer and wolf-whistles in return.

Three months, she thought, stepping back from the window. Three months we've worked like stink to get the place fixed. Now the buzz in the room and on the street told her every second of that time had been worth it. A little bubble of sheer pleasure and excitement burst in her chest. She turned back to the girls, who were noisily jostling for space, dressing, applying make-up and gossiping.

'There you are!' Ruby pushed through the throng of bodies and appeared at Violet's side, dressed in black men's trousers, a black tuxedo bodice and top hat. 'Wait until you see what Li Ling's made me. That woman is a bloody genius.'

Ruby reached for the baggy crotch of her trousers and gave them a yank and, by a miracle of hidden seams and studs, they came off in a single flourish, revealing a more Ruby-like ensemble of stockings and suspenders.

Violet clapped. 'It's perfect! I'm a little jealous. Li Ling has never so much as darned a sock of mine.'

'What, there's actually someone who's immune to your charms? I refuse to believe it. By the way, did Johnny help Albert with the curtain donated by Ashton's? I told him to roll his sleeves up.' Ruby lit a cigarette and blew smoke out the window.

Violet gave her friend's arm a squeeze. 'Oh, Ruby love, the curtains are perfect. We'll have to do a private show for the Ashtons one of these days to show our thanks. And yes, Johnny spent all afternoon in there with Albert.'

Ruby shook her head in wonder. 'I can't believe what you've achieved. The parlour is exquisite.'

Violet sighed. 'I only wish Madame were here to see it.'

'Oh, fiddlesticks, don't you worry about her. She's up there muttering and judging, waiting for the show like everyone else. She's going to hate all that fake blood.'

'I know! She'd never have allowed it.'

'You wait, she'll find a way of showing her scorn. Lights flickering, plates flying. Here, give us a hand with this, will you?' Ruby turned around and Violet took the stays of Ruby's vampish bodice and drew them in tight.

'Ouch. This'll teach me to keep away from the battered sausage cart next time I'm on tour.'

Violet pecked Ruby lightly on the back of her neck, where her red curls tumbled from beneath her top hat. 'Don't be ridiculous. A female Dracula should be voluptuous. You're just showing dedication to character!'

'Will I be rewarded with virgins in skimpy nightdresses? You know I like them.'

'Of course! No retelling of *The Brides of Dracula* would be complete without them.'

'Lucky me!'

'By the way, at least two of your brides will be hoisted by wires and will ascend to the ceiling, transported by your amorous attentions. Speaking of which, I should check Susan has gone through the rigging with Albert.'

'I ravish them and they float? We probably should have rehearsed that bit.'

'Yes, we probably should have.' They laughed.

'Have you opened a bottle of champagne?' asked Ruby, stooping to adjust her stockings. 'We should allow ourselves a tiny toast before curtain-up.'

Violet nodded. 'Good idea. I'll be back.'

She stepped out of the Rose Room and into the hallway, where she collided with Li Ling, who was making a final delivery of towels and sheets to the rooms.

'Oh goodness, sorry! Is the bar well stocked, Li Ling? I think we can expect a big crowd.'

'The bar is fine. Iris is down there now.'

'Good. I'll go and see her.' Violet continued down the hallway, leaving Li Ling to her laundry trolley.

As she turned into the main staircase and descended to the ground floor, she stopped and allowed the sight of the remade parlour to surprise her once more.

The peacock feather wallpaper had been Bunny's choice. The beautiful turquoise and violet shades formed a striking backdrop for the room's furnishings. The leather banquettes had been replaced by luxurious navy blue velvet armchairs and settees draped with dusky blue-and-cream shawls fringed with gold. The potted palms that had once stood against the parlour walls had been replaced with delicate Japanese screens of black lacquer and paper, each painted with kingfishers in blue and gold, and gold urns on lacquer plinths, spilling over with peacock feathers.

A mural of Botticelli's angels, painted with perfect accuracy by the talented Susan, adorned the ceiling. The eye was drawn upwards to this painted paradise of blue skies, gold-rimmed clouds and voluptuous flesh. Even Dido and Aeneas had been replaced, although not by a tiger. In a cage atop the beautiful sleek black piano curled a sleeping python, whom Iris had lovingly named Boris.

The stage curtain donated by Ashton's was a midnight blue velvet. It surrounded the new stage: a larger version than the original, with painted flats and footlights.

Coming upon the room like this never failed to make Violet want to close her eyes and give thanks: to Madame, of course, for giving her a home alongside Bunny and ensuring the two girls were joined for life. But also to Philip, whose money had allowed them to return La Maison des Fleurs to this state of grandeur.

She watched, unobserved, from the staircase as Iris and Albert entered the room together, each placing a tray of champagne flutes on the bar. Iris took up her place behind the bar and started polishing the glasses, lining them up ready for the guests. Albert, whistling, was winding the new gramophone.

Philip's money had allowed her to do all this. She had missed him fiercely in the weeks after his departure. Upon the arrival of his ship in Cape Town, he'd sent a letter informing her that Shen was safe and happy, and content to act the part of the nun. It allowed her to feel both invisible and accepted, he said. Shen had travelled with radish, cucumber and cress seeds from old Ming's market gardens and she had planted them in tin cans. She tended them with the ship's cook on the lower deck. He and Shen would travel on to Southampton together. Once they docked in England, he would put her in touch with an old friend who managed the staff in the kitchen garden at Hampton Court

Palace. What better place for the favourite of the emperor Pu Yi to end up than a palace?

Violet longed for Philip sometimes, the ache a reminder that he had, perhaps, glimpsed her loneliness, as she had glimpsed his. Every now and then her thoughts wandered to lobster in a bubble bath. She felt a tug in her heart.

'Penny for 'em?' It was Albert, peering up the stairs.

'Not worth even half that, I'm afraid.' She descended the stairs to meet him.

'I don't believe that for a second, Violet Kelly. Sometimes your face looks like your brain's working hard enough to set yer hair on fire.'

'Well, thank you, Albert, I'll remember that. My face being such an important asset to this business and everything. Are we all set for the Brides of Dracula to levitate?'

'Double-checked.'

'And what about your cameo?' She'd given in at last: Albert was finally allowed onstage, although only as the back end of Dracula's horse.

'Can't wait. I've been practising my canter. Want to—'

'Oh, good grief, no.'

Iris waved from the bar. 'Come and see the amount of champagne we've got on ice. I feel a headache coming on just looking at it!'

Violet planted a kiss on Albert's cheek. 'I'd better go; don't want to upset the boss.'

She joined Iris behind the bar and they stood side by side in silence, watching as Albert departed in the direction of the front door, to his new doorman's high desk and stool.

Iris nodded in Albert's direction. 'Are you sure he doesn't know?'

Violet propped her elbows on the bar and leaned her chin in her hand. 'Well, I haven't told him and you haven't.'

'So, you received another one this morning?' Iris fetched two glasses and poured them each a fifth of whisky.

Violet nodded and swallowed her drink. The ghost-man had resumed his haunting. Every few weeks, a pink rose would appear at La Maison des Fleurs: on the front step, tucked into the milk bottles; in the letterbox; once on the sill of Madame's office window. It was no surprise to Violet to see another rose this morning. It was tucked inside the folded newspaper that had been brought into the kitchen and placed on the table by an unsuspecting Charlie Han.

'The ghost-man wants us to know he's not finished with us.' Violet pursed her lips at the thought.

'And he wants to frighten us.'

'Which is why we have to keep it to ourselves. What do Arlo and Jeanie say?'

Iris had struck up a firm friendship with Jeanie, and the couple had been fixtures at the house during the months the team had spent refurbishing La Maison. Now Jeanie was a reliable source of information on the underground of Kings Cross.

Iris shrugged. 'Jeanie reckons the place has gone quiet again. Those guns are still out there, we know that. But whoever's in charge has gone below deck for a while. She hasn't seen a bust lip or a shanked face for weeks now.'

'I guess we can be grateful for that.'

'Yes, indeed.'

Violet stood up and placed the whisky glass in the sink behind her. 'Right. Are we ready to release the Brides of Dracula upon our unsuspecting guests?'

'Oh, Violet, you could hardly call *that* lot unsuspecting.'

'True. I'd better go and let the girls know.' Violet wriggled out from behind the bar.

Iris frowned at her. 'You're not wearing that, are you?'

'Oh, heck, no! I'd better get my lady-brothel-owner clothes on.'

Iris raised her glass and smiled affectionately at her twin. 'The Madame is dead. Long live the Madame.'

—

Smoke from buckets of dry ice drifted across the front of the stage and curled at the feet of the gentlemen in the front row. There was an excited coughing and clinking of ice in glasses as the velvet curtain lifted slowly to reveal a darkened cemetery at night. The cardboard headstones were frankly a work of art, thought Violet, from her place in the doorway. The curtain continued to rise to reveal a clever backdrop showing a moonlit landscape and the gateway to a castle, which glowed as if from firelight within.

Bunny appeared at her side and slipped her hand into Violet's. 'Here we go!' she whispered.

Theodora stepped out from behind the tallest headstone, carrying a candle in a glass case. She lit a match, and candlelight illuminated the stage. Violet felt a nudge in the ribs and the familiar sound of Bunny stifling a snigger: apparently unable to stand the lack of glamour in her costume, Theodora had hitched up her sack to reveal a flash of lace panties beneath.

'Ahhhhh,' said Theodora, in her best hunchback voice. 'My mathter will thoon return! But wait until he theeth what pleathures await inside the cathle!'

At this, the good-natured crowd gave a satisfied, 'Oooooh!'

We lure them with lace panties, thought Violet, but it's the pantomime that keeps 'em.

From somewhere in the hallway, she heard the clatter of coconut halves being clapped together to sound like hoofbeats.

Ruby Dracula, complete with blood-tipped fangs, cantered unsteadily into the room on the back of her two-person horse which, rather unexpectedly, executed a daring leap onto the stage. The back legs of the horse were working particularly hard, Violet observed.

Gramophone music began to play, filling the room with ethereal strings. Dracula was helped down from her horse by her loyal (if underdressed) hunchbacked butler. She paced the front of the stage in one direction, then the other, baring her incisors. The music swelled.

'I say, Ignacio?' shouted Dracula, untying the neck of her voluminous cape and flinging it aside.

Theodora-Ignacio, transformed by the audience's praise, was hamming it up. She lurched to Dracula's side. 'Yeth, mathter?'

'I say, Ignacio?' Dracula reached down and, with a single yank, whipped off her trousers. Every man in the audience was on his feet cheering.

Theodora rose to the moment. 'Yesssssth, maaasssssthter?'

Dropping ever so slowly into the splits, hands raised to the skies, Dracula yelled, 'I say, Ignacio—I am *thirsty* tonight!'

Violet smiled and closed her eyes, listening to the thunderous applause. When she opened them, she caught the special triumphant glance that Ruby sent her way. It said: Look out— La Maison des Fleurs is *back*!

ACKNOWLEDGEMENTS

THANKS FIRST TO THE PEOPLE who recognised a spark of life in a pretty rough draft of this novel and saw the book it might become . . .

Jane Palfreyman, publisher at Allen & Unwin: thank you!

Ali Lavau, editor at large: if this book works at all, it's thanks to your advice and your patient, meticulous care.

Jenny Darling and Anyez Lindop at the Jenny Darling Agency: thank you for excellent advice given with kindness, warmth and good cheer.

Now, to the people who came before . . .

Thanks to Emeritus Professor Brenda Walker at University of Western Australia: who once said to me, while supervising my *terribly serious* PhD: 'You're so funny in real life. Why isn't that on the page?' As I write this, I think it'll be thirty years since

I first encountered you as an undergraduate. How lucky I've been to have you as a mentor and guide.

Thanks to Paul, Shar, Dad and Alison, for sharing in my excitement. Paul, you were right to insist I keep writing. Dad, thank you for reminding me why I wrote this book in the first place (spoiler: it was to have fun).

Particular thanks to those friends who read and championed early drafts of this book: Chloe Britton, Paul Jones, Katy Jenkins, H Morgan-Harris, Jessica Douglas-Henry, Roswitha Adldinger, Alison Faure-Brac, Andrea Davies and Cassie Cochrane.